Witch Is Where Unicorns Cry

Published by Implode Publishing Ltd
© Implode Publishing Ltd 2021

Chapter 1

"Come on, be reasonable," Wanda said.

In case you're wondering, Wanda was the latest addition to the family Maxwell. Jack and Florence had won the goldfish on the hoopla stall at the village fête while I was on a fool's errand to rescue Buddy from meat-eating butterflies (yes, yes, we've already established I'm a gullible idiot—thanks, Grandma).

"What's wrong with the bowl you've got?" I sighed. Having a conversation with a disgruntled goldfish was not the way I'd envisaged starting my week.

"What's *wrong* with it?" She blew a couple of bubbles, which I was pretty sure was the goldfish equivalent of exasperation. "Just look at it. It's tiny!"

"So are you."

"Keeping me in a bowl this size is tantamount to goldfish cruelty, and unless the situation is rectified, I may be forced to submit a report to the authorities."

"Who are you talking to, Jill?" Jack shouted from the hallway, and then came through to the lounge.

"The fish."

"The *fish* has a name if you don't mind," Wanda said. "I don't go around referring to you as the *two-legged*, do I?"

"Sorry. She wants you to know her name is Wanda, Jack."

"Nice to meet you, Wanda. I really wish I could talk to animals. It must be great."

"Oh yeah, it's fantastic. I love having them moan and groan at me all day long."

"I am not *moaning and groaning*," Wanda insisted. "I am registering a legitimate complaint."

"What is she saying now?" Jack bent down and put his nose to the bowl.

"She reckons this bowl is too small for her and that we should buy her a bigger one."

"She has a point. It is a little on the small side."

"I like him." Wanda blew a few bubbles his way.

"Why don't you pop into that pet shop around the corner from your office and pick up a bigger one?" Jack said.

"How am I supposed to find time to do that?"

"Didn't you say you'd wrapped up all of your cases?"

"Yeah, but there's all the other things I have to attend to: Marketing and accounts and stuff."

"Doesn't Mr Bacus do your accounts?"

"Well, err, yeah."

"And I didn't think you did any marketing."

"Okay, okay. I'll buy the fish a new bowl."

"And not one of those cheapo ones," Wanda said.

Sheesh! My life wasn't my own.

***

"You're not Mrs V." I had a flair for stating the obvious.

The woman sitting behind the desk was about the same age as Mrs V, but there the similarity ended. She was much taller, and her hair was a peculiar shade of blue, which matched her dress.

"You must be Jill." She stood up and offered her hand. "I'm delighted to meet you."

"I'm sorry, but I'm a little confused. Are you here to talk to me about a case? Did my receptionist nip out somewhere?"

"None of the above. Please allow me to explain. Annabel and I have been friends for as long as I can remember."

"Is she okay?"

"She's fine, but that sister of hers has been taken ill."

"Again?"

"This time it appears to be genuine. Annabel is expecting to be down there for a week and maybe even two. She said she tried to call you, but she got your voicemail thingy. Anyway, she didn't want to leave you in the lurch, so she asked if I'd step into the breach, so to speak."

"I see. I'm sorry, I don't even know your name."

"Kay Kayfield, but you can call me Mrs K."

"And have you done this type of work before, Mrs K?"

"Oh yes, dear. Before I retired, I held similar positions in several blue-chip organisations." She glanced around. "This isn't exactly what I'm used to, but I'm quick to adapt."

"Okay. I'm grateful to you for stepping in at such short notice."

"Is there anything you'd like me to make a start on?"

"I — err —"

"What would Annabel be doing if she was in today?"

"Knitting, probably. Or crocheting."

"I was thinking more about what I could do businesswise."

"A cup of tea would be nice."

"Of course. Who do I call to arrange that?"

"Actually, there isn't anyone else. It's just you and me."

"I see." She took another look around and spotted the kettle and cups. "No problem. How do you take yours?"

"Milk, no sugar."

"I'll get straight on it. By the way, I can't seem to find Annabel's diary. Do you remember when your first appointment is today?"

"I — err — don't think I have any."

"What about tomorrow?"

"Tomorrow? Err, no."

"I see."

"The man is coming to repair the blinds on Wednesday, I believe."

"Right, well I'll get on with that tea, shall I?"

"Yes, please."

"Get me out of here!" Winky yelled.

"What are you doing in that cage?"

"Oh, I just thought it might be fun to try a taste of the prison experience. What do you think I'm doing in here? That crazy woman did it."

"Where did the cage come from?"

Before he could reply, Mrs K walked in behind me. "Ah, you've seen him. When I came in this morning, I found this young man wandering around the office. I assume he's a stray who must have come in through the open window. You really shouldn't leave it open all night."

"This is Winky. He's my cat."

"Oh? It never occurred to me that you'd allow a cat in your place of work. Isn't that a little unprofessional? What do your clients make of it?"

"No one has complained." Okay, maybe a few have. "Where did the cage come from?"

"I found a little pet shop, just around the corner. They were happy to rent out the cage for the day. I was going to take it back as soon as the cat people had taken him away."

"The *cat people*?"

"I called the cat rehoming place. They said they'd be here this afternoon."

"Right. In that case, could you call them back and tell them that there's been a misunderstanding and we won't be needing them."

"I'll get straight onto it." She made to leave the office.

"Before you do, Mrs K, do you have the key to the cage?"

"Of course. She fished it out of her pocket and handed it to me.

"Who's that old witch?" Winky said.

"She isn't a witch, she's a human."

"Never mind the semantics. Who is she and what's she doing here?"

"Mrs V has had to visit her poorly sister. Mrs K is standing in for her."

"Why didn't you call Jules, and get her to stand in for the old bag lady?"

"I didn't know anything about it until I arrived a few minutes ago. I can't throw Mrs K's kindness in her face."

"Are you actually ever going to let me out of here or what?"

"Sorry. There you go. What happened, anyway?"

"I was fast asleep, having a fantastic dream about Crystal-Bell. She and I were just about to—"

"I don't want to hear about your sordid dreams."

"Then the crazy woman walks in and freaks out. She yells at me for ten minutes, then disappears. Next thing I know, she's back with the prison. She's the one who needs locking up for animal cruelty."

"There's your tea, Jill." Mrs K appeared, cup in hand. "You enjoy that while I take this cage back. I'm sorry for the misunderstanding."

"No problem, Mrs K. It was an easy mistake to make. And don't worry about taking the cage back. I need to pay the pet shop a visit this morning, anyway, so I'll take it."

"Are you sure?"

"Positive. And thanks for the tea."

As soon as she was out of the door, Winky proceeded to mock me. "*Thanks for the tea.* You shouldn't be thanking her. You should be sending her packing after what she did to me. And what do you want from the pet shop? Something to compensate me for the trauma I've just been through, I hope."

"No chance."

"What then?"

"If you must know, I'm going to buy a fish tank."

"Are we going to have fish in the office? Cool, I love watching fish."

"No, we aren't having fish in here. It's for Florence's goldfish, Wanda."

"Seriously?" He laughed. "A fish called Wanda?"

"I didn't choose her name."

"When did you buy Wanda?"

"We didn't. Jack won her at the village fête."

"I shouldn't bother buying the tank, then."

"Why not?"

"Everyone knows that any goldfish won at a fair won't last the week. She'll be dead by the time you get the tank home."

"Rubbish. She looks perfectly healthy."

"Just make sure you ask what their returns policy is."

***

Although I'd paid many visits to pet shops in Washbridge, this was my first visit to Rue Pets, which was only a ten-minute walk from my office. Mrs K must have been fit for her age because I was shattered by the time I'd carried the cage back to the shop.

"Good morning, madam." The man behind the counter had a parrot on his shoulder.

"Hi. I'd like to return this cage. My PA hired it earlier today."

"Of course. Let me just put Buster back." After returning the parrot to his perch, the man came from behind the counter and took the cage from me. "Did the rehoming people collect the cat? The lady who hired this told me he'd sneaked into your office."

"Actually, there was a bit of a misunderstanding. Winky is my cat."

"I see. Well, there's nothing more to pay on this."

"While I'm here, I need a fish tank."

"In that case, you've come to the right place. Rue Pets has the largest range of fish tanks in Washbridge. I'm Rupert, by the way, I own this shop."

"I'm Jill."

"So, Jill, what kind of fish do you have? Temperate? Tropical?"

"A goldfish."

"I see. How many do you have?"

"Just the one."

"With only one fish, something like this should be

suitable." He pointed to a bowl that was practically identical to the one I already had at home.

"I think I need something a little bigger."

"Are you sure? This one should be more than big enough."

"You're probably right, but Wanda wants — err, that's to say, I'd still prefer something a little bigger."

"As you wish. How about this one?"

The second one was barely bigger than the first. I couldn't imagine it going down well with Wanda.

"What about that one?" I pointed.

"That's actually designed to hold up to a dozen tropical fish."

"How much is it?"

"Eighty pounds."

"Really?"

"The smaller one is only thirty-five."

Which left me in something of a quandary. Did I take the cheaper one and face more aggro from Wanda or did I fork out for the more expensive one?

"I'll take the bigger one." What price peace and quiet?

"Very well. And will you be needing anything to go inside the tank?"

"Like what? Water? I've got plenty of that in the tap."

"Very amusing, madam. I was thinking about a few ornaments to make the tank more interesting for your fish."

"Nah, I'll just take the tank, thanks."

"Very well, madam."

"Just one more thing, Rupert. What's your returns policy?"

"Any calls, Mrs K?"

"Just one. A woman wanted to know if you were Jill Maxwell the renowned clairvoyant. I told her that isn't you. I hope that's right?"

"I'm not at the moment, but who knows what the future might hold." I laughed.

Mrs K stared at me blankly. Clearly my razor-sharp wit was wasted on her.

"I feel as though I should be doing more, Jill. Is there anything else I can busy myself with?"

"Not really. The job is mainly answering phone calls and attending to visitors."

"You don't appear to have either of those."

"Not at the moment, but it can get really wild sometimes," I lied. "If you have any hobbies, I'm happy for you to spend time on those in between the busy periods."

"I actually do have a number of hobbies, but it wouldn't feel right doing that sort of thing during work hours."

"Don't be silly. You have my blessing."

"Very well. Thank you."

"I wish you wouldn't leave me alone with that old witch." Winky eyed the door. "Who knows what she might do next."

"I wish you wouldn't refer to her as an old witch. I keep thinking you're talking about my grandmother. And you don't have anything to worry about; I've explained that you're the office cat."

"That tank must have cost a small fortune."

"It did."

"How come you're willing to splash the cash on Wanda, but you won't buy me a new sofa?"

"Because, so far, Wanda hasn't conned me into paying ransom money."

"That was only a joke. There was a time when you would have found that funny."

Chapter 2

After leaving the pet shop, I made a quick detour to the car park, to put the fish tank in the boot before returning to the office.

"There was a phone call for you while you were gone," Mrs K said.

"Someone wanting their palm read?"

"Sorry?"

"Never mind. What did they want?"

"It was a young woman called Lorna Boone. She asked if she could make an appointment to come and see you. I knew you had nothing on today, so I said she could come this afternoon, at two o'clock. I hope that's okay?"

"That's fine. Did she say what it was about?"

"No, and she sounded a little upset, so I didn't like to press her for details."

"Very wise. Okay, thanks, Mrs K."

Winky spent most of the morning making passive aggressive comments about how I favoured all my other animals over him. Eventually, he returned to a familiar theme.

"The dog gets to share your house, and now the goldfish too, so why can't I?"

"We've had this conversation before. Florence is allergic to cat hair. Otherwise, I'd be more than happy to take you home with me."

"She might have outgrown her allergy by now. People do, you know. When was she last tested?"

"Err, only a couple of weeks ago. Still allergic. What can I do? My hands are tied."

It was obvious he had no intention of letting the issue lie, so to get some peace, I magicked myself over to Cuppy C for a coffee, and if someone happened to twist my arm, a muffin.

There was no sign of either of the twins, so I ordered my drink and muffin from the assistant behind the counter — and yes, she did twist my arm.

"Where are Amber and Pearl?"

"Upstairs, setting up the cork museum."

"Thanks, I'll go and see how they're doing." I made my way upstairs. "Hello, girls."

"What do you think of it, Jill?" Amber said.

"Credit where credit is due, you've made a really good job of this. It's a lot more professional than I was expecting."

"Thanks, Jill. We're really pleased with it." Pearl gushed.

"Where did you get all the display cabinets from?"

"We hired them."

The twins had installed glass-topped display cabinets along each wall. Inside them, the corks had been sorted by size and colour. I was pleasantly surprised to see that each cork had a little card next to it with details of its origin.

"What have you got left to do?"

"Not much. We just need to put up a few signs, which should be here later today. The grand opening is on Thursday. Make sure you come."

"I wouldn't miss it for the world."

Just then, there was the sound of footsteps on the stairs, and Aunt Lucy appeared. It was obvious from the expression on the twins' faces that they hadn't been expecting her visit.

"I just thought I'd pop over to take a look at this museum of yours."

"The girls have made an excellent job of it," I said, in a flagrant attempt to score a few brownie points with the twins.

"The display cabinets certainly make it look very professional." She walked over to the nearest one. "Why is the card for Billy's Bottom next to Daisy's Delight? And why is the card for Rab's Dingle next to Jeremy's Trick?"

The twins looked at one another, each of them clearly hoping the other would respond. It was Pearl who cracked first. "I suppose it's possible we could have mixed up a couple of the cards."

"A *couple*?" Aunt Lucy made her way from one cabinet to the next. "Ninety percent of these cards are next to the wrong cork. What was the point of me going to all the trouble of writing them out?"

"Maybe no one will notice?" Amber said.

"Of course they will. Just who do you think is going to visit this museum of yours?"

"*Corkers*?" I suggested.

"I told you I don't like that term, Jill, but you're right, they will be cork aficionados." Don't you think they'll realise these cards are all in the wrong place?"

"Will you help us to sort them out, Mum?" Pearl said.

"Please, Mum," Amber pleaded. "The museum opens on Thursday."

"It doesn't look like I have much choice, does it? But I expect you two to keep me supplied with tea while I'm doing it."

"Of course," Amber said. "And as many buns as you like."

The twins and I made our way downstairs, leaving Aunt Lucy with the unenviable task of sorting out the corks and cards.

"*And as many buns as you like,*" I mocked.

"Shut up, Jill!" Pearl snapped. "I might have known you'd think it was funny."

"If you recall, I did warn you about separating the cards from the corks, but did you listen? Of course not."

"Look who's over there," Amber said.

Martin was sitting by the window.

"Excuse me, girls, I need to have a word with my brother. Don't forget Aunt Lucy's bun."

Amber said something under her breath and Pearl stuck out her tongue.

"Jill." Martin stood up. "I was going to come and see you later."

"I've saved you the trouble."

"Why are the twins looking daggers at you?"

"Take no notice. They've got cork problems."

"*Cork* problems?"

"It's a long story. Do you have the name of the second guardian yet?"

"Yes, I do."

"Are you sure you haven't misheard it this time? I don't want another *Madam* Rodenia wild goose chase."

"I'm positive. The guardian of the East compass stone is called Ursula. And wait until you hear this: She's the queen of—"

"The unicorns."

"How did you know that?"

"I know Ursula well. I worked on a case for her, and she recently had Florence and one of her friends over there for a visit."

"That should make finding the second stone much easier."

"I hope so."

***

"Where did you come from?" Mrs K stared at me in disbelief.

She must have walked into my office for something, just as I magicked myself back there.

"I—err—"

"I came in to see if you wanted another drink, but you weren't here. But then you were?"

There was no good way to talk myself out of this, so I took the only option open to me, and cast the 'forget' spell.

"I—err—came in to ask you something." Mrs K looked a little disorientated. "But I can't for the life of me remember what it was."

"Maybe to ask if I wanted another drink?"

"That was it, yes."

"I think I'll wait until my visitor gets here."

"Very well." Still a little dazed, she backed out of the room.

"That one's even battier than the old bag lady," Winky said.

"To be fair, I did just use magic on her."

"I wish I could do magic." He sighed. "I'd put it to much better use than you do."

"Yeah? How?"

"I'd start by turning that old witch into a cockroach."

"Speaking of cockroaches, I had no idea that you had such rapport with the insect life in this office. When you pretended to have been catnapped, I got a right tongue-lashing from some old spider who thought I was responsible."

"That would have been Albert."

"That was him. How about the next time you see him, you tell him that I wasn't responsible for you ending up on the street?"

"I will if you buy me a new sofa."

"Forget it. I'd rather stay in Albert's bad books."

Mrs K came through to my office.

"Lorna Boone is here, Jill. I asked if she'd like a drink, but she said no."

"Okay. Send her through, would you."

The young woman was wearing a head scarf and sunglasses. Even though I couldn't see her eyes, her body language was that of a woman in torment.

"Thank you for seeing me at such short notice." Her voice cracked. "I really do appreciate it."

"No problem. Are you sure you wouldn't like a drink? Water maybe?"

"No, thanks."

By now, it was clear she had no intention of removing her sunglasses.

"What can I do for you—is it okay to call you Lorna?"

She nodded. "I'd like you to find my fiancé. You do trace missing persons, I assume?"

"Yes, of course." I waited for her to elaborate.

"Harry and I have been engaged for two years. We were due to get married last week, but then he disappeared."

"It's an obvious and not particularly nice question to have to ask, but is it possible he simply got cold feet and took off?"

"That's what everyone assumes, but it's not true. Harry would never have left me like that. Not on the eve of our wedding."

"When was the last time he was seen?"

"At the chapel. We'd just finished the final rehearsal." She took out her phone. "This is a photo taken on the day he disappeared."

Although the guy in the photo was smiling, the smile didn't seem to reach his eyes.

"Could you email me a copy of that?"

"Of course."

"And after the rehearsal, you went your separate ways?"

"No. We were on the way to the boat when Harry remembered he'd left his phone in the chapel. He went to get it, and that was the last time I saw him."

"Hang on. You said *boat*?"

"We were to be married in the small chapel on Randall's Island. Have you heard of it?"

"I can't say that I have."

"It's a small island on Wesmere Lake. The only thing on there is the chapel. We both thought it would be a romantic place to get married."

"Who else was there that day?"

"Harry and I, the best man and maid of honour, and the man who was going to perform the wedding ceremony. Oh, and the man who drove the boat of course."

"Let me make sure I've understood this correctly. The six of you were the only people on the island when your fiancé went missing?"

"That's right."

"What happened when he didn't turn up at the boat?"

"We all went to look for him. Except for Mr Bagshot. He stayed with the boat."

"Mr Bagshot is the boat owner, I assume?"

"That's right."

"So the rest of you searched the island but couldn't find Harry?"

"Correct."

"How big is the island?"

"Not very big at all. It took less than twenty minutes for us to search everywhere."

"What did you do next?"

"I wanted to stay on the island, but the others insisted I left with them. We almost didn't make it back, though."

"Why? What happened?"

"The motor started making a loud clonking noise, and the boat started to take on water. I couldn't believe it. First, Harry disappears, and then it looked like we were all going to drown."

"Good gracious."

"The guy managed to get us back to the shore, but only just. When I called the police to tell them about Harry, they weren't very interested at first, but I insisted they do something. They did eventually send one constable and he went over to the island, but he didn't find Harry."

"How did he get over there if the boat was out of action?"

"Another guy took the policeman across in a rowing boat."

"What do you think happened to Harry?"

"At first, I thought he might have tripped and fallen into the lake, but the police mounted an underwater search the next day, and they didn't find anything. Now, I don't know."

"Are the police still involved?"

"No. They reckon he must have lost his nerve about getting married and took off of his own accord."

"How do they explain how he got back from the island?"

"They say he must have arranged for someone to pick him up in another boat."

"Is that possible?"

"I have no idea, but it's irrelevant. Harry would never do anything like that. Something must have happened to him, and I want you to find out what."

***

"Is that tank for Wanda, Mummy?" Florence greeted me at the door.

"Yes, darling. Do you think she'll like it?"

"Yes. Can we put her into it now?"

"We can. Let's go through to the kitchen and I'll fill it with water."

"That's a much better size." Jack looked up from his stamp album.

"Will you go and get the fish while I fill this?"

"Will do."

By the time I had the water ready, Jack was back with Wanda.

"Tip her in," I said.

"Be gentle!" Wanda yelled.

"She says you should be gentle," I translated for Jack's benefit.

Once Wanda was in her new tank, Jack took her back through to the lounge. He and Florence seemed happy to watch the fish do circuit after circuit of her new home. I found it about as exciting as watching paint dry, so I left them to it and went back to the kitchen where I found Grandma sitting at the table. Normally, I would have had something to say about her letting herself into the house, but I was too mesmerised by her wig.

"Close your mouth, Jill, you'll catch a fly."

I knew I was staring at the wig, but I couldn't help myself. The last time she'd done this, and I'd mentioned it, she'd insisted it was her own hair. Surely, she couldn't deny it was a wig again.

"Isn't that a—?" I hesitated.

"A what?"

"Your hair. Isn't it—?"

"In a new style? Yes, it is, but I'm not here to discuss my hair. I'm here to tell you that your presence is required at the lido on Sunday."

"I don't understand."

"You must remember. It's that place with the swimming pool that you took a dip in fully clothed."

"I know what the lido is, but I thought it had closed down."

"And so it had, but it's going to re-open. Those Reptile people relinquished ownership after a little persuasion."

"What kind of *persuasion*?"

"Best you don't know the details. Suffice to say there's a grand re-opening this Sunday, and your presence is required."

"Because of the part I played in saving it?"

"No. To see them present me with an award for rescuing the lido."

"*You*? What did *you* do?"

"I hired you of course. It's at two o'clock. Don't be late."

Jack came through to the kitchen. "What's that on your grandmother's head?"

"How did you see her?"

"I was watching through the gap in the door."

"She reckons it's her new hairstyle."

"It's a wig, isn't it?"

"Of course it is, and a bad one at that."

"What did she want?"

"To send my blood pressure through the roof, and she succeeded."

Chapter 3

"What's wrong with it?" I demanded.

"It's fine." Wanda blew an unenthusiastic bubble. "I suppose."

"You asked for a bigger tank, and this is bigger. Much bigger."

This goldfish was seriously doing my head in.

"It is bigger, and I appreciate that. But—"

"But what? What's wrong now?"

"It seems so very bare. A few ornaments that I could swim around, and in and out of, would be nice."

"How many do you call a few?"

"Not many. Three or four should do it. Possibly five. You certainly don't need to buy more than six."

"And if I buy some ornaments, will that satisfy you?"

"Of course. My needs are very simple."

"Right. I'll pop into the pet shop later today."

"I really do appreciate it."

"Did I hear you talking to the goldfish?" Jack said when I joined him at the kitchen table.

"She wants ornaments now."

"That tank is a little spartan."

"How is it that you and Florence won the goldfish, but I'm the one who's become her personal shopper?"

Just then, Florence came in from the garden where she'd been throwing the ball, and Buddy had been ignoring it. "There's a new boy in my class, Mummy."

"What's his name?"

"Thomas. He's a wizard."

"Do you mean that he was pretending to be a wizard?"

"No. He's a real wizard. He told me so. He asked me which spells I knew."

I turned to Jack. "Did you know about this?"

"I saw a new mum at the school gates yesterday, but I didn't actually speak to her."

"Is she a witch?"

"I don't know. It's not like I have witch-dar."

"How old is she?"

"About our age, I guess."

"Does she live in the village?"

"I've no idea, Jill."

"You need to find out."

"And just how am I supposed to do that?"

"It shouldn't be all that difficult seeing as how all the mums have the hots for you."

"That's true."

"It had better not be. Find some excuse to strike up a conversation with her."

"What do you want me to say to her? *Are you a witch*?"

"Of course not. You could try to find out where she lives for starters."

"Okay, I'll try, but I'm not promising anything."

***

As soon as I walked into the office building, my ears were assaulted by an awful high-pitched noise, which appeared to be coming from upstairs. Had Winky got himself caught in the blinds again?

I hurried up the stairs, and found Farah, from Bubbles, staring at my office door.

"Is everything alright in there, Jill? I didn't know

whether I should go inside or not."

"It's okay. I'll sort it out."

In the outer office, I found Mrs K sitting at her desk, playing (and I use that term loosely), a violin.

"Good morning, Jill."

"Morning. You have a violin."

"This is my new hobby. You did say it was okay to indulge during quiet periods, didn't you?"

"Err, yeah, I did. The thing is, Mrs K, I was expecting your hobby to be a little quieter. I've just seen our neighbour, the lady who runs the dog grooming parlour down the corridor, and she told me the noise — err — music was upsetting the animals."

"I'm so sorry, Jill, I should have realised."

"Perhaps a quieter hobby if you have one?"

"Don't worry. I have plenty to keep me occupied. Should I go and apologise to the lady down the corridor?"

"That won't be necessary. Have there been any calls?"

"Just the one. Someone wanting to know how much our creosote was. I told them they must have the wrong number."

"Right. I'll be going out later, to follow up on the Boone case, but a cup of tea would be most welcome in the meantime."

"I'll get straight onto it."

"Kill me!" Winky said. "Just kill me now and put me out of my misery."

"What are you talking about?"

"Crazy witch lady and that cello of hers of course."

"It was a violin."

"Cello, violin, same difference. Do you know how long I've had to listen to that awful row? My ears may never be the same. I've a good mind to register a claim for injury in the workplace."

"A workplace is only a workplace if you actually do some work in it. Sitting around on your backside all day, eating salmon, doesn't qualify."

"I might have known I wouldn't get any sympathy from the person who won't even buy me a new sofa for my poor aching limbs."

"Jill?" Mrs K popped her head around the door. "I could have sworn I heard you talking to someone."

"It was no one; just the cat."

"I see. I'll just go and make that drink."

"So, I'm *no one* now." Winky gave a dramatic *woe is me* sigh. "Nice to know."

Give me strength.

Before I started work on the Boone case, I wanted to arrange to visit Ursula who I'd discovered was the guardian of the second compass stone.

"Queen Ursula's phone, Ronald speaking."

"Ronald, it's Jill Maxwell. Is the queen there?"

"She isn't here at the moment. After that business with her brother, she felt she needed to get away for a few days, so she's gone on a retreat. She thought it better not to take her phone with her."

"I see. I was actually hoping to come and see her sometime. When will she be back?"

"On Thursday."

"Okay. I guess it can wait until then. I'll call again on Thursday."

"Did your little girl enjoy her visit?"

"She loved it. She's already counting the days until she

can visit again next year."

"When the queen gets back, I'll tell her you called."

"Thanks, Ronald."

***

To better understand the Boone case, I wanted to pay a visit to the scene of the 'disappearance'. Until Lorna Boone came to see me, I'd never heard of Randall's Island. Apparently, though, I was in the minority because when I'd spoken to Kathy the previous evening, she'd told me she'd once attended a wedding there. Even Jack had heard of it.

Wesmere Lake was located twelve miles south of Washbridge. I had definitely visited the lake as a kid, but I didn't recall any mention of an island. There were very few cars in the car park and the guy in the small refreshment kiosk looked terminally bored.

"Hi." I flashed him a smile. "Lovely day."

"Not in here it isn't. If you're after a cold drink, you're out of luck. The fridge is on the blink."

"Actually, I just wanted to ask you about Randall's Island."

"What about it?"

"I assume that's it over there?" I pointed. "It's much smaller than I expected."

"That's what everyone says."

"I understand there's a chapel on the island."

"The chapel is the *only* thing on there."

"Do many people get married in the chapel?"

"Yeah, but I don't for the life of me understand why. All that faffing about ferrying the guests back and forth, and it's not cheap either."

"Can I get across to the island today?"

"You need Matty. Do you see the path over there? Walk along that for about five minutes and you'll come to his mooring."

"Thanks."

I was a little surprised to find that the only boat at the mooring was a small rowing boat. Sitting on the decking, pipe in mouth, was an old guy with a bushy beard. He'd been reading a book, which had dropped onto his lap when he dozed off.

"Excuse me."

"What?" He sat up so quickly that the book fell onto the floor.

"Sorry, I didn't mean to make you jump."

"I wasn't asleep."

"Right." I gestured to the rowing boat. "Are you open for business?"

"Yes, until four o'clock. It's five pounds for the round trip. I can take three at a time."

"It's just me."

"The price is the same regardless."

"Fair enough." I handed over the cash.

"The name's Matty." He stepped into the boat, then took my hand to help me aboard.

"I'm Jill." I took a seat while Matty cast us free and began to row across the lake.

"Do you use this boat for wedding parties?"

"No." He laughed. "It would take all day to get them all across there, and I don't reckon they'd want to sit in this thing, dressed in their smart clobber. They use a launch for the wedding parties."

"Do you own that?"

"Nah, that's got nothing to do with me."

"Who does it belong to?"

"A guy called Norman Bagshot. He keeps it in a small boathouse on the opposite side of the lake."

"Is the launch only used for weddings?"

"Nah, he'd go broke if that was the case. He hires it out for trips around the lake during the spring and summer."

"Did you hear about the man who went missing?"

"I certainly did. I had to take the policeman across to the island because the launch was damaged and taking on water. They sealed off the lake the next day while they searched it, which cost me a day's earnings. The whole thing was ridiculous."

"What makes you say that?"

"Obvious, isn't it? The guy must have got cold feet and done a runner. Wish I'd done the same twenty-four years ago, but don't tell my missus I said that."

"My lips are sealed."

"Here we are. How long are you planning to stay on the island?"

"How long do you reckon it will take me to look around?"

"You can walk around the whole island in twenty minutes."

"I want to take a look at the chapel too."

"You won't be able to go inside. They keep it locked most of the time."

"Thirty minutes ought to be long enough."

"Okay. I'll be back over for you then."

Although the island was only small, it wasn't possible to see from one side of it to the other because it was covered in tall trees and dense bushes. A few yards from where Matty had dropped me was a narrow path that disappeared into the trees. I followed that for a couple of minutes before coming to a clearing, in the centre of which was the chapel—a small white-stone building. It was undoubtedly an unusual setting, but I failed to see the appeal. And yet, according to Matty, the chapel was booked several months in advance.

The doors to the chapel were locked, but there was a small sign that gave contact details for anyone interested in booking it for their wedding. After making a note of the telephone number, I walked around the building, stopping to look through the tiny windows. Although quite basic, the interior looked to be immaculately maintained.

Standing back from the building, I tried to picture what had happened on that day. According to Lorna, they'd been there for the final rehearsal. Once that had finished, they started back to the boat, but then Lorna's fiancé realised (or at least, claimed) that he had left his phone behind. He had returned alone to the chapel to retrieve it, but was never seen again.

Wow! Where did I even start with this one?

***

"Jill, thank goodness you're back." Mrs K looked a little spooked.

"What's wrong?"

"I had two very strange people in here about twenty

minutes ago: A man and a woman, both wearing catsuits. They said they were friends of yours. They did tell me their names, but they were very strange. Beige and Dade, I think."

"Daze and Blaze."

"That's it. You do know them, then?"

"I do indeed."

"Why do they dress so strangely?"

"It's just their thing. Did they say what they wanted?"

"No, the woman said it wasn't urgent and that they'd be in touch."

"Okay, thanks. Anything else?"

"I meant to mention earlier that I have an appointment at the opticians this afternoon. I made it before I knew I'd be standing in for Annabel. Is it okay if I nip out for a while?"

"Of course. Take as long as you need."

"This is your chance," Winky said. "Change the locks while she's out."

"Do you have to be quite so melodramatic? Mrs K is perfectly nice."

"My eardrums will never be the same after having to endure that awful double bass."

"It was a violin, and it wasn't all that bad — okay, it was that bad, but it's done now."

"She'd better not be rude to my cousin when he arrives."

"*Cousin?*"

"Jimmy. Don't tell me you've forgotten."

"I haven't forgotten because you didn't tell me."

"Your memory is getting worse, Jill. My cousin Jimmy is

coming up from down south. I asked you if it was okay if he stayed here for a couple of days and you said yes."

"I said no such thing. I'm not running a cat boarding house. You'll have to tell him that he can't come."

"It's too late now; he's already on his way. Jimmy isn't well, and this might be my last chance to see him before—" Winky wiped his eye.

"Two days, you said?"

"Yeah."

"Okay, but no longer than that."

"I promise. Thanks, Jill. You're the best. Haven't I always said so?"

Winky was fast asleep, and I was just wondering what to do about lunch when a little voice made me jump.

"Hi, it's me again."

"Albert?"

The last time I'd seen this spider, he'd given me a tongue lashing.

"I just wanted to apologise, Jill. When we spoke before, I said things I shouldn't have said."

"You were very quick to judge."

"I know, and when I found out Winky had stolen that yarn, I let him know how disappointed I was in him. Anyway, like I said, I just wanted to apologise."

"That's okay."

"I'm forgiven?"

"Of course."

"Thanks, Jill. I hope this means we can be friends."

"Err, yes. Of course."

Chapter 4

After grabbing a sandwich for lunch, I paid my second visit of the week to Rue Pets.

"Back again?" It was Rupert, who had sold me the fish tank the previous day, and he had a stick insect on his head. "I wasn't expecting to see you again so soon."

"I wasn't expecting to be back so soon. I have to ask, why have you got a stick insect on your head?"

"That's Bert."

"Right. Aren't you afraid he might fall off?"

"Not at all. Bert has a great sense of balance, but it is time I put him back." He gently lifted Bert and put him into a glass cage. "Now, what can I do for you today?"

"Wanda says she needs some ornaments."

"*Wanda*?"

Oh bum! Why didn't I think before I opened my mouth?

"Wanda's my daughter. She wants some ornaments to put in the tank that you sold me yesterday."

"Your daughter sounds like a very sensible young lady. Goldfish thrive on stimulation. Did you have anything in particular in mind?"

"Something Wanda can swim around and through."

"Sorry?"

"Did I say *Wanda*? I meant — err — Goldie."

"You called your goldfish Goldie?"

"Yeah. What's wrong with that?"

"Nothing. Nothing at all. It's inspired. We have a wide selection of ornaments that would be suitable. Do you have a budget?"

"No, and I don't want one. I've got more than enough animals with my two dogs, cat and goldfish. I don't want a bird too."

"I said *budget*. Not *budgie*."

"Oh? Right. Err, what would be a reasonable amount to spend?"

"Ten pounds should be sufficient."

"That sounds okay."

"For each ornament."

"Ten pounds each? That's fifty pounds."

"Nothing is too good for Goldie," Rupert said. "Am I right?"

"I'm not sure about that. Where are these ornaments?"

"Over there, on that far wall. Would you like me to help you to choose?"

"No, it's okay. I'll go and pick some."

The ornaments were stacked on top of cupboards that ran the length of one wall. There were hundreds of them, ranging in price from a fiver to twenty-five pounds each. I picked up one in the shape of a barrel with a hole through the centre.

"You don't want that one."

I turned around, expecting to find Rupert standing behind me, but he was at the other side of the shop, attending to another customer. Was I hearing things?

"The hole isn't big enough."

Only then did I realise that the advice was being dispensed by one of the goldfish in the tanks mounted on the wall above the display of ornaments.

"What do you mean?" I said.

"Those things are a disaster. Look, there's one of them in here." He used his fin to point to an identical barrel in his tank. "A couple of guys have damaged their fins swimming through that hole."

"I wouldn't want that. Which ornaments would you recommend?"

"The green castle is very good."

"It's a bit expensive, isn't it?"

"What price health and safety?"

He went on to recommend another four ornaments, which came to a total of seventy-three pounds.

"Good choices," Rupert said, as he charged my card.

"I just hope Wanda—err—I mean Goldie appreciates them."

I'd just dropped the ornaments off at the car and was on my way back to the office, when who should I bump into but Rita, AKA RiRi, who was walking arm in arm with a man. It was a man I recognised. And, judging by the look of recognition on his face, he remembered me too.

Oh bum!

"Hi, Jill. I really enjoyed our night out," Rita said.

"Me too."

"We must do it again soon. This is my hubby, Charles."

"Hi."

"We've met, haven't we?" he said.

"I don't think so."

"Yes, at the hotel in Middle Tweaking, but I thought your name was Vanessa? You're Mirabel's assistant, aren't you?"

Double bum!

"No, darling," Rita said. "Jill is a private investigator. Her office is just around the corner."

"Oh?" He was understandably confused. "I could have sworn—you don't have a twin, do you?"

"No, but I've been told by a few people that they've

seen someone who looks just like me. A doppelganger, I suppose."

"That must be it." He nodded.

Phew! That was a close call.

"But don't you live in Middle Tweaking, Jill?" Rita said.

Triple bum!

"Err, yeah."

"It's strange you haven't seen this other woman. The one who looks like you."

"It is, isn't it? I'll have to keep my eyes peeled for her. Anyway, I must be making tracks. I have a client coming to see me in a few minutes. It was lovely to meet you, Charles."

And off I scurried before they could ask any more awkward questions. At least now I knew what Rita's husband's super-secret job was. He worked for DOPA.

***

Mrs K wasn't back from the opticians, and I could hear Winky laughing in my office. What could be tickling him so much?

I found him on his back on the floor, holding his sides. "Stop it, Jimmy."

On the sofa was a brown and white moggie who was chuckling to himself.

As neither of them seemed to have noticed me, I cleared my throat to get their attention.

"You must be the famous Jill," the moggie said. "I'm very pleased to meet you at last. Winky speaks very highly of you."

"I very much doubt that. You're his cousin, Jimmy, I

assume."

"At your service."

"I was sorry to hear about your poor health."

"My poor—?"

"I told Jill how ill you've been, Jimmy," Winky said.

"Oh yeah, that's right. At death's door, I was." He coughed rather unconvincingly. "I'm on the mend now, though."

"So I see."

"Thank you for allowing me to stay here, Jill."

"Let's get a couple of things straight: First, this is for two days only."

"No problem. I'll be out of here first thing Thursday morning."

"That's three days."

"It's only two nights," Winky said.

"Okay. Thursday and you're gone."

"And the second thing?"

"Any trouble from you. Absolutely anything, and you'll be out on your ear straight away. Understood?"

"Absolutely." He turned to Winky. "You were right. She is a tough cookie."

"Come on, buddy, I'll show you around the neighbourhood." Winky jumped onto the windowsill, Jimmy followed, and the two of them disappeared outside.

***

Emilia Flint was to have been Lorna Boone's maid of honour. She was one of the six people on Randall's Island on the day that the groom-to-be disappeared. She worked in Washbridge, and when I called her, she suggested we meet at a coffee shop near to her offices.

It seemed like a new coffee shop popped up every day, so I wasn't too surprised that I'd not heard of the one Emilia suggested. Rub Together was only a few doors down from Kathy's shop, and yet I hadn't noticed it before. As soon as I walked through the door, I could tell this wasn't going to be my kind of place. The walls were covered in decorative plaques with 'profound' and/or 'inspirational' quotes on them.

There is always something to be grateful for.

Live simply. Laugh Often.

It was enough to make you vomit.

I was a few minutes early, so I grabbed an overpriced coffee (I guess they had to pay for all those plaques somehow) and took a seat on the world's most uncomfortable chair while I waited.

"Jill?"

"Emilia? Thanks for agreeing to meet me at such short notice."

"No problem. I work flexitime, so I can get out pretty much whenever I like. Would you like a top-up?"

"No, I'm fine, thanks."

Judging by the way Emilia chatted to the barista, she was clearly a regular.

"Have you been here before, Jill?" She took the seat opposite me.

"No. This is my first time."

"I love to read all the plaques. They're so inspiring, don't you think?"

"Absolutely, and so very profound."

"I have several in my flat."

"Me too."

"Such a terrible business with Lorna and Harry." Emilia took a sip of her latte. "I feel so sorry for her."

"I know you were to be the maid of honour, but I don't know what your relationship with Lorna is."

"Friends. Best friends, I suppose. We met at prep school, and we've been close ever since."

"What about Harry? Have you known him long?"

"Err, yeah. Didn't Lorna tell you?"

"Tell me what?"

"He and I used to be a thing."

"Oh? No, she never mentioned that, but then she was quite distraught when she came to my office. Wasn't that awkward?"

"Not really. I was only with Harry for a few months. He and Lorna didn't get together until a year after we'd split up."

"Still, it must have been a bit weird?"

"At first, maybe, but it soon became a non-issue. I was already with someone else by the time Lorna and Harry got together. I honestly couldn't have been happier for them."

"Can you tell me everything you remember about the day Harry went missing?"

"We'd already had one rehearsal the day before, but Lorna insisted we have another because she wanted everything to be perfect on the day. To be absolutely honest with you, I never understood why she wanted to get married on that awful island. Not when there are so many other places she could have chosen."

"Do you know why she was so keen?"

"She'd visited the island as a child, and since then had

always dreamed of getting married there. Travelling back and forth on that boat was beyond awful." Emilia hesitated. "Sorry. Listen to me complaining about the boat when poor Harry is missing."

"You were telling me about the rehearsal."

"It didn't go well."

"What happened?"

"It was all Robert's fault. He was playing around with a video on his phone during the ceremony."

"He was the best man, right?"

"Yeah. Harry's best friend from Uni. He's a really funny guy, but Lorna can't stand him."

"Did anything else unusual happen during the rehearsal?"

"Not really. We were all on our way back to the boat when Harry realised that he'd left his phone in the chapel. Apparently, Lorna had made him put it down, so he wouldn't get distracted."

"If it was in the chapel, how did he expect to retrieve it? Wouldn't the chapel have been locked?"

"I don't know. I suppose so."

"You didn't see him ask for the key before he went back?"

"No, but then the first I knew about it was when he walked past me in the opposite direction. I suppose he must have had it."

"Then what?"

"Nothing, really. When he didn't show up, we all went looking for him, but he'd vanished into thin air."

"Were Lorna and Harry having any issues that you're aware of?"

"Not really. The stress of the wedding was getting to

both of them, but no more than other couples in the same situation."

"Do you have any theories as to what happened to Harry?"

"None. It doesn't make any sense whatsoever."

***

Jack was in the kitchen with Oscar.

"Hi, Oscar."

"Hey, Jill."

I turned to Jack. "Where's Madam?"

"She and Wendy are upstairs. They're playing unicorns."

"We're just finalising details for our visit to StampCon this Saturday," Oscar said. "Are you sure we can't persuade you to join us? The village hall is still out of commission, so you wouldn't be missing dance class or basket-weaving."

"Tempting as that is, I thought I might take Florence to the seaside if the weather holds up."

"That's news to me," Jack said.

"I only decided this afternoon."

Oscar stood up. "I'd better get back. It's my turn to make dinner. I'll see you on Saturday morning, Jack."

"Yeah. See you." Jack waited until he heard Oscar leave and then turned to me. "Seaside?"

"Why not?"

"While I'm stuck at some boring stamp convention?"

"It's not my fault you signed up to go there. And besides, you'll have all your stamper friends to talk to."

"You're enjoying this."

"I am, actually."

"You'll be pleased to know that I managed to grab a word with Thomas' mum."

"Who?"

"The boy wizard. Apparently, they live next door to the rectory."

"When did they move in? What do they do for a living?"

"I've no idea. I only spoke to her for a minute. I didn't give her the third degree."

"I need details."

"Then you'll have to get them yourself. She's more likely to open up to a fellow sup than she is to me."

"I suppose you're right. Oh, I nearly forgot."

"What?"

"Hold on." I hurried out to the car, to retrieve the bag of fish tank ornaments. "I bought these for Wanda."

Jack peered into the bag. "They look okay."

"They came highly recommended by one of the resident goldfish, and they cost a small fortune, so they'd better be."

"Your grandmother popped by earlier. She was wearing a brunette wig today."

"What did she want?"

"To bring us a present."

"Really? What is it? Where is it?"

"It's in the lounge. On the wall."

Chapter 5

"Thomas is really funny, Mummy," Florence said over breakfast. "Miss kept writing words on the blackboard, and he made them go."

"What do you mean, *go*?"

"They disappeared. Puff!" She giggled.

"Did he rub the words off with the board eraser when the teacher wasn't looking?"

"No, silly. He magicked them gone. It was funny."

"Doesn't Thomas know that he shouldn't use magic when there are humans around?"

"Don't know." Florence shrugged. "If Thomas can use magic, why can't I?"

"Because we have to keep it our secret. You know that."

"It's not fair."

"You mustn't use magic outside this house, and that's final."

"Not fair!" She got down from the table and stomped upstairs.

"Do you think his mother knows what he's up to?" Jack said.

"I don't know, but if Florence sees him getting away with it, sooner or later, she's going to do the same thing. I think I need to have a word with his mother."

By the time I was ready to leave for the office, Florence had got over her little strop.

"Be a good girl at school today, darling." I gave her a kiss on her head.

"I will, Mummy."

"And no magic. Promise?"

"I promise."

"Good girl."

"Jill!" Jack called from the lounge. "I think you should see this."

I found him staring at the goldfish tank.

"What's wrong?"

"Look at the fish. She's been doing that for the last five minutes."

Wanda was blowing a stream of bubbles, clearly trying to get Jack's attention.

"What is it, Wanda? I have to go to work."

"These ornaments."

"What's wrong with them? They came highly recommended."

"The colours don't work."

"They look fine to me."

"That's as maybe, but then you don't have tetrachromatic colour vision."

"Tetra what?"

"It means that we goldfish can see four primary colours."

"So what? I can see hundreds of colours."

"I don't think you quite understand how the eye works."

"Of course I do."

"Then you'll know that the human eye can only see three primary colours. All the colours you see are a mix of those."

"That's what I meant. Obviously."

"The point is that to my tetrachromatic eye, these colours simply do not go together."

"I don't know what you expect me to do about it."

"Fortunately, the solution is very simple. You need to change that arch. The green doesn't work. Did they have that same arch in another colour?"

"I think so. Blue and red from memory."

"Red. That would work."

"You want me to swap the green arch for a red one?"

"If it isn't too much trouble."

"If I do that, do you promise that you'll be happy?"

"Absolutely. I'm not one to complain unnecessarily."

I stuck my hand in the water and retrieved the green arch. Jack was looking on with a huge grin on his face.

"What?" I challenged him.

"I never said a word." He shrugged.

"You didn't need to. I'm a slave to this goldfish."

"You should read that." He pointed to the plaque on the wall. "It'll cheer you up."

Grandma's present had been one of those stupid inspirational plaques, but this one changed message every few hours.

"*Love your pet and it will come back tenfold.* What hogwash."

"Still, it was nice of your grandmother to buy it for us."

"She didn't do it to be nice. She did it to mess with my head."

***

I decided to call at Rue Pets before going into the office, but when I tried the door it was locked. The sign on the door showed that they would open in ten minutes, so there was little point in going to the office only to have to come back. To pass the time, I imagined all the things I could do to Grandma as payback for the plaque. Maybe I should buy her a subscription to Wigs Monthly.

"Hello again." It was Rupert. "I hope you haven't been waiting long."

"Only a few minutes."

He unlocked the door, disabled the alarm, turned on the lights and beckoned me inside.

"What can I do for you today?"

"I'd like to swap this arch." I took it out of my bag and placed it on the counter.

"Is it damaged?"

"No, it's just that Wanda—err—I mean, Goldie doesn't like the colour."

"How can you possibly know that?"

That was a very good question. "I—err—can just tell by the way she refuses to interact with it. I'd like to exchange it for a red one."

"Hmm." He shook his head.

"What's wrong?"

"We don't actually offer exchanges. Not after an ornament has been used."

"But it was in her tank for less than twenty-four hours."

"Company policy, I'm afraid. I could do part-exchange."

"How does that work?"

"I'll take this one off you and give you a fifty percent discount on the red one."

"Okay, I suppose that will have to do."

***

I took one step into the outer office and almost slipped.

When I looked down, I saw that the floor was covered in splodges of something grey and sticky.

"Sorry about the mess, Jill," Mrs K said. "This is much more difficult than it looks."

On her desk was a small potter's wheel, on top of which was a large lump of clay.

"Pottery?"

"It's another one of my hobbies, although I did only start last weekend. I haven't actually made anything yet."

"And that is—?" I gestured to the lump of clay.

"It's supposed to be a vase."

"Right."

"You don't mind me doing this while things are quiet, do you? You did say it was okay."

"Err, it's fine. I'm just a little concerned that someone might slip and injure themselves."

"You're right. Maybe this wasn't such a good idea. I'll tidy it away and clean the floor."

"Thanks."

And I'll come up with something different to keep me occupied tomorrow. Something a little less messy."

"That would be good."

"I told you that you should have brought Jules back." Winky smirked.

"Mrs K is doing a good job."

"If you say so. I'm sure your clients are going to be very impressed by a pot-throwing violinist."

"Where's your cousin?"

"He's catching up with a few old friends, and then he's taking me out for a slap-up meal tonight."

"It's alright for some."

A few minutes later, Mrs K, who was still wearing a smock covered in clay, popped her head around the door. "The man is here about the blinds, Jill."

"Send him through, would you?"

"Hello, duck." The man was wearing a blue uniform with the words Blinding Blinds on his breast pocket.

Duck?

"Hi."

"First time I've seen someone throwing a pot in an office. And judging by that monstrosity she's making, it could do with throwing." He laughed. "Out of the nearest window."

"I don't think you should be—"

"Relax, duck, I'm only pulling your leg. What's the story with that little guy?"

"That's Winky."

"*Winky?*" He laughed. "I don't reckon he does much winking, does he, duck? Not with just the one eye."

"I assume you are here to see to the blinds."

"You assume right. Connor Conway at your service." He glanced at the windows. "How long have you had these up?"

"I'm not sure. Quite a while."

"I can tell that." He walked over to the window and began to play with the cord. "These are well past their sell-by date."

"Can you mend them or not?"

"*Not* would be my guess but let me take a closer look." He fiddled about with them for a couple of minutes. "Nah. You'd be throwing good money after bad. You need to replace these."

"How much would that cost me?"

"I'm the wrong person to ask. I'm strictly maintenance, but I can get someone from our sales team to drop by if you like."

"Okay. When?"

He took out his phone and tapped away for a couple of minutes. "I can have someone with you tomorrow if you like, duck? How does ten-thirty sound?"

"Ten-thirty will be fine."

***

Mrs K came through from the outer office.

"Jill, what is your policy on receiving visitors without an appointment?"

"That all depends on who the visitor is. If it's the tax inspector, my policy is to pretend I'm not in. If it's someone with a big box of chocolates, my policy is to welcome them with open arms."

"It's a man who says he needs the services of a private investigator. A Mr Song."

"In that case, my policy is to ask you to send him through."

"Right you are."

It wasn't every day that I received a visitor wearing a kilt and a cowboy hat. In fact, I'd go as far as to say that this was a first.

"Orlando Song." He marched into the room and gave me a firm handshake. "Thank you so much for taking the time to see me without an appointment."

"I'd normally be too busy to see you," I lied. "But you caught me at a fortuitous time." I desperately wanted to ask about the kilt/cowboy hat combo, but I wasn't sure how to slip it into the conversation, so I gestured for him to take a seat.

"I'm the proud owner of Wash Sounds. You may have heard of it?"

"Err, I don't think so. Is it a record shop?"

"No. A recording studio."

"I had no idea there was one here in Washbridge."

"It's actually on the outskirts of the city. I opened it almost twenty years ago. I've been in the business for over twenty-five."

"I would never have guessed there was enough demand around here."

"You'd be surprised. Most of our clients are newcomers to the business, just starting out. Some of those who went on to make it big still come back to us."

"That must be rewarding."

"It's the best part of the job."

"What brings you here today? Is it okay to call you Orlando?"

"Of course. I'm pretty much at my wits' end, Jill. The business I've dedicated most of my life to is in danger of being destroyed." He reached into his jacket pocket and brought out an iPod. "May I?"

"Sure."

He pressed the play button, and the most awful sound filled the office. Out of the corner of my eye, I spotted Winky under the sofa with both paws over his ears. It wasn't long before I could stand no more, so I gestured for Orlando to stop the torture.

"This is what I'm up against, Jill."

"Sorry, but I don't understand. What was that?"

"That was Harry Jones and the Defenders."

"They're awful."

"Actually, they're one of the best bands to ever grace my studio."

"I think we'll have to agree to disagree on that."

"I can understand you doubting my word, but it's true. The problem is not with the artist but with the recording."

"I assume there must have been some kind of problem at the studio for it to sound like that?"

"Not at the time it was recorded. We played back the session on the day and it was perfect. One of their best."

"In that case, I'm really confused."

"Someone is sabotaging the recordings. A couple of days after the initial session, I was due to make a few minor edits. Nothing major, just a few tweaks I'd talked through with Harry. When I loaded the session, that's what I heard."

"Obviously, I know next to nothing about the recording process, but isn't this stuff all digital now?"

"It is."

"Don't you have some kind of backup system? Isn't it on the Cloud?" Whatever that means.

"We do, but all the versions are the same. They all sound like that."

"What do you think happened?"

"I can only assume someone managed to hack into the system and corrupted the recording."

"Could it have been an accident? A power surge or something like that?"

"Definitely not. This isn't the only time it's happened. The last five sessions have all gone the same way, leaving me with some very unhappy customers. Word is starting to get out, and unless I can find out what's going on and put a stop to it, this may be the end of Wash Sounds."

"I take it from the fact that you're here, you think this is a deliberate act of sabotage."

"There's no doubt about it."

"Okay. Do you have any suspicions as to who might be behind it?"

"None. It has me totally flummoxed."

"Is it possible that it's an inside job?"

"No."

"You sound very sure about that."

"I am. Ours is a very small team; there's just three including me: My receptionist, Claire, and Roy, the sound engineer. He's been with me for more years than I care to remember."

"What about your competitors?"

"There are two other recording studios in Washbridge."

"There are? I'm amazed."

"Washbridge Studios has been around for almost as long as we have. The owner is a guy called Roger Tunes. I'll be honest, there's no love lost between the two of us, but I can't believe he'd resort to something like this."

"But am I right in thinking that he would have the knowhow?"

"I guess so."

"What about the other studio?"

"They're brand new. I don't know much about them at all."

"Name?"

"Kaleidoscope."

"Who owns it?"

"No idea. Like I said, they've only been open for a few months."

"Okay. You said you're sure your current employees aren't behind this. What about ex-employees? Any disgruntled ones?"

"There is one, but she wouldn't have a clue how to do something like this."

"Tell me about her anyway."

"Her name is Joyce Keys. She worked for me for about eighteen months on reception. Petty cash started to go missing, and it soon became obvious that she was helping herself to it, so I let her go."

"When was that?"

"Just over a year ago."

"And have you heard from her since?"

"Not a word, and like I said, she wouldn't be capable of doing anything like this."

"What about unhappy clients? Did you have any before this all started?"

"No." He hesitated. "Well, there was one, I suppose, but he really had no reason to be unhappy."

"Tell me about him."

"The guy's name is Arnold. He was the lead singer — if you could call him that — of Arnold and the Armchairs."

"Seriously?"

"If you think the name is bad, you should have heard the guy sing. He was the worst. Tone-deaf and flat as a pancake."

"Did you tell him that?"

"No. If someone is prepared to put up their money to make a recording, then I don't stand in their way."

"What happened?"

"When he heard the finished product, he insisted that we had ruined his performance. He couldn't accept that it was his voice that was the problem."

"Did he refuse to pay?"

"He didn't get the chance because all sessions have to be paid for in advance. All he could do was make lots of silly threats."

"What kind of threats?"

"He said he'd leave bad reviews for us everywhere and that he'd write to the music press."

"And did he?"

"Not that I ever saw."

"I'd like to start by paying a visit to your studio. Would that be okay?"

"Sure. You can come by whenever you like."

"I'd prefer to do it undercover, if that's alright with you?"

"If you think it will help."

"I do. What about if I posed as a journalist, doing an article on the recording business?"

"That should work. When do you plan to drop by?"

"I'd like to do it when you're recording a session if possible."

"I have an artist booked in the day after tomorrow."

"That would be perfect."

Chapter 6

Expense and more expense. If I wasn't buying ornaments for the goldfish, I was forking out for new blinds. At this rate, I would have to get a second job.

I needed something to cheer me up, and one of Aunt Lucy's cupcakes was bound to do the trick. I called ahead to make sure she was free and then magicked myself over there.

"Go and sit in the lounge, Jill. I'll bring the tea through."

"And cakes?"

"Of course. I made some cupcakes yesterday."

"Yummy."

There were so many of them that I was spoiled for choice. "Lemon. No. Strawberry. No. Maybe, blackcurrant."

"Shall I choose for you, Jill?"

"I think you'd better."

She handed me the strawberry one. "You can always have another afterwards if you like."

"Thanks. How did you get on at the cork museum?"

"Those girls drive me to distraction. What were they thinking, separating the cards from the corks?"

"I did try to warn them."

"I managed to sort it out, but it took forever. I've told the girls that if they get them mixed up again, I'm not going to bail them out."

"It's the grand opening tomorrow, isn't it? I assume you'll be there?"

"I'm not going anywhere near the place. I know what cork collectors can be like. They'll take great pleasure in finding fault with my collection, and I'd prefer not to be there to hear it."

"You don't have a very high opinion of your fellow corkers."

"What did I tell you about using that word? But you're right. They can be quite vicious when they put their minds to it. I've told the twins that on no account must they allow anyone to touch my precious collection. Hopefully, they'll heed my words this time."

"Let's hope so. By the way, you never told me how you got on at the Candlefield Corks competition."

"It was very disappointing. Blue Sue came fourth."

"Fourth isn't bad."

"I was hoping for at least a second, but then I didn't allow for Norah Mellow."

"Who's she?"

"One of the judges. The woman has always had it in for me, ever since my Olive Green beat her Diamond Arrow into second place a couple of years ago."

"Olive Green and Diamond Arrow? I take it those are the names of corks?"

"That's right."

"So this Norah Mellow woman—she enters the competitions too?"

"Not since she became a judge."

"How come you aren't a judge?"

"I've been asked a couple of times, but I declined. I prefer the excitement of the competition."

We were interrupted by the sound of paws on the stairs. They were much slower than usual, and the reason for that soon became obvious. When Barry pushed the door open and made his entrance, balanced precariously on his back was Rhymes.

"Hello, you two," I managed through a mouthful of cupcake.

"Hi, Jill." Barry's tail wagged a greeting. "Rhymes asked me to bring him downstairs. I was very careful, so I didn't drop him."

"Good boy. You're a good friend to him, Barry."

"I wanted to make sure we're still on for Friday," Rhymes said.

"Oh yes." Aunt Lucy grinned. "I'd forgotten that you were taking Rhymes to his recital."

"I hadn't." Although, goodness knows I'd tried. "What time do you have to be there?"

"It starts at seven o'clock. Will we be able to get in some sightseeing first, Jill?"

"I'm afraid not."

"Aww."

"I'm sorry, Rhymes, but I'm working on a big case, so there won't be time for that."

"Are we going on the train?"

"There won't be time for that either. I shall have to magic us there."

"*Magic*?" Rhymes looked horrified. "I've never been magicked anywhere. Will it hurt?"

"It's okay," Barry reassured him. "I've been magicked, and it doesn't hurt one little bit."

Rhymes looked unconvinced.

***

I was back at Wesmere Lake because I'd arranged to meet Warren Hole. He both owned the chapel, and conducted the wedding ceremonies. I didn't think he would have agreed to talk to me if I'd told him the real reason for my interest in seeing the chapel, so I'd said that I was thinking of getting married there.

Am I a genius or what?

Warren Hole was a short man with a dubious taste in footwear: the sandals simply didn't work with the grey suit. I was a little concerned that Matty might blow my cover, but on the short trip over to the island, he didn't mention our conversation of the previous day.

Once Matty had dropped us on the island, Warren led the way to the chapel.

"When were you planning to get married, Tuppence?"

I'd always liked the name Tuppence, ever since I'd worked on a case for Tuppence Farthing, the owner of a thimble shop in Candlefield. This was my opportunity to be Tuppence for the day.

"Next summer, hopefully."

"We're completely booked up until the end of July next year, so it would have to be August onwards."

"That should work."

"What's your fiancé's name?"

"Jack."

Warren took the keys from his pocket, pushed open the door, and gestured for me to go inside.

"Stunning, isn't it?"

"Err, yeah. It's fantastic, but it's a little smaller than I expected."

"Which makes for a more intimate atmosphere."

"I guess."

"How many guests will—?" He stopped midsentence, and for a moment I thought he'd taken ill. "You're wearing a wedding ring?"

Oh bum! I'd totally forgotten about that.

"This was my mother's wedding ring. She died several years ago."

"I'm sorry to hear that. You wear it on your ring finger?"

"Err, yes. Silly really. I'll have to swap it when I marry." It was time to change the subject. "What's through there?" I pointed to the door behind the altar.

"Nothing. It's just storage."

"Could I see?"

"I don't see why not." He took out his keys and unlocked the door to reveal a room containing old furniture and several wooden crates. "Is there any reason you wanted to see in here?"

"I'm very safety conscious. I just wondered if there was another exit."

"No. Just the main doors."

"How do guests get across the lake on the day of the wedding?"

"We use a launch, which can carry a couple of dozen people at a time."

"I think I've seen everything I need to. Thank you for taking the time to show me around."

"My pleasure. Do you want to make a provisional booking today?"

"I'll need to speak to my fiancé first, but he usually goes along with what I suggest."

"Excellent. Can I ask how you heard about the chapel?"

"Actually, I saw an article in the paper about the man who disappeared on the eve of his wedding."

"Oh." Warren's face fell.

"Such a strange story."

"Quite."

"I assume you were there that day?"

"Yes, it was the final rehearsal."

"What do you think happened to him?"

"I have no idea." Warren made a show of checking his watch. "I really must get back now because I have a meeting in fifteen minutes."

"Of course." We made our way back to the mooring where Matty was waiting to take us across the lake.

Warren had been quite talkative on our trip to the chapel, but he hardly said a word on the way back.

***

Thankfully, by the time I returned to the office, Mrs K had cleared away the potter's wheel and cleaned up the floor.

"Crosswords these days are way too easy, don't you find, Jill?" She gestured to the newspaper on her desk.

"I never do them."

"You really should. When you get to our age, it's important to keep the grey matter active."

Our age?

"The two women who run our village store are always doing crosswords. In fact, I believe they're in some kind of crossword club."

"You should ask them to take you with them."

"Maybe." Not a chance. "Have there been any calls while I was out?"

"There was one, but I think it may be another wrong number. Some crazy woman was asking about anti-witch crystals. There are some very strange people around, don't you find, Jill?"

Never had a truer word been spoken.

Jimmy was back.

"Hello again, Jill. You're looking even more beautiful today." He flashed me a toothy smile.

"Whatever it is you're after, the answer is no."

He turned to Winky. "She's very mistrustful, isn't she?"

"I have good reason to be. I've lived with Winky for a long time now."

"I resent that remark," Winky said.

"I hear you're treating Winky to dinner, Jimmy."

"You're welcome to join us. Winky tells me you make a really hot kitty."

"I'd rather poke myself in the eye with a sharp stick."

"I can see you're on the fence about it, so if you change your mind, the offer still stands."

"Don't hold your breath."

Mrs K came rushing into my office and closed the door behind her. "She's here."

"Who's here?"

"That crazy woman."

"You're going to have to elaborate. I get a lot of visitors who could easily fall into that particular category."

"It's the woman who called about the anti-witch crystals. Do you think we should call the police?"

"That won't be necessary. I'll have a quick word with her."

"Are you sure, Jill? She sounds unhinged to me. She seems to think she's an orange."

"I'll be fine. Send her through, would you?"

"I'm sorry to turn up without an appointment, but this is a matter of some urgency."

"That's okay. Why don't you take a seat, Mrs Orange?"

"Thank you. And you must call me Rosemary."

"Okay, Rosemary, what's the nature of this emergency?"

"I don't know if you recall, but some years ago you were kind enough to provide me with—" She glanced around to check that no one was listening. "With some anti-witch crystals."

"Let me think." I scratched my chin for effect. "Yes, it's all coming back to me. Did they do the trick?"

"They most certainly did. In fact, they have been nothing short of miraculous. We've had no trouble from that neighbour of ours since I started using them."

"Excellent."

"The problem is that I've almost run out, and I'm terrified of what she might do once I don't have that protection. I'm hoping you could let me have some more."

"Unfortunately, I no longer have any of the crystals I gave you before."

"Oh no. This is terrible news."

"However—"

"Yes?"

"I do have some new ones which will have the same effect. In fact, if anything, they're even stronger."

"Really?" Her face lit up. "Do you have them with you?"

"As luck would have it, I do." I opened my drawer, took out a white paper bag, and handed it to her. "These are much stronger than the last ones. A single one of these will keep witches at bay for a whole year."

"That's fantastic. Thank you so much. How much do I owe you?"

"Nothing. They're on the house."

"I wouldn't hear of it." She took out her purse, pulled out three twenty-pound notes, and dropped them onto my desk.

"Really, Rosemary, I can't accept this much."

"I insist." She stood up. "These are worth their weight in gold. Thanks again." And with that, she made her exit.

"And you accuse *me* of being a scam artist," Winky said.

"I am not a *scam artist*," I protested. "I told her I didn't want anything for them."

"You can give me the money if that will ease your conscience."

"No chance."

"What was that you gave her, anyway?"

"Boiled sweets."

"Genius." Jimmy nodded his approval.

***

With my unexpected windfall, I decided to treat myself to coffee and cake at Coffee Animal.

What do you mean it wasn't a windfall, but ill-gotten gains? I did my very best to refuse payment. What more could I have done? And more to the point, why am I justifying myself to you? Sheesh — give a woman a break.

Dot's beauty spot was on her left cheek today, and the time had come to ask her about it.

"Dot, I'm curious. How come your beauty spot changes position?"

"What do you mean?"

"Some days it's on your left cheek. Others it's on the right one. And, at least once, there was one on both cheeks. And one day, it disappeared altogether."

"You say some weird stuff, Jill." She laughed.

"I'm serious. How do you do it?"

"I've no idea what you mean. It's always right here, in the same place." She touched her left cheek.

"Are you sure?"

"I think I would know."

"Okay. Sorry, it's just that—err—never mind. I'll have my usual, please."

Was I losing my mind? Had I really imagined that her beauty spot changed places? Maybe I was overworking.

"There you go, Jill." She handed me my drink and blueberry muffin.

"Thanks, and sorry about the beauty spot thing."

"That's okay. Just a minute, you need your animal."

"What is it today?"

"You probably won't have heard of it." She placed a glass cage on the counter.

"An axolotl."

"I'm impressed. You're the first person to recognise it. Most people have never heard of them."

"I'm something of an expert when it comes to the axolotl."

I found a quiet spot and placed the cage on the table.

"Is that right?" The little voice came from inside the cage.

"Sorry?"

"Are you really an expert on us?"

"Not really. I once worked on a case where one of the people I interviewed had a thing about axolotls."

"Whoever it was clearly had good taste. We're very much under-represented when it comes to household pets. Why anyone would choose a cat or a dog over us is beyond me. I'm Axel, by the way."

"Jill. Nice to meet you."

"Who are you talking to, Jill?" Mad had appeared at my table.

"Axel the axolotl. He was bemoaning the fact that cats and dogs are more popular than the axolotl."

"He has a point. Do you mind if I join you?"

"Of course not. Your lips don't seem quite so—err—"

"Enormous? They're shrinking slowly, thank goodness. I've warned Mum to keep Nails away from me because I won't be responsible for my actions if I get my hands on him."

"Your mum tried to persuade me to have my lips done. She even offered me a discount, but I didn't fancy it."

"Wise decision. By the way, Lizzie started her course yesterday."

"I told you. I don't want to know anything about that. If Kathy finds out about it, I don't want my fingerprints anywhere near it."

"Fair enough. I will just say she's a natural."

"Mad!"

"Sorry, I won't say another word. Do you remember I told you my boss had warned me that I was going to be busy soon?"

"Yeah."

"He wasn't kidding." She glanced around to check no one was in earshot. "Apparently, the ghouls are plotting something big."

"*Ghouls*? What are they exactly?"

"Loathsome creatures that like to feed on human flesh."

"Like a zombie?"

"Not really. Zombies are the undead. Ghouls are just—err—horrible things."

"I don't understand why you're involved. They're not ghosts, are they?"

"They're certainly not. I said exactly the same thing to my boss. I don't see why we have to deal with them. The trouble is that no one wants to take ownership of the problem. The rogue retrievers insist they aren't sups, and they've washed their hands of them. Organisations like Z-Watch won't get involved because, as they have rightly pointed out, they aren't zombies. That just leaves us. I honestly think the only reason we get lumbered with them is because ghosts and ghouls both start with G-H."

"You should ask for more pay."

"Don't worry. I've already told the boss I want double time for all the hours I put in on this."

"What exactly are the ghouls planning?"

"I wish I knew."

"Is there anything I can do to help?"

"Not unless you can track them down. I've had no luck so far."

***

"Mummy!" Florence threw herself at me as soon as I walked through the door. "Daddy said I can have a kite."

"Did he?"

Jack came out of the kitchen. "Wendy has got one, so I said you'd get her one this weekend."

"Me?"

"I'll be at StampCon, remember."

"Can I have one, Mummy?"

"I suppose so."

"Yay! I bet mine will be better than Wendy's. I want a big red one."

"We'll have to see what they have in the shop. Have you played ball with Buddy yet today?"

"He doesn't like to play ball."

"Maybe not, but he needs the exercise. Go and play with him before we have dinner."

"Aww. I'm too tired."

"Go and play with him or there'll be no kite."

"Not fair." She pulled that sour face of hers, as she went in search of Buddy.

"Did you go and see Thomas' mother?" Jack said.

"I didn't get the chance. I'll do it in the morning.

Chapter 7

The next morning, Florence was running around the garden, dragging behind her what appeared to be a sheet of A4 paper with a length of string attached to it.

"She was driving me mad," Jack said, by way of explanation. "So, I made her a temporary kite to keep her going until you take her to buy one on Saturday."

"Is it supposed to keep falling to the ground like a stone?"

"I never claimed to be an expert in aerodynamics."

"Do we have any jam roly-poly?"

"That's a strange question. What made you think of that?"

"I had a dream that I was perched on a step ladder, eating a giant roly-poly pudding, and I tripped and fell into the bowl of custard."

"You have the weirdest dreams. I suppose I could try the village store later, but I wouldn't get your hopes up. Incidentally, I've been meaning to ask. Where have you put the compass stone?"

"I'm not telling you."

"Why not?"

"I'm not going to tell anyone. The only thing I will say is that this time it's somewhere that no one will ever find it."

Before going into the office, I wanted to visit the mother of the young boy who had joined Lizzie's class. She was probably oblivious to the fact that her little boy, Thomas, was using magic in the classroom. Although I'd been to the rectory before, I hadn't really taken much notice of the small cottage next door. The iron gate creaked open. A mosaic path led the way to the front door, and it was only when I was halfway along it that I realised its pattern depicted a night sky full of stars. At its centre was a full moon partially hidden by a silhouette. The silhouette was unmistakeably in the shape of a witch on a broomstick. I was still trying to come to terms with that when I spotted the large planters, which were clearly cauldrons, at either side of the door. That's when I spotted the plaque on the wall next to the door – the house was called The Coven.

Was this woman insane?

I rapped on the door using the broom-shaped door knocker.

I half expected the door to be answered by someone wearing a traditional witch's hat and gown, but the young woman who stood in front of me was wearing skinny jeans, and an off-the-shoulder top. Her hair, which was an unnatural yellow colour, was in a ponytail.

"Yeah?" She said while blowing a gum bubble.

"Hi. Are you Thomas' mum?"

"What's the little toerag done now?"

"He hasn't done anything – err, well that's not entirely true. Do you think we could go inside to talk?"

"Who are you, anyway?"

"My name is Jill Maxwell. I live at the old watermill, just across the village. My daughter, Florence, is in your son's class."

"You'd better come in, then. I can't offer you a hot drink because the leccie is off. You can have a beer if you want one, though?"

"Err, no thanks. Has there been a power cut?"

"Nah, I just need some change to feed the meter. I don't suppose you could lend me some pound coins, could you?"

I took out my purse. "I only have these two."

"Ta, that'll do." She snatched them from me. "You're a love. I told Ricky to leave me some this morning, but he never did."

"*Ricky?*"

"My hubby. Useless lump."

"I'm sorry, but I don't know your name?"

"Cindymindy."

"Cindy Mindy?"

"It's just one name. My Mum couldn't make up her mind whether to call me Cindy or Mindy, so she joined the two together. Are you sure you don't want a beer?"

"I'm sure."

"I didn't realise there was another witch living in the village. I've seen the werewolves with the little girl, Wanda."

"Wendy."

"Sorry?"

"The little girl's name is Wendy."

"Right. I've never been very good with names, Janet."

"It's Jill."

"Course it is. Sorry."

"I couldn't help but notice your mosaic path."

"Nice innit? It ought to be. Cost a small fortune."

"I was a little surprised you included the witch silhouette."

"That's the best part of it."

"And you're using cauldrons for planters."

"I got'em cheap on eBay."

"Right. And your cottage is called The Coven."

"Ricky wanted to call it Dunroaming, but I wasn't

having any of that nonsense. Just wait until I tell him that there's another wizard in the village, he'll be made up."

"There isn't."

"Oh? Are you a single mum?"

"No. Jack, that's my husband, is a human."

"Blimey, that must be a bit weird. How do you keep it from him?"

"It's not easy."

"I couldn't do it, but then I never could keep a secret. Anyway, what was it you came to see me about?"

"I thought you'd want to know that Thomas has been using magic in the classroom."

"Says who?"

"Florence."

"Who's she?"

"My daughter. I did say."

"Sorry, told you I was hopeless with names. What did Thomas do?"

"Apparently he kept wiping the blackboard clean after the teacher had written on it."

She laughed. "The little monkey."

"I'm worried that if he continues to use magic in class Florence might do the same."

"Your daughter is a sup like you, then, is she?"

"Yeah, and I've always taught her not to use magic when humans are around."

"Quite right too."

"So, you'll have a word with him?"

"Who?"

"Thomas. About not using magic in the classroom."

"Of course. I don't want those rogue retrievers and their stupid catsuits paying me a visit."

"Exactly."

"I could make you a cup of tea now that I've got money for the meter."

"Thanks, but I really should get going."

"Okay. Nice to meet you, Janet."

***

"Where did you get that?" I screamed.

Winky and Jimmy were playing hockey across the office floor, and they were using the compass stone as the puck.

"Quiet!" Winky said. "There's a fiver riding on the result.

"I don't care." I dropped to my knees and grabbed the 'puck'.

"Hey!" Jimmy yelled. "That was a certain goal."

"Tough." I checked the stone for damage. Fortunately, it looked intact. "I asked where you got it from?"

"The 'not-so-secret' drawer in your desk."

"You had no right to go in there."

"Why are you so worked up about some old stone?"

"This isn't any old stone. This is the north compass stone. It's invaluable."

"How are we supposed to finish our match without a puck?"

"You aren't. You shouldn't be playing games in my office. A new client might turn up at any moment."

"Look up there!" Winky pointed to the open window.

"I don't see anything."

"You missed it. A group of flying pigs just went by."

"Haha. You're hilarious. Not!"

So much for securing the compass stone. I needed to put

it somewhere that no one would ever find it, but where?

Without warning, Winky and Jimmy both shot underneath the sofa.

"I've already told you that I can look after that stone for you." Grandma had appeared behind me. No wonder the cats had been so spooked.

"Thanks, but no." I was doing my best not to stare at her blonde wig. "I'm perfectly capable of keeping the stone safe."

"You've certainly done a cracking job so far."

"I don't need your help."

"Please yourself, but if it's stolen, don't come crying to me."

"I won't. Anyway, I have to ask, what's going on with all the wigs? And don't try to tell me that it's your hair."

"I've bought a fifty per cent share in a business called WFW."

"WFW? What's that?"

"Wigs For Witches, obviously."

"Where's that based?"

"In Candlefield, but I plan on opening a branch in Washbridge."

"I thought you'd retired. Isn't that why you sold all your other businesses?"

"I could never retire. I've still got a few centuries left in me. I just fancied a change. That's why I bought the hotel, and it's why I'm moving into wigs."

"You can't open a shop called Wigs For Witches in the human world."

"Of course not. This branch will be known as WiFY. *Wigs* For You."

"Will you be selling them to sups and humans?"

"Of course, and I have just the one for you."

"I don't need a wig."

"Everyone should have a wig in their life. I'll expect to see you at the grand opening next Wednesday."

"Where is WiFY?"

"Next door to the new coin shop that opened recently. Be sure to tell all your friends. So, do you want me to take that stone for safekeeping or not? This is your last chance."

"No. It's fine."

"As you wish." She disappeared.

Winky and Jimmy crept slowly out from under the sofa.

"That's one scary lady," Jimmy said.

"With a bad taste in wigs." Winky laughed, but not for long because a tiny wig appeared on top of his head. "Hey, get this thing off me."

Mrs K chose that moment to come through the door. "I thought I heard you talking to someone, Jill?"

"Err, just to the cats."

"Right." She glanced at Winky. "Is that a wig on his head?"

Before I could respond, someone shouted hello from the outer office. While Mrs K went to see who was there, I told the two cats to get under the sofa and stay out of sight.

"What about this thing?" Winky pulled at the wig, but it wouldn't budge.

"It's your own fault for annoying my grandmother."

"I can't walk around with this thing on my head."

"Get under the sofa, and I'll ask Grandma to reverse the spell later."

"You better had."

"It's the salesman from the blinds company," Mrs K said.

"Right. Send him through, would you?"

The salesman was wearing a silver-grey double-breasted suit. It was the same man who'd come to repair the blinds the day before.

"Good morning, duck. Nice to make your acquaintance."

"You were here yesterday."

"That wasn't me, duck. That was Connor Conway, the maintenance guy. I'm Billy Bestway."

"You look exactly the same."

"A few people have remarked on that, but I don't see it myself." He glanced around. "Where's that one-eyed cat of yours?"

"How do you know I have a cat?"

"Connor must have mentioned it." He crouched down. "There he is, and he has a little friend with him. What's that on his head?"

"That? Err, that's a bandage."

"It looks like a wig."

"Well, it isn't. He cut his head."

"It must have been a big cut."

"Can we get on? I am rather busy."

"Of course, duck. I just need to take some measurements."

***

In a moment of weakness, I'd agreed to attend the grand opening of the cork museum, and it was too late to back out now. Still, maybe it would take my mind off the cost of the replacement blinds. Billy, Connor or whatever his name was, had assured me I wouldn't find better for the price, and as I couldn't face the prospect of having to shop around, I'd signed the order. At least I wouldn't have to wait long for them to be fitted; he'd promised they'd be installed next Monday.

I don't believe it!

The queue outside Cuppy C stretched all the way back up the street. Surely all of these people weren't here for the cork museum, were they?

"Excuse me," I said to the witch and the wizard who were at the back of the queue. "Is this the queue for the cork museum?"

"Yes, it is," the witch snapped. "I told him we should have come earlier."

"I've said I'm sorry, Chrissy." He shrugged. "How was I supposed to know it would be so popular?"

I had no intention of waiting in the queue, so I made my way to the front.

"Hey, you!" an angry witch yelled at me. "There's a queue here, in case you hadn't noticed."

"I'm staff."

"A likely story. Get to the back of the queue."

Ignoring the growing discontent, I knocked on the window, and when I eventually managed to catch Pearl's eye, she came over and unlocked the door.

"Jill, we weren't sure if you'd come."

"Let me in before this lot lynch me, would you? I wasn't expecting this kind of turnout."

"We told you, didn't we?" Amber had come over to join us. "Those corkers are crazy for it. We're going to make a killing today."

The queue was growing longer by the minute. "I don't see any of your regulars out there."

"That's the whole point. We're trying to attract new customers," Pearl said. "It's a good job we trebled our normal cake order today."

A wizard rapped on the window and pointed to his watch.

"It's time," Amber said. "I'll open the door and you two get behind the counter."

"Me?" It was ages since I'd worked behind there. "I'm not sure I can remember what to do."

"It's like riding a bike. You'll be fine," Pearl assured me. "Come on, we're going to need all the help we can get to serve this lot."

"Okay, then."

Amber waited until we were behind the counter, and then she began the countdown. "Three, two, one. The cork museum is now officially open." It was a good job she stepped aside, otherwise she'd have been trampled underfoot as the corkers pushed inside.

I was looking at the coffee machine, desperately trying to remember how to work it, when I heard the twins groan. I turned around to see Amber and Pearl standing there, but there were no customers at the counter or seated in the shop.

"Where is everyone?" I said.

"They all went charging upstairs," Amber sighed. "Not one of them ordered anything."

"They're probably all eager to see the corks."

"You're right," Pearl said. "Once they've had a good look around, they'll be down for refreshments."

"Defo!" Amber seemed reenergised.

"I'm sorry, girls, but I can't hang around until then."

"Aren't you going to take a look upstairs, Jill?"

"I think I'll give it a miss. I've already seen the exhibits, and it'll be rammed up there."

I was just about to leave when Grandma walked through the door and glanced around at the empty tables. "Looks like this has been a roaring success."

"Everyone is upstairs looking at the corks," Amber said.

"Yeah, there's loads of them," Pearl added for emphasis.

"And I assume you've charged them all an entrance fee?" She turned to me. "Where are you rushing off to?"

"I have work to do."

"That must be a novel experience for you."

"Before you disappear, I need you to reverse the wig spell."

"I have no idea what you're talking about."

"Don't play the innocent. I'm talking about the wig you stuck on Winky's head."

"That cat needed teaching a lesson."

"Okay, you've made your point. Now, will you reverse it?"

"No, but it will wear off at midnight."

"Do you promise?"

"Yes, I promise. You can put it down to me getting soft in my old age."

Chapter 8

Robert Tonking, who was to have been the best man at the wedding of Lorna and Harry, was the assistant manager at Wash Bowl, one of Jack's favourite haunts. It was some time since I'd visited that particular establishment, and I was pleasantly surprised by the facelift it had received.

I always felt sorry for the unlucky individual who got stuck on the shoe-exchange desk. Having to spend all day in close proximity to so many stinky shoes made my job look like a breeze. The guy who'd drawn the short straw today was a young man who looked eighteen going on sixty.

"Excuse me," I said.

"What size?"

"Sorry?"

"What size shoes do you want?"

"I don't want any shoes."

"You can't bowl in your own shoes."

"I'm not here to bowl."

"Take a wrong turn, did you?"

Although I sympathised with his malodorous working conditions, it didn't excuse such smartassery. "I'm here to speak to Robert."

"I've got an uncle called Robert, but we call him Uncle Bob."

"Yes, yes, that's all very interesting, I'm sure. I'm here to speak to Robert, the assistant manager."

"That's him." He pointed. "He's working on lane twelve."

"Thanks."

"Hold on. You can't go down there in your own shoes."

"I'm not going to be bowling."

"It doesn't matter. You can't go beyond those steps unless you're wearing bowling shoes."

"Fine. Give me some shoes. Size six."

He leaned over the counter. "Are you sure about that? Your feet look much bigger."

"Just give me the shoes. And can you pick a pair that doesn't smell, please?"

"Sure. Would you like a pair that has been treated with our odour-killing floral spray?"

"Yes, please."

"Unlucky. There's no such thing."

I so wanted to slap that stupid grin off his face.

"Robert?"

The young man looked up. "That's me. Are you Jill?"

"Yeah."

"Sorry, I thought I'd have finished this by now. Do you mind if I carry on working while we talk?"

"That's fine."

"How's Lorna holding up?"

"Haven't you spoken to her?"

"She won't speak to me or return my messages. I'm pretty sure she blames me for what happened. I assume you've heard all about it?"

"I'd prefer to hear your version of events, starting with your relationship with Harry."

"He and I met at university where we kind of hit it off straight away. Lorna never seemed to take to me, and she wasn't very pleased when Harry asked me to be his best man. I know for a fact she tried to get him to change his mind, but credit to Harry, he stuck to his guns. On the day he went missing, I messed up big time. We'd already had one rehearsal, which went fine, but then Lorna insisted on having another. I wasn't best pleased because I had to take time off work. Anyway, while the two of them were running through their vows and stuff, I sneaked a look at my phone. Someone from work had sent me an email, which I clicked on without thinking. The next thing I knew, a video of a cat started playing. I stopped it as quickly as I could, but it was too late. Lorna went ballistic at me and Harry. Things kind of went downhill from there."

"What do you remember about what happened after the rehearsal was over?"

"Needless to say, neither Lorna nor Harry were talking to me by then, so I hung back as we walked to the boat. We'd almost reached the moorings when Harry came darting past me on his way back to the chapel."

"To get his phone?"

"I didn't know that at the time, but yeah, apparently. Anyway, we all got in the boat and waited. And waited. All the time, Lorna was staring daggers at me. Anyway, eventually, someone suggested we'd better go and see what Harry was doing, but there was no sign of him, and his phone was still in the chapel."

"How do you know that?"

"We went inside and found it there."

"Was the chapel locked?"

"I'm not sure."

"Try to remember. It's important."

"Err—it couldn't have been because Lorna was the first one to reach the door, and she just pushed it open. It was

Lorna who found Harry's phone where he'd left it."

"Right. How had Harry and Lorna been getting along in the days leading up to the second rehearsal?"

"I spoke to Harry a couple of times on the phone, and he sounded totally stressed out, but I guess that's par for the course, isn't it?"

"Did he ever say anything to suggest he might be getting cold feet? That he might be thinking of calling it off?"

"No. I told him he should do a runner, but I was only joking. I didn't think he actually would."

"And is that what you think happened? That he bailed?"

"I hope so because the alternative is too horrible to think about."

***

"Be careful, Jill, please." Mrs K appeared to be building something from matchsticks. "Don't cause a draught or you might knock it over."

"What's that you're making? A boat?"

"It's an aeroplane."

"Right. Is this another one of your hobbies?"

"Yes. I've been building models from matchsticks for years. I've made dozens of them over that time, and although I say so myself, I'm something of an expert." She took out her phone. "Look, these are some of my favourites."

"Very impressive. A spaceship?"

"It's the Eiffel Tower."

"Oh yes. I see it now. I like that lighthouse."

"That's Big Ben."

"Right. Of course. Have there been any calls for me?"

"Someone wanted to know if we sold ball bearings. I told him that we were out of stock."

On first glance, my office appeared to be cat-free, but then I heard Winky grumbling under the sofa.

"Are you alright under there?"

"No, I'm not." He scrambled out. "How can I possibly be alright with this thing stuck to my head?"

"I think it suits you." I laughed.

"I'm glad you find it so funny."

"Where's Jimmy?"

"I kicked him out."

"How come?"

"He was making fun of the wig, so I told him to sling his hook. Can't you get this stupid thing off my head?"

"I've had a word with Grandma, and she promised it will disappear on the stroke of midnight."

"That's hours away."

"I'm sorry, but it's the best I can do. Hopefully, this will teach you a valuable lesson. Don't mess with my grandmother."

"Pah!" He slunk back under the sofa.

Poor old Winky. Snigger.

My phone rang.

"Jill, it's Ursula." She sounded dreadful. "I understand from Ronald that you were trying to get hold of me earlier in the week."

"I was, yes. Are you okay? You don't sound well."

"I'm fine. What can I do for you?"

"I'd rather talk face to face if that's possible. Are you free for a few minutes now by any chance?"

"Err, yes, I suppose so. Pop over and I'll have someone make us a nice cup of tea."

Ursula certainly hadn't sounded her usual bubbly self, and I was worried that I might have chosen a bad time, but it was important that I collect the four compass stones as soon as possible for Florence's sake.

Ronald met me at the doors to the palace, and he too wasn't his usual jovial self. In fact, he was in tears.

"Ronald? Are you okay?"

"I'm fine."

"You don't look it. Why are you crying?

"I'm not." He managed a weak smile.

"Yes, you are. What's wrong, Ronald?"

"It's U-fever season."

"*U-fever*?"

"It's similar to hay fever in the human world, and it's particularly bad this year. Follow me, please. The queen is expecting you."

It was the same story in the throne room: The queen and her three ladies-in-waiting were all dabbing their puffy red eyes.

"I apologise for my appearance, Jill. I hate this time of year." Ursula gestured to the table. "Let's talk over there."

"Ronald tells me you're suffering from U-fever."

"The whole city is down with it. If it carries on like this for much longer, there'll be a city-wide shortage of tissues."

Ronald returned a few minutes later with tea and a tray of custard creams.

"Thank you. You're spoiling me."

"I'm getting a taste for these biscuits myself. Now tell me, what brings you here today?"

"I understand that you're the guardian of the East compass stone."

She almost spat out her biscuit. "Did you just say *compass stone*?"

"Yeah. Have I got it wrong? Aren't you the guardian?"

"Yes, I am. It's just that I never expected anyone ever to say those words to me. My family have been guardians for generations, but as far as I'm aware, no one has ever asked us to produce the clue. May I ask why you're looking for it, Jill?"

"I'd rather not go into the details right now, but I can tell you that Florence's safety depends on me finding all four of them."

"That isn't going to be easy."

"I know, but I do already have the North stone."

"Wait here, please." She wiped her eyes again. "I'll go and get the clue for you."

Ursula returned a couple of minutes later with a small golden chest, which she placed on the table. Clearly, she took her role as guardian rather more seriously than Adam Rodenia, my least favourite bingo caller. Ursula opened the chest, and took out a golden envelope, which she passed to me.

"Thank you. Is it okay if I open it?"

"Of course. I'm keen to learn what it says after all this time."

I tore open the envelope, pulled out the slip of paper, and read the clue out loud, "This bird is too valuable to kill."

Ursula shrugged. "Any ideas what that means?"

"None. Whoever came up with these clues was obviously a sadist."

Ursula sneezed three times. "I'm really sorry, Jill, but I need to have a lie down if you don't mind. All this sneezing and blowing my nose has worn me out."

"Of course. I appreciate you sparing the time to see me."

"No problem. Good luck with finding the stones."

***

Back at the office, Winky was still under the sofa.

"That wig really suits you." I chuckled. "Do you want me to ask Grandma to leave it there?"

"No, I don't. I just hope no one that I know sees me."

The words were no sooner out of his mouth than who should appear at the open window than his ex, Mimi.

"Where is he?" she demanded.

Winky was desperately waving his paws around and shaking his head at me.

"Who?" I said, all innocent-like.

"You know who. Where's Winky?"

"He—err—he's gone away for a few days. Can I give him a message?"

"You can tell him I don't appreciate him bad-mouthing me on feline media."

"Are you sure it was him? That doesn't sound like something he'd do." It so did.

"Of course I'm sure. I know he's annoyed because I dropped out of the pirate fancy-dress competition, but that's no excuse for—"

And that's when it happened: Winky sneezed.

"Is that him?" Mimi glared at me.

"Is what him?"

"Where are you, Winky? Come out here and face me like a tom."

Winky didn't move a muscle.

"He's not here," I said to no avail.

Mimi jumped down from the window, and before I could object, she shot across the room.

"There you are! Come out here, you coward."

"I'd rather not if it's all the same to you."

"Come out here before I drag—what's that thing on your head?"

"Err—it's nothing."

"You're wearing a wig."

"No, I'm not. This is a—err—"

Mimi produced her phone and proceeded to snap photos of him. "This is priceless."

"Please, Mimi." Winky came out from under the sofa. "You can't post those online. I'll never live it down."

"You've got that right." She grinned. "See ya, lover." And with that, she headed back out of the window.

"Just kill me now." Winky sank to the floor and put his paws over his eyes.

Why do staplers hate me? What? It's a serious question. Every stapler I've ever owned has caused me grief. If they're not getting jammed every five minutes, they refuse to staple anything thicker than a couple of sheets of paper. I should invent a new type of stapler. One that, and here's a novel idea, actually works. I'd be a millionaire. How difficult could it be?

My stapler ruminations were interrupted by a phone

call from a number I didn't recognise.

"Jill Maxwell."

"Ah, Mrs Maxwell, I'm very pleased to have caught you. My name is Ponsonby Pond-Senby."

"Ponsonby Ponsonby?"

"No, you misheard. It's Ponsonby Pond." He hesitated. "Senby. The Pond and Senby are hyphenated."

"I see. What can I do for you Mr Pond-Senby?"

"Please call me Ponsonby."

"Okay. How can I help you, Ponsonby?"

"I'm sure you'll have heard of WWW."

"Is that something to do with wrestling?"

"No."

"Pandas?"

"No. It stands for Witch Who's Who. It's one of the most prestigious publications in the paranormal world. As you can imagine, being included in WWW is a high honour, which is why I'm delighted to confirm that we intend to include you in the next edition."

"Me? Really?"

"Yes. The committee reviewed the list of possible new additions last week, and you were unanimously accepted."

"*Unanimously*, eh? How very exciting. I can't wait to tell —"

"I'm sorry to interrupt, but that won't be possible. It's a strict condition of entry to WWW that you do not tell anyone until the new edition has been published."

"Surely, I can tell my family?"

"I'm afraid not. I hope you understand."

"Fair enough. When will it be published?"

"In a few months, but someone will need to interview

you first. It's important we get all your details correct."

"Okay. Do you need me to pop into your offices?"

"There's no need. Someone will pay you a visit, either at your home or place of work, whichever is most convenient."

"My office might be best."

"Excellent. As I mentioned, secrecy is of the utmost importance, so the interviewer will pretend to be from the tax office."

"Fair enough. When will this be?"

"Let me check the diary. The first date I have is a week tomorrow, in the afternoon. Are you free then?"

"I can be. What time?"

"How about two-thirty?"

"That's fine."

"What are you looking so pleased about?" Winky said when I'd finished on the call.

"I can't tell you."

"Why not?"

"Because it's top secret. Let's just say I'm going up in the world."

"Meanwhile, my reputation is going to be trashed and all because of this stupid wig."

"You did rather bring it on yourself by insulting my grandmother."

"I was only joking. Has everyone in your family had a sense of humour bypass?"

"Grandma certainly has. By the way, are you any good at crossword clues?"

"I'm a crossword master. Why?"

"I'm stuck on one particular clue."

"I didn't know you did crosswords."

"I don't usually, but the women at the village store have asked me to join their crossword club."

"They must be desperate for members if they've asked you. What's the clue you're stuck on?"

"This bird is too valuable to kill."

"How many letters?"

"Err, I don't remember."

"It doesn't matter. It's obvious anyway."

"Not to me it isn't."

"Have you never heard the fable of the goose that laid the golden egg?"

"Actually, yeah, I do remember that. I think you might be right."

"Of course I'm right. I'm always right."

***

"Mummy, Thomas was floating at school."

"What do you mean, *floating*?"

"He was using the left tator spell."

"The what? Oh, you mean the 'levitate' spell."

"Everyone laughed at him."

"Did the teacher see him?"

"No. Miss was writing on the board. When she turned around, he was back in his chair. I wanted to do it too."

"I hope you didn't."

"No, but it would have been fun."

"Where's your daddy?"

"In the garden, playing with Buddy."

"Would you go and tell him I'm home, and then you can give Buddy his dinner."

"But Mummy, his food smells."

"I don't want to hear any complaints, Florence."

"Okay." She gave a huge sigh for such a little girl.

When Jack appeared, I took him through to the lounge. "Did Florence tell you what Thomas was up to today?"

"She did. Did you speak to his mother?"

"Cindymindy? Yeah, I did."

"Cindy Mindy? Is that her name?"

"Yeah, and it's one name. Cindymindy not Cindy Mindy."

"What a weird name."

"Never mind her name. It's clear our little talk didn't do any good. Cindymindy is four sheets to the wind."

"It's three."

"What is?"

"The saying is *three* sheets to the wind."

"Whatever. She seems totally oblivious to the risks she's running. There's witch paraphernalia all over the garden and her cottage is called The Coven."

"I'm not sure what else we can do."

"We have to do something because if this carries on, it's only a matter of time before Florence joins in, and then we really will be in trouble. I'll have another word with Cindymindy, but this time I'll make sure she knows I mean business."

"Don't do anything you'll regret later."

"When do I ever? By the way, did you manage to get any jam roly-poly from the village store?"

"What do you think? The Stock sisters reckoned they had some under P for poly, but there was just a space where it should have been. I got you some rice pudding instead."

"I hate rice pudding."

"Do you? I could have sworn you loved it."

"You're the one who loves rice pudding."

"Oh yeah, you're right. I guess I'll just have to eat it all."

It was Jack's turn to read Florence her bedtime story. While he was upstairs, I was thinking about my upcoming elevation to the elite of Candlefield. Once I was in WWW, people would have to show me the respect I deserved. I might insist that everyone, starting with the twins, referred to me as Mrs Maxwell.

"Why are you looking so pleased with yourself?" Jack said when he joined me in the lounge.

"I don't know what you mean."

"You were grinning like a Cheshire cat when I came in."

"No, I wasn't. Did Florence go off okay?"

"Yeah, she was whacked. Isn't it tomorrow night you go to London with Rhymes?"

"Don't remind me."

"You might enjoy it."

"Listening to a bunch of tortoises, reciting awful poetry? What could be more enjoyable?"

"Did you get the compass stone clue from Ursula?"

"I did, and this one is really tough, but I managed to figure it out."

"What's the clue?"

"You'll never work it out. It took me ages."

"Try me."

"This bird is too valuable to kill."

"That's easy. The goose that laid the golden egg."

Chapter 9

The next morning, I deliberately got up early because I wanted to catch Cindymindy before I headed to the office. I'd finished my breakfast before Jack and Florence sat down to eat their sawdust. I'd just kissed them both goodbye, and I was headed out of the door when Kathy called.

"Good morning, Jill."

"Morning. Can this wait? I'm just on my way out of the house."

"I was going to ask if you'd like to call in for a coffee on your way to the office. I have some exciting news."

"Can't you tell me now?"

"No. I want to see your face when I tell you."

"You're not pregnant, are you?"

"No, of course not."

"Okay, but there's something I have to do first. I can be there in about three-quarters of an hour."

"Okay, I'll see you then."

Kathy might think her news was exciting, but I bet she hadn't been invited to be included in Who's Who. It was just a pity that I couldn't tell her my news, not even after the new edition of WWW was published. That's the problem with having a human for a sister.

I left the car outside the old watermill and made my way to Cindymindy's house on foot. Craig Orange was outside Oranges' Oranges, arranging the display of fruit and veg.

"Hello, Jill!"

"Hi, there."

"Mum tells me you gave her some more anti-witch crystals." He gave me a knowing wink.

"I did, and I tried to tell her I didn't want any money for them, but she insisted."

"Don't worry about it. She's thrilled to bits, and so far, she's still had no problem from the neighbours."

"As long as she's happy."

"Can I interest you in any fruit this morning? Pears are on special offer."

"Not today, thanks. Maybe this weekend."

I rapped on the door with the broom-shaped knocker.

"What?" The wizard who answered the door was wearing a string vest tucked into his trousers. He had shaving foam on one half of his face, and two small pieces of paper stuck to his chin.

"Is Cindymindy in?"

"She's visiting her mum. Have you got a pound coin for the electric? I can't see what I'm doing in here. I've cut myself twice already."

"Err, let me check. I've got a couple."

"They'll do, thanks." He snatched them from me and was about to disappear back inside.

"Hold on. Are you Cindymindy's husband?"

"Yeah. Ricky. Who are you?"

"I'm Jill Maxwell. We live in the old watermill."

"Right. CM said you'd been around."

"CM? Oh, you mean Cindymindy."

"She said something about your girl being in Thomas' class."

"That's right. I came to see Cindy—err—CM because Thomas has been using magic in the classroom."

"The kid's a chip off the old block." He laughed. "I was always getting sent to see the headmaster for messing around."

"Yeah, but that was different."

"How do you mean?"

"I assume you went to school in Candlefield?"

"Yeah. Candle Lane Juniors. I had a great time there."

"The difference is that Thomas goes to school in the human world. He can't be allowed to perform magic spells in a classroom full of humans, or the rogue retrievers will get to hear about it."

"Those catsuit-wearing nutters don't worry me."

"They should because if you're not careful, you'll find yourself and your family being dragged back to Candlefield."

"Wouldn't bother me. It was CM's idea to come here. I've never known what she sees in the human world. Except for the internet of course. That's pretty cool."

"Will you have a word with your son."

"What's he supposed to have done, anyway?"

"Apparently, yesterday, he used the 'levitate' spell to float around the classroom."

"Did he?" Ricky clearly found that hilarious. "What a kid."

"You need to tell him to cut out the magic when he's around humans."

"Okay, I'll have a word with him."

"Promise?"

"Sure. Look, I need to finish shaving because I'm going for a job interview down the bus depot later."

"Okay. Thanks, and good luck with the interview."

Wow! Just wow!

I had thought Cindymindy was bad, but Ricky took bad to a whole new level. I wasn't convinced he would speak to Thomas and, even if he did, I doubted it would do much good. If Florence came home with yet another tale of Thomas using magic in class, I would have to take more decisive action.

***

Kathy couldn't have looked any smugger even if she'd had the letters S-M-U-G tattooed across her forehead.

"I thought we'd have our tea in the orangery," she said.

"Where's that?"

Ignoring my quip, she led the way to the *conservatory*. "I've had the most exciting news ever."

"Let me guess. Peter has bought you a subscription to Gnome Monthly."

"Why can't you ever be serious about anything, Jill?"

"Sorry. What's your big news?"

"Guess who has been nominated as a finalist for Washbridge Businesswoman of the Year?"

"Your next-door neighbour?"

"See what I mean. You can't be serious even for five minutes."

"I'm sorry. Congratulations. What do you stand to win?"

"The prize is unimportant. It's the recognition, and of course the prestige."

"You can't spend prestige."

"I wouldn't expect you to understand, but I think it's a great honour."

"When do you get to find out who's won?"

"Next week. The final is being held at the town hall a week on Saturday."

"And I suppose you want me to be there?"

"Actually, no."

"Oh?"

"You can't come. The numbers are limited and it's invitation only. Pete is coming, obviously."

"Right. Well, I wish you the best of luck."

"I hope my success doesn't make you feel bad, Jill."

"Why should it?"

"It can't be easy to have such a dynamic, entrepreneurial sister."

"You forgot to mention modest." I would have given anything to tell her that I was about to be included in WWW.

"Thanks, Jill."

I glanced out the window and caught sight of Henry and Henrietta, who were cosying up to one another near to the summerhouse.

"By the way, did you have any more trouble from your jazz-loving neighbours?"

"Not a peep, thank goodness. I'm glad I didn't go around there with all guns blazing. Hey, by the way, will you be taking Florence to Kids' Music Fest next weekend."

"What's that?"

"Haven't you seen the posters? They're everywhere. We had a flyer through the door too. I'll see if I can find it." While she was gone, the gnomes and elves all gave me a little wave.

I took the flyer from her. "Florence might be too young

for this."

"Nonsense. It says it's suitable for kids three and over, and besides, Florence loves to dance, doesn't she?"

"I guess so. I'll ask her if she wants to go."

"It'll be great, you'll see."

***

The matchsticks had gone, but Mrs K wasn't done with her models just yet.

"That looks very difficult, Mrs K."

"Not when you've been doing this for as long as I have. There's a knack to it." *It*, in this case, was putting a model ship into a bottle. "I'm at the crucial stage. Would you like to watch?"

"Err, sure."

Inside the bottle was a block of wood, with lots of smaller pieces of wood attached to it. Some of the small pieces of wood had squares of cloth tied to them.

"I just need to pull on these strings to finish. Are you ready?"

"Absolutely."

She pulled the strings gently. "Hey presto! What do you think?"

I actually thought it still looked like a pile of wood and cloth. "It's—err—very impressive."

"It's the Cutty Sark, but I probably didn't need to tell you that."

"Err—right. Yes, I can see that now. And you say you've been putting ships in bottles for some time?"

"Many years." She took out her phone. "Look."

I watched as Mrs K flicked through photo after photo of

bottles, each one full of wood, string and cloth. Not one of them was recognisable as a ship.

"They're amazing."

"This one is my favourite. The Mary Rose."

"And where do you keep all of these?"

"In my dining room."

"Out on display?"

"Of course. They're quite the conversation piece."

"I'll bet they are. You seem to have an awful lot of hobbies, Mrs K."

"I always have had. I like to keep busy. I'm not one for watching TV."

"How do you find time for them all?"

"I have a whiteboard in the kitchen that I use to keep track of all my hobbies. That way I don't neglect any of them."

"What does your husband think of that?"

"Mr K has his own whiteboard of hobbies."

"And do the two of you share any?"

"Hardly any, dear. We mostly have very different interests." She picked up the 'Cutty Sark'. "I'd like you to have this, Jill."

"I couldn't possibly accept it. Not after you've put so much work into it."

"I insist. I already have two Cutty Sarks at home. Please say you'll take it. It would give me great pleasure to know you have it on display in your home."

"Err, okay. Thanks."

Winky was sans wig.

"What's that hot mess in your hand?" He laughed.

"Shush! Mrs K will hear you."

"What is it supposed to be?"

"The Cutty Sark."

"*Cutty Sark*?" He was bent double with laughter. "Why do you have it?"

"She gave it to me as a present."

"The bin's over there."

"I can't throw it away. Mrs K probably spent days on this. Maybe even weeks."

"I assume that's her first ever project?"

"No. She's been making them for years, apparently. She showed me the photos."

"Were they any better than that monstrosity?"

"Not really."

"I could do better than that, blindfolded, with one paw tied behind my back."

"I'd like to see you try. It takes a lot of skill."

"Do you want to have a wager that I can't do better?"

"I'm not having any more bets with you. You always cheat."

"Rubbish. I might make one just for the fun of it."

"If it keeps you quiet for a few days, I'm all in favour. Anyway, I'm glad to see you've cheered up now the wig has gone."

"Your grandmother has a lot to answer for. I'm getting tons of stick online after Mimi posted those photos."

"She didn't."

"She did, but don't worry, I'll have the last laugh."

"What are you planning on doing?"

"That would be telling."

***

Wash Sounds was based in what had obviously once been a church hall. From the outside, the only clue to its current role was a small brass plaque next to the door. I rang the bell twice but there was no response, so I tried the handle; the door was unlocked. Inside, the reception desk was deserted, and I was beginning to wonder if I'd got the wrong day, when Orlando appeared through a door to my right.

"Jill, I do apologise. My receptionist, Claire, called in sick this morning."

"Call me Roberta."

"Sorry?"

"I'm Roberta Truman, the journalist."

"Oh yes, of course." He winked. "Welcome to Wash Sounds, *Roberta*. We're due to start in about thirty minutes. Why don't you come and see where the magic happens?"

"Sure."

He led the way down a short corridor to the studio, which was smaller than I'd imagined it would be. Seated behind a sound desk was a man, in his late thirties, who was wearing a Hawaiian shirt, shorts and flipflops. Clearly, the music industry attracted some eccentric characters.

"Roy, this is — err —"

I could see Orlando had already forgotten my cover name, so I stepped forward. "Roberta Truman."

"Roy Jones." He stood up, shook my hand, and then yawned. "Sorry about that. I had a late night."

"Roberta is a journalist," Orlando said. "I have some paperwork to catch up on. Is it okay if I leave you with Roy, Ji — I mean, Roberta?"

"Sure." It was obvious from Roy's puzzled expression that Orlando hadn't thought to mention my visit ahead of time. "I'm doing a piece on the recording industry, focussing on smaller outfits such as yours."

"What's the name of your publication?"

An excellent question, and one I wished I'd anticipated earlier.

"It's called — err — Music — err — Tech Monthly."

"I can't say I've heard of it, and I take all of the industry mags."

"It's new. Brand new. This article will be in the launch issue."

"Right. How exciting. What's the angle of your article?"

"The angle? Err, I — err — "

"The tech side of the business, I guess."

"That's right. Definitely the tech."

"What do you think of this bad boy?" He gestured to the sound desk. "I put most of this together myself."

"Very impressive."

"I can talk you through it if you're interested, but it may be a little too technical for you."

"Not at all. The more technical, the better." I took out the notepad that I'd bought at the newsagents on my way to the studio. "Fire away."

He didn't need asking twice, and for the next twenty minutes, he described the setup in tediously boring detail. None of which I understood, but I nodded, and scribbled on the pad. At one point I saw him grab a quick look at my 'notes', so by way of explanation, I said, "Shorthand."

"Right. I think that's covered everything. You've probably got lots of questions for me?"

"I — err — " I was beginning to think this particular cover

story hadn't been such a good idea.

Fortunately, Orlando reappeared just in the nick of time. "Troy's here. He's just getting a drink. Are we ready, Roy?" Roy didn't respond. "Roy!"

"Sorry, what?"

"Were you asleep?"

"Of course not." He yawned. "What did you say?"

"I said Troy is here. Are we ready?"

"Yep. All set."

Moments later, a young man, dressed from head to toe in denim, walked into the studio. "You didn't tell me you'd got yourself a new receptionist, Orlando."

"This is Roberta. She's a journalist."

"Really?" Troy's eyes lit up. "Troy Total. A pleasure to meet you." Before I could stop him, he'd planted a kiss on the back of my hand. "You've probably heard of me?"

"I don't think—"

"I'll be recording for the next couple of hours, but I can give you an interview afterwards."

"Actually, I write for Music Tech Monthly. We cover the techie side of the business."

"Oh." His smile evaporated, as he realised that I would be of no use in furthering his career. "I guess we'd better get this show on the road."

For the next two hours, I watched Troy perform a number of R&B tracks. The man might be a bit of a prat, but he had a fantastic voice, and I found myself boogying along while watching Roy do his thing.

When the session was finished, Troy came through to join us.

"Superb, Troy," Orlando said. "One of the best yet."

"I thought so too." Troy clearly didn't suffer from a lack

of confidence. "Let's give it a listen."

Roy cued up the recording and played it back. After listening to it a couple of times, Troy signalled his approval with a thumbs up. Afterwards, Troy and Orlando arranged to reconvene at the studio in two days' time, to lay down a couple more tracks.

Once Troy had left, Orlando took me through to reception.

"That seemed to go okay," I said.

"It did, but then so did the others. I'm terrified that the same thing is going to happen again."

"I'll do my best to see that it doesn't."

Chapter 10

I thought I'd better give Aunt Lucy a call, to firm up the details for collecting Rhymes later that day. She usually picked up on the first or second ring, but the call rang out for the longest time and I was just beginning to think she wasn't going to answer.

"Jill, hi. I'm sorry for taking so long. I was just signing an autograph."

"*Autograph?*"

"Yes, I'm in the cork museum at the moment. Is it urgent because I have a queue of people waiting for selfies and autographs."

"I didn't think you intended to go?"

"I hadn't planned to, but then lots of people called and asked if I'd attend so I could answer their questions about my collection."

"Right. I was just calling to ask what the arrangements are for collecting Rhymes."

"Goodness, I'd forgotten all about that. He asked me to get in touch with you to tell you it starts at seven, but the poets have to be there for six-thirty."

"Okay. I'll come over to your place at six to be on the safe side."

"I'll tell him. Sorry, Jill, but I really must go now."

"Okay. Bye."

Curiosity got the better of me, so I magicked myself over to Cuppy C where I found the twins leaning on the counter, waiting for someone to serve.

"I expected this place to be buzzing," I said.

"Doesn't look like it, does it?" Pearl sighed.

"This is the most people we've had in here all day."

Amber gestured to the three old witches who were seated next to the window. "And they've been nursing those same drinks for the best part of an hour."

"What about all the corkers? I've just spoken to Aunt Lucy; she said she had a queue of people waiting for selfies and autographs."

"Those corkers are all tight-wads," Amber said. "We're lucky if they buy as much as a cup of tea."

"Yeah," Pearl snapped. "Some of them even have the cheek to bring their own flasks."

"Have there been many visitors to the museum?"

"Yeah. It's non-stop."

"It sounds like Aunt Lucy has become something of a celebrity."

"She's loving every minute of it. She's even taken to sending down for drinks, like we're her lackies."

"I think I'll go and take a look." I started for the stairs. "Before I do, I have a puzzle for you two."

"What kind of puzzle?"

"It's a crossword clue."

"Go on, then. It's not like we've got anything better to do."

"Okay. It's very difficult, so see if you can work it out before I come back downstairs. Ready?"

"Yeah."

"This bird is too valuable to kill."

"The goose that laid the golden egg," Pearl said.

"I thought you said it was difficult." Amber rolled her eyes.

In complete contrast to the tea room, the museum was crammed full of corkers who were either staring in awe at the display cabinets or queuing to see the star of the show. Aunt Lucy was sitting at a small table, posing for photos and signing autographs. In between selfies, I managed to catch her eye.

"Hi, Jill!"

"What's it like to be famous?"

"Don't be silly." She blushed, but I could tell from her smile that she was enjoying all the attention.

"I thought I'd better see the cork phenomenon for myself. I'll leave you to it."

"Would you do me a favour on your way out? Ask the girls to bring me a cup of tea, please. I'm parched. And a cupcake wouldn't go amiss."

Back downstairs, the twins were still waiting for their next customer.

"I have to give you credit, girls, the museum is a runaway success."

"We should have listened to you," Amber said. "It's a complete dead loss. The only person who has benefitted is Mum."

"Speaking of whom, she asked if you'd take a cup of tea and a cupcake upstairs for her."

**

I had planned on having a drink in Cuppy C, but I didn't fancy listening to the twins moaning and groaning, so instead I magicked myself over to Washbridge, with the intention of paying a visit to Coffee Animal. On my way down the high street, however, something caught my eye. Or to be more precise, *someone* caught my eye.

On the opposite side of the street, a young boy was

skipping along the pavement. There was something familiar about him. Where did I know him from? And then it came to me. The last time I'd seen him, he'd been dressed in a scout's uniform, selling cookies outside my office building. I'd unknowingly handed him a rare ten-pence piece that turned out to be worth twenty grand. The lucky blighter. No wonder he looked so happy. I was just about to go into Coffee Animal when the young boy disappeared into a shop called On A Sixpence. That name rang a bell—it was Rita's coin shop. Perhaps the boy had sold his valuable coin to her. Before grabbing a coffee, I decided to nip across the road to say a quick hello and take a look around her shop. As I walked by the window, I glanced inside and saw Rita and the boy in conversation. The next thing I knew, she gave him a hug and a peck on the cheek, as though she knew him, and then he left the shop.

That was kind of weird.

I waited until the boy had disappeared down the high street, then I stepped into the shop.

"Jill! It's great to see you again," Rita said. "Welcome to my little empire. What do you think of it?"

"It's great. You've done a fantastic job. How's business?"

"Incredible. I expected it to be a slow burn, but people around here seem really interested in coins. I've had a steady stream of visitors ever since I opened."

"Did you do a lot of advertising?"

"None. It's so expensive, isn't it?"

"You're not kidding. I have to rely on word of mouth. Still, the recent story in the press must have helped."

"Which story was that?"

"You must have seen it. A young boy found a rare ten-pence coin that was worth a small fortune."

"Now that you mention it, I think I did hear something about that." She quickly changed the subject. "Isn't it weird that Charlie thought he had already met you?"

"Yeah, that was strange. What exactly is it your husband does again?"

"You know I can't tell you that." She smiled. "It's top secret."

"Sorry. I hope it isn't anything to do with UFOs."

"Of course not." She laughed.

"Or the paranormal. That kind of stuff freaks me out."

"I—err—I've just remembered that I promised to phone one of my clients. Sorry, Jill."

"No problem. Nice to see you again, Rita."

Snigger.

That short visit had proven to be very interesting indeed. Rita had clearly become uncomfortable when I'd mentioned the story about the rare ten-pence piece; she obviously knew the young boy who had 'discovered' it in his change. Call me cynical if you like, but I was beginning to question the whole rare coin thing. It was all rather convenient that the story hit the local headlines just as Rita was opening her coin shop. A coincidence? Very unlikely. As I left On A Sixpence, I noticed that shopfitters were hard at work next door on Grandma's new shop, WiFY. They still had an awful lot of work to do if it was going to be ready in time for the grand opening next Wednesday.

***

Back at the office there was no sign of Winky; maybe he was making a ship in a bottle somewhere. I'd only been at my desk for a matter of minutes when the door burst open, and in rushed Farah, followed closely by Mrs K.

"Jill, you have to help me!" Farah was close to tears.

"What's happened?"

"Logan has gone missing!"

"Slow down. Take a deep breath, and then tell me who Logan is."

"A Bichon Frise. I'd just finished trimming him. His owners will be here any minute now. What will I tell them?"

"Did Delilah leave the cage door open again?"

"Delilah isn't working today. It's just me, and I know I fastened the cage because I always check and double-check. What am I going to do, Jill?"

"Don't panic. We'll find him." I turned to Mrs K who was still standing in the doorway. "Would you go and look outside for him, please?"

"Of course." She headed straight out of the office.

"Okay, Farah. Show me where you last saw Logan."

"This could be the end of my business." She sobbed.

"Don't be silly. Everything's going to be alright, I promise. Come on, let's go."

I practically had to drag her along the corridor to Bubbles.

"Where was he when you last saw him?"

"Through the back. All the cages are in there." She led the way into the back room, but then stopped dead in her tracks. "I don't believe it!"

For a moment, I feared the worst, and I half expected

her to say the other dogs had disappeared.

"He's back." She pointed to the cute Bichon Frise, sitting patiently in the cage. "I don't understand it, Jill. He wasn't there five minutes ago."

Clearly, dog-grooming was a much more stressful occupation than I'd imagined. The cage was fastened, so unless Logan had learned how to open and close the latch, Farah had clearly imagined it all.

"Why don't you take a seat, Farah. I'll ask Mrs K to bring you a nice cup of tea."

***

Norman Bagshot ran the launch that was used by wedding parties to cross Wesmere Lake. I'd decided to use the same approach I'd employed with Warren Hole, by posing as a bride-to-be, who was considering having my wedding at the chapel on the island.

The launch's mooring was on the opposite side of the lake from Matty and his rowing boat. Next to the mooring was a small boathouse, inside which was an office; it was in there that I found Norman Bagshot, who was busy with paperwork.

"Mr Bagshot?"

"Yes. How can I help you?"

"My name is Tuppence Farthing."

"What a lovely name."

"Thanks. I'm considering booking the island chapel for my wedding, and I understand that you have a launch that you use for such occasions?"

"That's correct."

"I was hoping I might be able to see it."

"Regrettably she's out of commission at the moment, undergoing some minor repairs." He pointed to a huge tarpaulin. "That's her over there."

"I'd still like to see her if possible."

"Unfortunately, I've had to strip her down to carry out the repairs; that involved removing all the seats too. I can show you some photographs, though." He took out a photo album and handed it to me. There were numerous photos of the launch, including many taken when it was being used for weddings. "What do you think?"

"It's very pretty. How long will it be out of action?"

"Not too long."

"Maybe I could come back and see it when it's back in service?"

"Of course."

I made to leave, but then hesitated. "Incidentally, didn't I see something about a guy disappearing from the island on the eve of his wedding."

"That's right."

"What happened?"

"I've no idea. I suppose he must have got cold feet at the last minute."

"But how did he—?"

"Sorry, Tuppence." He took out his phone. "There's an urgent call I have to make."

"Right, okay. Thanks."

***

When buying a pet, it inevitably comes with certain responsibilities, but there are limits, and having to take your tortoise halfway across the country, to take part in a poetry recital was surely over and above the call of duty.

And yet, there I was, waiting downstairs at Aunt Lucy's house for Rhymes.

"My wrist aches with all the autographs I've signed today," she said.

"I hope you charged them."

"I couldn't do that, Jill. It was an honour to be asked."

"Rhymes does know that I'm here, doesn't he?"

"Yes, I told him what time you were coming when he was with the turtle makeover lady."

"The who?"

"She came earlier to get him ready for tonight."

"Unbelievable."

The door creaked open and in walked Rhymes. "What do you think, Jill?" He did a little twirl for me.

"I had no idea you could do that with a shell. What colour is it?"

"Aquamarine."

"Won't the colouring damage your shell?"

"No. It isn't permanent, and it's completely safe."

"And there's glitter on it."

"You don't think I've overdone it, do you? I wasn't sure about the sparkle."

"Err, no. It's fine."

"Just *fine*?"

"I meant nice. Very nice. Isn't it, Aunt Lucy?"

"You look fantastic, Rhymes," she reassured him.

"Come on, then." I picked him up. "Or we'll be late."

"I'm still worried about this magic thing. Are you sure it won't hurt?"

"You'll be fine. Let's go."

Shell Hall was located behind the Globe Theatre. It was a tiny grey building, with a roof shaped like a tortoise shell.

"That wasn't so bad," Rhymes said, as we landed a few yards from the entrance. "Come on, let's get inside."

"Why don't I wait for you out here?"

"I want you to see my performance."

I was afraid he might say that. "I won't fit through those doors."

"Use your magic."

"I'm not turning myself into a tortoise."

"You don't need to. Just shrink yourself."

"Okay." I did as he said, and we made our way inside.

"Poets to the left, guests to the right," said the tortoise doorman.

"Wish me luck, Jill."

"Break a leg."

"That's not very nice."

"No, I didn't mean — err — good luck. You'll be great."

I took the right-hand corridor that led to the main auditorium, which to my surprise was full of witches and wizards. I was beginning to think I wasn't going to find a seat when a witch on the fifth row beckoned to me. "This seat is free. My friend couldn't make it."

"Thanks. I'm Jill."

"Kirsty."

"It's much busier than I expected. I thought I'd be the only one here."

"It's like this every year. That's why Shelly is so nervous."

"Shelly? She's — ?"

"My tortoise."

"Right. I'm here with Rhymes."

"What a great name, and so appropriate too."

"Is Shelly here to listen to the recitals?"

"No. She's giving a recital too."

"How many recitals will there be?"

"At least fifty, I'd guess."

"Really? I assumed it would just be Rhymes and that we'd be in and out in an hour, tops."

"We'll be lucky to get away before midnight, I reckon."

"Great." I sank into the seat. "Have you heard any of Shelly's poems?"

"Of course. She reads them all to me. She's so talented. What about Rhymes?"

"If I'm honest, his are awful."

"I'm sure they aren't all that bad."

"You're right. I'm probably being unfair." I most certainly wasn't.

"I can't wait to hear the other poets, can you, Jill?"

"No, I'm on the edge of my seat."

For the next three hours, I was forced to endure a slew of terrible tortoise poetry.

"That's Shelly." Kirsty stood up and cheered.

Any hope that Kirsty had been objective about her tortoise's poetry was soon shattered. This little classic was entitled My Best Friend is a Witch.

My best friend is a witch called Kirsty,
I'm glad she's not a vampire,
Because they're all bloodthirsty,
Kirsty loves my work,
And is always so encouraging,
She's never a jerk,
She's just kind and nurturing.

While the rest of the audience could manage only polite applause, Kirsty was on her feet, whooping in appreciation. After Shelly had left the stage, Kirsty turned to me, with tears in her eyes. "That was so beautiful, wasn't it?"

"It was very touching."

"I told you she was good, didn't I?"

"You did tell me that."

"I can't wait to hear Rhymes."

"Me too."

Unfortunately, we didn't have too long to wait.

"I love what he's done with his shell," Kirsty said. "What colour is that?"

"Aquamarine, apparently."

"And is that glitter?"

"Yeah. He had a makeover especially for tonight."

"He and Shelly should exchange numbers. I'm sure they could be best friends."

"Hmm." There was one slight flaw with that plan. It meant that I'd have to put up with more of Kirsty's inane ramblings, which was a definite no-no.

Centre stage, Rhymes took a deep breath and then held forth with this masterpiece.

My shell is my friend,
It's tough, and rigid and never will bend,
Everywhere I go, it goes too,
It fits just like a cosy shoe,
You could say my shell makes me serene,
Especially today when it's aquamarine.

"That was brilliant!" Kirsty was up on her feet, shaming me into joining in her enthusiastic applause. "You must be so proud of him, Jill."

"Err, yeah. Very."

It was just after eleven o'clock when the last poet exited the stage, by which time I had lost the will to live.

"It was so lovely to meet you, Jill." Kirsty gave me a hug. "Tell Rhymes I thought his poem was excellent."

"I will." She seemed to be waiting for something, and then I realised she expected me to return the compliment. "Likewise, with Shelly. Tell her I thought her poem was delightful."

I made my way outside, reversed the 'shrink' spell, and waited for Rhymes to appear. It was another thirty minutes before he came through the doors.

"What did you think, Jill? Be honest."

"It was your best poem yet." Which wasn't saying much.

"Do you really think so? I was going to read Ode to Toast, but I changed my mind at the last minute and wrote that while I was waiting to go onstage."

"It was the right decision. Come on, it's late. We'd better get home."

I was surprised to find Aunt Lucy waiting up for us.

"Hello, you two. How did it go?"

"It was fantastic," Rhymes gushed. "Wasn't it, Jill?"

"Unbelievable."

"I forgot to tell you, Jill." Rhymes beamed. "I've already been invited to perform there again next year."

"Oh goody."

Chapter 11

It was Saturday morning. Over breakfast, I'd made the mistake of reciting Rhymes' terrible poem to Jack and Florence. Jack's reaction had been much the same as mine—an uncontrollable desire to tear off his ears. Unfortunately, Florence had immediately pronounced it her favourite poem, and insisted that I recite it several more times until she had learned it. Now she was walking around the house, reciting it over and over again.

My shell is my friend,
It's tough, and rigid and never will bend,
Everywhere I go, it goes too,
It fits just like a cosy shoe,
You could say my shell makes me serene,
Especially today when it's aquamarine.

After each recital, she giggled.

"This is your fault," Jack whispered to me.

"Don't you have to get ready for StampCon? Oscar will be here in twenty minutes."

"Can't you tell him that I'm feeling under the weather?"

"No, I can't. If I can endure hours of the Tortoise Poets Society, I'm sure you can manage to look at a few stamps."

"But the place will be full of stampers."

"*You're* a stamper now, remember."

My shell is my friend,
It's tough, and rigid and never will bend,
Everywhere I go —

"I think we've heard that poem enough times now, Florence."

"But I really like it."

"I know you do, but Mummy has a headache."

"Where are we going to buy my kite?"

"I'm not sure. One of the toy shops, I suppose."

"You should go to Kite Kite," Jack said.

"Where?"

"Kite Kite. It's near the police station."

"Is it new?"

"No, it's been there for years."

"I can't say I've ever noticed it."

"It's only a small shop. It's next door to Feet Feet."

"*Feet Feet*? You've just made that up."

"No, I haven't. It's a podiatrist."

"Let me get this straight. Kite Kite is next door to Feet Feet?"

"Correct. And you'll never guess what's on the other side of Kite Kite."

"Sandwich Sandwich? Coffee Coffee? Cheese Cheese?"

"No, it's the post office." He grinned.

"It looks like we're going to Kite Kite, Florence," I said.

"Yay! I want a yellow kite."

"Okay, but only if you promise not to recite that poem again today."

***

"Have a lovely time," I shouted to Jack, as he climbed into Oscar's car.

He made a gesture, which I think meant: *You too.*

"Are we going to get the kite now, Mummy?"

"Only if you've fed Buddy."

"I fed him last night. I don't think he's hungry again yet."

"Is that why he's circling your legs? Feed him, and then we'll go."

"Not fair." She huffed.

I'd just picked up my handbag when Kathy called.

"Has Jack gone to that stamp thing?"

"Yeah, he's just left. Why?"

"I've decided to give myself the day off. I thought we could do something together."

"I've got Florence."

"I know. I meant the three of us. What time does she finish her dance class?"

"There isn't one today. They had a burst water pipe in the village hall."

"Great. What do you fancy doing?"

"I've already promised Florence that she can fly a kite."

"Great. It's years since I've done that. We could get lunch afterwards."

"Okay, but I have to go and buy the kite first."

"Why don't I meet you in the park? I assume that's where you're going?"

"Yeah. Will Mikey and Lizzie be with you?"

"Mikey won't want to come. He spends every Saturday morning playing some weird Dungeons and Dragons thing. I'll ask Lizzie, but it's hard to tear her away from her studies these days. Which park and what time?"

"I have to go into Washbridge to buy the kite, so we might as well make it Washbridge Park. Shall we say ten-thirty by the main entrance?"

"Sure. See you then."

"I've fed Buddy." Florence appeared by my side.

"Good girl. Your Auntie Kathy is going to come kite-flying with us."

"Is Lizzie coming too?"

"I don't know. I don't think so. Come on, let's go and get you that kite."

***

Jack was only partially right. The shop next-door to Kite Kite was indeed a podiatrist called Feet Feet, but like many other post offices across the country, that had closed down. In its place was a shop called Cupcake Cupcake Cupcake. Talk about one-upmanship.

"Come on, Mummy!" Florence tugged at my sleeve.

"Those cupcakes look yummy, don't they?"

"No. I want a kite."

"Okay." I sighed. "Let's go and see what they have."

I was surprised to find that the man behind the counter was an elderly vampire, who greeted us with a fangy smile.

"Well, well, what do we have here? Two beautiful witches. I don't get many sups in the shop these days. Are you on a day trip from Candlefield?"

"No, we live here in the human world. In Middle Tweaking."

"That's a beautiful little village. I went to the annual festival there several years ago. Remind me what they call it."

"Freaking Tweaking."

"That's the one."

"I see your next-door neighbour has gone one better with the shop name."

"Hmm." He scowled. "I don't know why they can't come up with their own ideas instead of stealing mine. It was bad enough when the foot guy put up the Feet Feet sign, but now I have Cupcake to the power of three to contend with. I'm Mortimer, by the way, but everyone calls me Morty."

"I'm Jill. And this is my daughter, Florence."

"And would you be here to buy a kite, young lady?"

"Yes, I want a yellow one."

"What should you say, Florence?"

"Please!"

"Yellow is a very good choice." Morty came from behind the counter. "Did you know that yellow kites fly higher than all the other colours?"

Florence was thrilled by that 'revelation', and she eagerly followed Morty to the other side of the shop.

"Look, Mummy, there are so many of them."

While Florence was looking at the kites, Morty came over to me and whispered, "Do you want it with or without?"

"Sorry? With or without *what*?"

"Magic of course. I have regular kites and enchanted ones. The enchanted ones are a little more expensive, and I keep them in the back."

"What do they do that the regular ones don't?"

"Basically, they're much easier to fly. Kite flying with a regular kite can prove quite difficult for the novice."

Difficult? How difficult could it be to fly a kite?

"I'm sure a regular one will be fine." I turned to Florence. "Have you seen one you like?"

"This one, please." She held up a yellow kite with white spots.

I checked the price, and it wasn't too outlandish. "Okay, we'll take that one, please."

It was only a ten-minute walk from Kite Kite to Washbridge Park. As we made our way there, I reflected on Morty's attempts to upsell me to an enchanted kite. Why would anyone waste their money on one of those when kite flying was so simple? You held the string and ran — that's all there was to it.

"Look, Auntie Kathy's over there!" Florence pointed. "Lizzie isn't with her."

"She probably had lots of homework to do. Why don't you go and show Auntie Kathy your kite?"

"That's lovely, Florence." Kathy nodded her approval. "Did you pick it?"

"Yes, I wanted a yellow one."

"It's just as well you didn't let your mummy choose one. She was hopeless at flying kites when she was a little girl."

"Were you, Mummy?"

"Of course I wasn't. Auntie Kathy is just being silly."

"Yes, you were," Kathy insisted. "Don't you remember when Dad bought us a kite each at the seaside, and yours ended up in the sea?"

"No, I don't." Even as I denied it, I remembered staring out to sea as my kite disappeared over the horizon.

"Will you show me how to do it, Mummy?" Florence said.

"Of course I will, darling. It's really easy. Just watch me carefully." I took it out of its packaging, unwound the string, threw the kite into the air and then began to run.

"It isn't flying, Mummy."

She was right; it was just being dragged along the ground behind me. "It will in a minute." Undaunted, I continued to run even faster, but the stupid kite refused to do any more than bounce along the ground.

Florence came running to me. Kathy followed at a more leisurely pace; she had a stupid smirk plastered across her face.

"Why won't it fly, Mummy?"

"I think it must be a dud. The man in the shop must have given me a broken one."

"Let me have a try." Kathy held out her hand.

"It's no good. It's clearly broken."

"There's no harm in my giving it a go."

"Please yourself." I handed her the kite.

"Run with me, Florence." Kathy set off back the way I'd come, and within a few yards, the kite was soaring high above her.

"Look, Mummy!" Florence shouted back to me. "Auntie Kathy made it fly."

"The wind must have picked up."

"Can I have a go, Auntie Kathy?" Florence held out her hand.

"Of course you can. Grab the string and run as fast as you can."

Not wanting Florence to be too disappointed, I cautioned, "You might not be able to do it straight away. It's quite difficult."

I needn't have worried because within a few yards the kite was flying high in the sky.

"She's a natural," Kathy said. "She must get it from Jack."

"Anyone can fly a kite when the wind gets up. It was completely still when I tried."

"Sure."

"It's true."

"Why don't you have another go when Florence is done? The wind is quite strong now."

"I—err—I will, but I need to nip to the toilet first. Are you okay here with Florence?"

"Of course."

That sister of mine was such a smarty-pants. I'd show her. As soon as I was out of Kathy's field of vision, I cast the 'faster' spell and headed back to Kite Kite.

"Back so soon?" Morty was clearly surprised to see me. "If your kite has blown away, I'm afraid I can't give you a refund."

"No, it's not that. I want one of your enchanted kites."

"Oh? I thought you said that—"

"Quick. I have to get back."

"What colour?"

"It doesn't matter."

"Okay." He disappeared into the back and returned with a red kite, which was twice as large as the one Florence had chosen. "This one is thirty-five pounds."

"How much? Are you serious?"

"I did warn you that the enchanted ones were more expensive."

"Are you absolutely sure this one will fly for me?"

"Positive. You'll look like a kite master."

"Okay, I'll take it."

After paying, I rushed back to the park. I could see Kathy in the distance, watching Florence running around with the yellow kite, which was swooping high and low.

I took my kite from its packaging, grabbed the string, threw the kite into the air, and began to run towards them. This time, the kite soared high into the sky.

"Where did that come from?" Kathy looked agog.

"I told you I could do it."

"I like your kite, Mummy," Florence started to run alongside me.

"Let's show Auntie Kathy how it's done."

The two of us spent the next fifteen minutes running back and forth while Kathy looked on.

"Would you like a go with this one?" I said to Kathy, once Florence and I had run out of steam.

"Sure. Watch and learn."

What I learned was that a human cannot fly an enchanted kite, no matter how hard she might try.

"Having a problem, Kathy?"

"There's obviously something wrong with this kite."

"You know what they say about a poor workman, don't you?"

After we'd decided to call it a day, we headed for the gates at the opposite end of the park.

"What's going on over there?" I pointed to a gang of men who appeared to be constructing some kind of stage.

"That must be for the Kids' Music Fest," Kathy said.

"What's that, Mummy?"

Before I could respond, Kathy got in, "It's a music show for children. Would you like to go, Florence?"

"Yes, please. Can I?"

"I suppose so."

"Is it today, Mummy?"

"No, it's not until next weekend."

"Can Wendy come with us?"

"I'll have to ask her mummy."

As we walked by the workmen, I happened to catch a

snippet of their conversation.

"When do the ghouls arrive?"

"Friday night. That's what I heard, anyway."

Mad had told me that they were expecting a major incident involving ghouls. Were they planning to attack the audience at the music festival?

"Jill, are you coming?" Kathy shouted.

"Yeah, sorry."

***

It was almost six o'clock when Jack finally arrived home.

"If I ever have to look at another stamp, I'll scream."

"I take it you had a good time?"

"I thought Oscar was bad, but his friends, Phil and Natalie, are absolutely obsessed. They insisted we visit every exhibit in the place, and they never stopped talking about stamps. I thought my head was going to explode. What about you and Florence? Did you have a nice day?"

"Daddy!" Florence came running into the hall and gave Jack a hug. "I've got a yellow kite and Mummy has a red one."

Jack turned to me. "You bought two?"

"In for a penny, in for a pound."

"Mine flew really high, didn't it, Mummy?"

"It did, darling. You were very good at it."

"What about your mummy?" Jack grinned. "Could she make her kite fly?"

"Yes, her kite went really high too. Auntie Kathy could fly my kite, but she couldn't fly Mummy's."

"Oh? How come?"

I shrugged. "Kathy never was very good with kites, even as a kid."

Chapter 12

It was Monday morning and Florence was outside in the garden, trying to fly her kite. That was despite my having told her there wasn't enough room out there for her to get it off the ground.

Jack and I were still eating breakfast.

"Jill, calm down, you'll blow a gasket."

"You didn't hear what Grandma said at the re-opening of the lido yesterday."

"Maybe not, but you've told me a dozen times, so I'm pretty sure I've got the gist of it by now."

"She took all the credit for rescuing that place."

"What else did you expect from her?"

"I thought I might at least get a mention."

"Surely the main thing is that the lido is going to stay open?"

"Of course it is, but she had the nerve to stand there, and make a long speech about how she had worked tirelessly, to ensure the lido would be available for generations to come. The *only* thing she did was to tell me to sort it out."

"Which you did. And knowing that should be reward enough for you."

"They gave her flowers and chocolates."

"Yes, you said."

"There's even talk of them putting up a plaque to recognise what she did."

"You have to let this go, Jill."

"If they do put up a plaque, I'm going to scribble out her name and write mine on there."

"You don't think that might be a little petty?"

"That was fun, Mummy." Florence came back into the house.

"Did you manage to get the kite to fly, pumpkin?" Jack said.

"The yellow one wouldn't fly, but the red one did. It was easy."

Oh bum! I hadn't realised Florence had taken the red kite outside too.

"Really?" Jack eyed me suspiciously. "Don't you find that strange, Jill?"

I shrugged.

"Can I play some more?" Florence said.

"You can play for another twenty minutes and then you need to get ready for school." Jack turned to me. "Is there anything you want to tell me?"

"Like what? I don't know what you mean."

"Don't you find it curious that the yellow kite won't fly but the red one will."

"Not in the least." I stood up and took the breakfast pots over to the sink.

"I wondered why you'd bought two kites. The red one is magic, isn't it?"

"I have to get ready for work."

"You're busted, Jill."

"I still have no idea what you're talking about."

***

As I made my way upstairs, I heard music coming from the outer office. It was a strange tune, kind of folksy, dominated by the sound of bells. Since Mrs K had stepped in for Mrs V, she'd indulged in a number of weird hobbies, but the sight that greeted me took it to another level.

She was dressed as a Morris dancer, complete with straw hat, wooden clogs, and leg pads full of bells. Oblivious to my arrival, she was dancing (if that's what you could call it) while swinging a small wooden stick around.

"Mrs K!"

"Jill, I didn't hear you come in." She stooped down to turn off the music (and I use that term loosely). "You did say I was okay to practise my hobbies while we were quiet."

"You're a Morris dancer?"

"Yes. I started not long after I met the future Mr K. He was already heavily involved in the scene."

And yet, you still married him? "That's nice. Do you and Mr K go Morris dancing often?"

"Not as often as we'd like because we both have so many other hobbies. Do you think you might like to do it, Jill?"

"Me? No, I don't think so."

"It's something you and your husband could do together."

"My ankle isn't up to it."

"What's wrong with it?"

"It's an old injury. I don't like to talk about it. Have there been any calls?"

"Someone from the blinds shop called to confirm that a man will be coming to install your new blinds today."

"I'd forgotten all about that. Anything else?"

"Someone rang to ask why their taxi hadn't turned up."

I was beginning to think Mrs K was making up these

calls.

You cannot be serious!

I stared in disbelief at Winky who was dressed in an outfit not dissimilar to that being worn by Mrs K. He too had bells on his legs and was dancing around the office.

"What are you doing, Winky?"

"Meowis dancing."

"Don't you mean Morris?"

"Nah, we felines came up with this tradition long before you two-leggeds decided to copy it, and it's always been called Meowis."

"That's utter nonsense."

"Why else do you think it ended up being called Morris dancing? Whoever nicked the idea obviously misheard the name."

"Are you any good at it?"

"Of course I am. I've won awards for my Meowis dancing."

"How come you've never mentioned it before?"

"I'm not one to blow my own trumpet. Would you like to join me in a dance?"

"No, thanks. I have a missing bridegroom to track down and a compass stone to find."

"Haven't you found that goose yet?"

"Not yet. I've been really busy."

"Good one." He laughed.

"You'd better take that ridiculous outfit off because the guy will be here to fit the new blinds anytime now."

The words were no sooner out of my mouth than the door opened behind me. Fortunately, I was able to react quickly enough to stop Mrs K coming into the room and seeing Winky.

"The blinds man is here, Jill."

"Okay, give me one minute and then send him through, would you." Once she'd closed the door, I turned to Winky. "You'll have to go outside until he's gone."

"I'm not going out there. It's raining."

He was right; it was pouring down. "Get under the sofa, then, and stay right at the back so he can't see you."

"I'll get my costume dusty under there."

"I don't care. Get under there now or I'll throw you outside, rain or no rain."

"Alright, but I'm going to send you the dry-cleaning bill."

Connor Conway walked through the door. Or so I thought.

"Hello, duck. I'm here to fit your new blinds."

"Hello again."

"*Again*? Have we met before?"

"You came to try and repair the old blinds."

"That wasn't me, duck. That was Connor. I'm Raymond Raynard."

"You look a lot like Connor."

"Don't say that." He laughed. "Connor is an ugly devil."

"How long is this likely to take?"

"Shouldn't be more than an hour. Do you mind if I ask you a question?"

"What's that?"

"Why is your receptionist Morris dancing?"

"It's her hobby."

"And you don't mind her doing that during work

hours?"

"Not while it's quiet."

"I wish my boss were as understanding as you. Is she single?"

"Sorry?

"Your receptionist. Is she single?"

"No, Mrs K is married."

"Pity. She looks really hot in that get up. I was thinking of asking her out on a date."

"Do you think you could get on with fitting the blinds? I am very busy."

"Of course, duck. I'll get straight on it."

I swore if that guy called me *duck* just one more time, I'd turn him into one.

What? I was only joking. I would never do something so reckless.

"Excuse me, duck, I don't suppose there's any chance of a cup of tea, is — ?"

"What have you done?" Winky rushed out from under the sofa.

"He was asking for it."

"Quack, quack," said Raymond, as he waddled around the room.

And of course, Mrs K chose that very moment to walk into the office. "There's a duck on your desk, Jill."

"He just flew in through the window."

"And why is your cat wearing a Morris dancer's costume?"

There was simply no good way to explain away the scene that now confronted Mrs K, so I did the only thing I could: I cast the 'forget' spell, led her back into the outer office, and put her into her chair. Back in my office, I reversed the 'duck' spell, and then cast the 'forget' spell on Raymond. While he was coming around, I told Winky to get out of his costume.

Raymond shook his head. "Do you think I could have a glass of water, duck? I've come over all unnecessary."

"Of course." I stuck my head out of the door. "Mrs K, could you get the blinds man a glass of water, please?"

"Err, yes, of course."

Back in my office, Raymond was sitting on the sofa.

"Are you okay?" I asked.

"I think so. I reckon I must have blacked out for a moment, and I had the weirdest dream. I was a duck, and there was a cat dressed as a Morris dancer standing next to me."

"That is weird. Are you sure you're okay to carry on?"

"I'll be fine once I've had a drink of water. There's no need to worry about me, duck."

***

I could stand no more of that insanity, so I left Raymond to install the new blinds, and headed down to Coffee Animal. I'd no sooner walked through the door than my ears were assaulted by the sound of quacking. I couldn't believe it; this could not be happening. Of all the animals they could have chosen, why did the animal of the day have to be a duck? I'd had more than my share of those for one day, so I magicked myself over to Aunt Lucy's house.

I wasn't sure if she'd be in because it was quite possible that she'd still be signing autographs and taking selfies with her corker fans at Cuppy C.

But for once, I was lucky.

"Jill, how lovely to see you."

"I wasn't sure you'd be in, Aunt Lucy."

"I had no choice." She held up her arm to show me her bandaged wrist.

"What happened? Have you had a fall?"

"No. It's the result of signing all those autographs. I've told the girls I need a break." She looked me up and down. "What about you? Are you okay? You look frazzled."

"I'm fine. Apart from the waterfowl."

"*Waterfowl?*"

"I had a run-in with a duck this morning, and I have to find a goose, but I don't have a clue where to look."

"The butcher down the street usually has a few."

"No. I mean a specific goose."

"I think I'd better put the kettle on while you explain."

As Aunt Lucy made the tea, I told her that I needed to track down the goose that laid the golden egg, but I didn't mention the compass stones or Braxmore.

"I always thought that was just a fable." She handed me the tea and we sat at the kitchen table. "Custard cream?"

"If you're twisting my arm. Thanks."

"I suppose you've already tried Goose Island."

"No. Where's that?"

"I'm not exactly sure. I've never been there myself, but I've heard a few people mention it over the years. I'll get the Candlefield map. It's upstairs, I think." She returned a couple of minutes later and placed the map on the table.

"Why do they call it Goose Island, Aunt Lucy?"

"Take a wild guess."

"Sorry. Silly question."

"There it is." She put her finger on the map. "It's near to Dozy Dale."

"How far is that from here?"

"About half an hour on foot, I'd guess."

"In that case, I'll finish my tea, and then take a walk over there."

I could have saved time by magicking myself to Goose Island, but I figured the walk would help me to wind down. Aunt Lucy had been kind enough to lend me her map, but I couldn't make head nor tail of it, so after a couple of wrong turns, I approached an elf who was passing by.

"Excuse me, sir."

"I don't want to buy any of your potions."

"I'm not selling potions."

"Are you sure?"

"Positive."

"Every time I walk along this road, I get accosted by one of your lot, selling potions, charms and the like."

"*My lot?*"

"Witches. And wizards. I made the mistake of buying a get-taller potion a month ago."

"Did it work?"

He gave me a look. "What do you think?"

"I'm sorry about that, but I can assure you that I'm not selling potions."

"Charms?"

"I'm not selling anything. I was hoping you could direct me to Goose Island."

"Why didn't you say so? You're in Dozy Dale. If you continue down this road for about a mile, you'll come to

Dozy Lake. Goose Island is in the centre of that lake."

"Thanks. Just one more thing. How do I get over to the island?"

"Swim?"

"Isn't there a boat I could hire?"

"Not that I know of." He checked his watch. "I really must be going. I have an appointment with my chiropractor."

"Okay, thanks for your help."

Goose Island was much smaller than Randall's Island, and just as the elf had said, there was no sign of a boat to take me across the lake. I certainly had no intention of swimming, so I cast the 'levitate' spell and floated slowly across the short stretch of water. I was halfway across when a shark popped its head out of the lake and blocked my way.

"Do you mind?" I snapped.

"Not at all."

"What are you doing in this lake anyway? Shouldn't you be in the ocean?"

"What business is that of yours?"

"Just get out of my way."

"I won't. If you want to get past me, you'll have to jump over me."

What a thoroughly unpleasant individual.

"Fine." I levitated a little higher in order to bypass him and then continued towards the island. As I got closer, I expected to see the geese who gave the island its name, but there was no sign of them. I was beginning to fear this might be yet another dead end.

When I reached the island, I lowered myself gently to

the ground.

"Geese! Oh geese!" I shouted. "Where are you?"

Nothing.

Why call it Goose Island if there isn't a single—

The air was suddenly full of honking noises, and from nowhere a huge gaggle of geese appeared. They were headed straight for me. I'd never been a big fan of geese; I found them quite intimidating, particularly in such large numbers, so I started to back away.

I was just about to set off back across the lake when the goose at the front spoke.

"Please don't leave. We get so few visitors out here."

"I'm not surprised. You probably scare them all away by making that awful noise."

"That's our welcome song."

"You could have fooled me."

"It's true. It's called Welcome to Goose Island."

"Oh? Do you think you could get your friends to stop— err—singing for a while."

"This is the Goosey Choir."

"Right. Maybe you could just have them pause for a few minutes?"

"Sure." He made a gesture to the others with his wing, and the 'choir' fell silent.

"I'm Gander," the talkative goose said.

"As in Goosey Goosey?"

"Sorry?"

"You know. Goosey Goosey Gander."

He shrugged. "I have no idea what you're talking about."

"Never mind. I'm Jill."

"Would you like to join us for a drink?"

"Sure. What do geese drink?"

"We have tea, coffee or hot chocolate. Unless you'd prefer a soft drink?"

"Tea will be fine."

Gander led the way to the centre of the island and a few minutes later, one of his feathery colleagues brought us both a cup of tea.

"This is delicious. Is it a special goose brew?"

"No, it's Earl Grey. What brings you to Goose Island, Jill?"

"I'm hoping you might be able to help me find a particular goose."

"We will if we can. Do you have a name?"

"Err, no. Actually, I'm looking for the goose that lays the golden eggs."

"You mean Freda."

"Do I?"

"Definitely. She's been doing that for years. It's kind of her party piece."

"Does she live here on the island?"

"No. The last I heard she was living in Down Court, but let me check with Lucy, she's Freda's niece." Gander honked at the top of his voice and a few moments later, a small white goose came rushing forward. "Lucy, this is Jill. She wants to speak to your Aunt. Does Freda still live in Down Court?"

"Yes, she does."

"Do you know Down Court, Jill?" Gander asked.

"No, but I'm sure I'll find it."

"I could take you there if you like," Lucy offered.

"That would be great. If it isn't too much trouble."

"No trouble at all. It's been a while since I visited my

aunt. When did you want to go?"

"No time like the present."

After I'd finished my tea and said my goodbyes to Gander and the Goosey Choir, I followed Lucy back across the lake.

"Is your Aunt's place far from here?"

"It's over an hour on foot."

"What if you flew?"

"That would only take a few minutes."

"How would you feel about flying with me on your back?"

She looked me up and down and gulped. "I'm not sure I'd be able to carry you."

"I didn't mean in my present form." I cast the 'shrink' spell. "How about like this?"

"That, I can manage. Climb aboard."

It was a little scary, but I managed to keep a grip on Lucy's feathers as we made our way back to the city.

"That's it down there." She gestured with one wing, almost causing me to lose my balance. "Sorry, Jill."

"I'm okay."

"Going down."

After a remarkably smooth landing, I reversed the 'shrink' spell, and then Lucy led the way to her aunt's apartment.

"I had no idea that geese lived in places like this."

"The island is okay when you're young, but it can be rather cold for the elders."

"Are all the residents of this apartment block geese?"

"Geese and ducks. There are a couple of swans too, but no one likes them." Lucy stopped outside a red door.

"This is it." She knocked and went straight in. "Auntie! It's Lucy."

A larger goose, wearing reading glasses, appeared at the other end of the hall. "Lucy, what a lovely surprise. Who's your friend?"

"This is Jill, Aunt Freda. She asked me to bring her to see you."

"You'd better both come in. The kettle has just boiled."

And so it was that I had my second cup of tea in the company of geese, in the space of an hour.

"You're the first two-legged that's been inside this apartment. To what do I owe this honour?"

"Gander suggested that you might be the goose I've been searching for."

"Me? Why would you be looking for me?"

"Gander said you can lay golden eggs."

"Oh that." She sighed. "Blooming nuisance, is all that is."

"It's true, then?"

"Oh yes, it's true."

I didn't understand it. The apartment at Down Court was nice enough, but if she was able to lay gold eggs, why wasn't she living in a huge mansion?

"May I ask what you do with them?"

"The egg man buys them from me." In fact, he should be here any time now for today's batch."

"There are some here now?"

"Yes. They're in the kitchen."

"Could I see them?"

"I suppose so, but there's not much to see. Follow me." She led the way into the kitchen where there was an egg box containing six eggs on the table.

"They really are gold."

"That's right. No one seems to know why. The doctor thinks it may be something to do with one of my genes. They taste fine, though. Or so I'm told."

"Can I pick one up?"

"Of course."

As soon as I picked it up, it was obvious that it wasn't real gold because it was much too light.

"I thought they were — err — "

"Were what, Jill?" Lucy said.

"*Real* gold."

Freda and Lucy looked at one another and began to laugh.

"Why on earth would you think that?" Freda said.

"It doesn't matter. Can I ask, Freda, are you one of the guardians?"

"*Guardians*? What do you mean?"

"Have you ever heard of the compass stones?"

"No. What are they?"

"It's a long story. Too long to go into now. I'm trying to track them down, and to find the next one, I have to find the goose that laid the golden egg."

"But there's no such thing, Jill. That's just a fable."

Nice as Freda, Lucy and Gander were, the whole thing had been a colossal waste of time. Freda did indeed lay golden eggs, but they were gold-coloured eggs, which meant she couldn't possibly be *the bird that was too valuable to kill*. Perhaps the clue meant something else entirely.

But what?

Chapter 13

I'd arranged to meet with Harry's sister, Gloria, at two o'clock. It was only one-thirty, but rather than hang around, I decided to take my chances by turning up early. She lived in a terraced house in Tall Trees, a suburb of Washbridge. As I approached the door, I heard raised voices coming from inside: A man and a woman. As soon as I rang the doorbell, the voices fell silent, and moments later, a young woman answered the door. She was red in the face and looked upset about something.

"Gloria?"

"Yes?"

"I'm Jill Maxwell. I phoned yesterday."

"I thought we said two o'clock?"

"Yes, sorry. I can come back in half-an-hour if you have company."

"I don't. There's no one else here. You'd better come in."

"Okay, thanks." I would have liked to ask her about the man's voice, but I didn't want to upset her ahead of our discussion.

"Through here." She led the way into the lounge, which was on the front of the house.

As I took a seat, I thought I heard a door close somewhere in the house. "I'm sorry for arriving early."

"That's okay. Would you like a drink?"

"No, thanks. I've just had one with the geese."

"Sorry?"

Oh bum! Failure to engage brain again.

"Mr and Mrs Geese. They're clients of mine on another case."

"I see. Do you have any idea what happened to Harry yet?"

"Not yet, I'm afraid. Are you and Harry close?"

"Of course. He's my brother."

"Not all siblings get along. My sister and I have always argued."

"Harry is my best friend as well as my brother."

"In that case, I assume you and he must have discussed the wedding. How was he feeling about it? Was he having second thoughts? Getting cold feet?"

"No, nothing like that. He was excited."

"What about his relationship with Lorna? Had there been any signs of stress that you noticed?"

"No. And none that he mentioned to me."

"How do you get on with her?"

"Lorna? Fine."

I waited for her to elaborate, but she didn't. "You weren't at the rehearsal on the day your brother went missing?"

"There was no reason for me to be there. It's not like I was the maid of honour or even a bridesmaid."

"How did you hear of his disappearance?"

"Robert, his best man, called me."

"When?"

"When it became obvious that Harry wasn't on the island. I'm not sure of the precise time."

"When was the last time you spoke to your brother?"

"The night before he disappeared. He phoned me."

"Does he call you often?"

"Most days. Like I said, the two of us are very close."

"Are you married, Gloria?"

"Yes, why?"

"No reason. Is your husband at home?"

"No, I told you that I'm here alone. He's at work." She made a show of checking her watch. "There's somewhere I need to be in half an hour. Will this take much longer?"

"No, I'm all done, thanks."

I couldn't shake the feeling that Gloria wasn't telling me everything she knew. There was no doubt in my mind that I'd heard her arguing with a man when I arrived, and yet she'd insisted she was alone in the house. When I'd asked how she got along with Lorna her response had been underwhelming to say the least. Clearly, she wasn't a fan. I definitely sensed some bitterness about not being asked to be the maid of honour or a bridesmaid. And why had she been so eager to cut short our discussion? Her excuse that she needed to be somewhere didn't ring true because I'd arrived much earlier than arranged, and I'd only been there for a matter of minutes. Throughout our discussion, she'd seemed nervous. Did she know more than she was saying?

***

There was no sign of Winky when I got back to the office, but there were a couple of hats on the sofa. Very strange.

I'd only been at my desk a few minutes when the door flew open and in charged Farah. It would have been a case of déjà vu, except this time Delilah was by her side. They were both clearly distressed.

"It's happened again, Jill," Farah said. "Another dog has gone missing."

"Are you absolutely sure? It's just that last time—"

"I'm positive. Tell her, Delilah."

"Farah's right," Delilah confirmed. "One minute Hug was in the cage, and the next he'd gone."

"*Hug?*"

"He's a pug."

"Right, let's go find him, then."

I despatched Mrs K to look down on the street. Despite protests from Farah and Delilah that I was wasting my time, I insisted that we check Bubbles.

"He's not there, Jill," Farah said. "We both checked this time."

"How many pugs do you have in for grooming today?" I asked.

"Just the one. Just Hug."

"And does Hug look anything like him?" I pointed to the pug sitting in the cage.

"It can't be," Delilah said. "That's him."

"I'm beginning to think you're doing this for a laugh, Farah," I said.

"Honestly, Jill. He wasn't there before. The cage was empty, wasn't it, Delilah?"

"Definitely. I don't understand it."

That made three of us. Perhaps the fumes from the shampoo were causing them to hallucinate.

"Not to worry. All's well that ends well. I'd better get back to my office."

"Sorry to have wasted your time," Farah called after me.

"No problem."

"There's no sign of him out there, Jill." Mrs K was on her way back up the stairs.

"It's okay. He's back, safe and sound."

I'd just sat back at my desk when Winky came through the window and rushed over to the sofa.

"Which one of these do you like?" he said.

"You're a cat. You shouldn't be wearing a hat."

"Why not?"

"Because — err — just because."

"How about this trilby?"

"No."

"Okay. How about the fedora, then?"

"Definitely not."

"Are you sure? I think I look good in it."

***

I hadn't exactly covered myself in glory when pretending to be a journalist, so I planned to use a different cover story for my visit to Washbridge Studios. I was going to pretend to be the lead singer of a band, looking for a studio where we could record our next album.

Washbridge Studios were located in a modern building on a small industrial estate just off the main Washbridge to West Chipping road. The woman behind reception looked familiar, but I couldn't place her.

"Jill, it is you, isn't it?"

"Err, yeah."

"How are you?"

"Fine, thanks."

"How long has it been?"

"I — err —"

"It must be at least five years. More even."

"I guess so."

"What brings you here?"

"I have an appointment with Roger Tunes."

"You do?" She checked her computer. "I don't see anything."

"I booked it under my stage name."

"Vicky Voss?"

"That's it."

"I always said you should have joined us."

Us? Who was *us*?

"We split up you know."

"You did?"

"Pity really. The usual story. Artistic differences."

"Of course."

"Things might have been different if you'd taken up our offer to be the *The*."

It all came flooding back to me. Brenda had been a member of the sensation that was The Coven. Famous, amongst other things, for their routine where they went down on one knee, and then jumped up, announcing: We. Are. The. Coven. I'd been invited to join them and become the The, but I'd declined. Not long afterwards, Brenda had struck out on her own under the name 'We'. As a solo artist, she'd really hit the big time. The last time I'd seen her was when Jack, Kathy, Peter and I had seen her in concert.

"How come you're working here, Brenda?"

"My management turned out to be scumbags. I had no idea what I was doing when I signed with them. By the time I realised what was going on, it was too late, and I was left with nothing."

"But you were so talented. Couldn't you have started again?"

"Probably, but the whole affair left me totally jaded. Maybe I'll go back to it one day."

"How did you end up here?"

"I knew Roger Tunes from the time when we recorded our album here. He heard what had happened and offered me this job. But enough about me, tell me what you're up to."

"I — err —"

Just then, a tall, bald man with a goatee walked into reception.

"Vicky? I'm sorry if I've kept you waiting. I'm Roger Tunes."

"It's okay. I've only just arrived."

"Why don't I show you around?"

"That would be great."

"See you later, Jill," Brenda said.

"See you."

"Do you know Brenda?" Roger asked.

"Yeah. We go way back."

"Did she call you Jill?"

"Yeah, Vicky is my stage name."

"Of course. How do you know Brenda, if you don't mind my asking?"

"Not at all. She once invited me to join The Coven."

"It's so sad what happened to them." He opened a door and gestured for me to lead the way inside. "This is our main studio. We do have another, smaller one, but that's being upgraded at the moment. What do you think of it?"

I looked around slowly, pretending to study the equipment. "Very impressive."

"The 645 True Sound desk was only installed last year. It's top of the range, but I'm sure I don't need to tell you that."

"Quite."

"What's the name of your band, Vicky?"

"*Band*? Err, the Witches."

"Vicky Voss and the Witches. Very catchy. I don't remember seeing any of your albums. What kind of music do you play?"

"Rock. Hard rock."

"My favourite." He pointed to the room on the other side of the glass. "Why don't you go through there and give her a test drive?"

"Sorry?"

"You'll want to test the acoustics. Which instrument do you play?"

"Err, none. I'm the singer."

"Of course. Well, the mic is primed and ready to go. If you nip next door and give us a few bars, you'll get a feel for the place."

"I'd love to, but I'm under strict orders to rest my vocal cords for two weeks." I rubbed my throat. "Nodules."

"Nasty. When are you hoping to record your album?"

"In a couple of months."

"You've left it rather late. We have very few free slots available, but we should be able to sort something out. Would you like me to book you in now?"

"Not yet. I'm going to take a look around Wash Sounds first. I'll make a decision after I've seen what they have to offer."

"Orlando and I go way back. Our setup is far superior to his, in my opinion." He grinned. "But then I would say that, wouldn't I?"

"Are the two of you friends?"

"I wouldn't call us friends, exactly."

"I heard a rumour that he'd had some problems over there."

"I heard the same thing, but I wouldn't take much notice of rumours. I never do. By all means, go and take a look around Orlando's place. I'm confident that you'll choose us in the end. When you do, give me a call and we'll set up a date."

Brenda was on the phone when I returned to reception, so I gave her a quick wave and was on my way. Maybe he was just an accomplished actor, but Roger Tunes had come across as a genuine kind of bloke. When I mentioned that I'd heard rumours of problems at Wash Sounds, I'd opened the door for him to stick the boot in, but he hadn't done so. Instead, he'd encouraged me to check out the competition before making my decision. He was clearly confident in the quality of his offering.

***

We were almost out of dog food, so I called in at the village store.

"I'm so glad you agreed to take part, Jill," Marjorie Stock said.

"Take part in *what*?"

"The crossword competition on Sunday."

"I didn't."

"But your grandmother put both of your names down for it."

"Grandma?"

"Yes. I had no idea that the lady who ran the hotel was

your grandmother. Such a lovely woman. Did you know she's opening a wig shop in Washbridge?"

"Err, yeah. When did she do this? Sign me up, I mean?"

"This morning."

"I'm sorry, but I don't think I can make it on Sunday."

"But you have to. The names have been submitted now. Please don't withdraw, Jill. Cynthia and I have been looking forward to this all year."

"I—err—okay."

"You'll take part?"

"It doesn't look like I have a choice. Where do I find the dog food?"

"Under 'F' for food."

I was still spitting feathers when I got back to the old watermill, where Jack met me in the hallway.

"You'll never guess what that woman has done now!"

"Slow down, Jill. What's wrong? Which woman?"

"Grandma. Who do you think?"

Jack just shook his head.

"Not satisfied with taking all the credit for rescuing the lido, now she's roped me into some stupid crossword competition."

He shook his head again and seemed to be gesturing towards the kitchen.

"What's wrong? Where's Florence?"

"In the kitchen. With your grandmother."

Oh bum!

"Why didn't you warn me?" I whispered.

"You didn't give me the chance."

Florence came through the kitchen door, holding a huge toffee lollipop. "Look what Great-Grandma bought for me. It's yummy." Before I could stop her, she threw her arms around me, leaving sticky handprints on my jacket, and then she gave me a sticky toffee kiss.

"That's lovely. Why don't you and Daddy go and play a game in the lounge? Mummy needs to speak to Great-Grandma."

"What's that all over your face?" Grandma said. "That jacket of yours could do with dry cleaning."

"Never mind that. What gives you the right to sign me up for a crossword competition?"

"You might enjoy it."

"You should have asked me first."

"You'd have said no."

"That's precisely why you should have asked."

"I hear you're looking for a goose."

"Sorry?"

"Lucy tells me you're looking for a goose."

"Well, yes. I went to Goose Island earlier."

"Did the choir sing to you? Such lovely voices they have. Did you find the goose you were looking for?"

"No."

"Pity. You weren't by any chance searching for the goose that laid the golden egg, were you?"

"I thought I was, but now I'm not sure."

"Oh." She stood up. "In that case, you won't be interested in what I came to tell you."

"Hang on. What do you mean? What did you come to tell me?"

"That I know where you can find the goose that laid the golden egg."

Chapter 14

Over breakfast, Florence was in a contemplative mood.

"Mummy, why do spiders have eight legs, but we only have two?"

"I don't know, darling. They just do."

"I'd like to have eight legs. Why do fish live in water?"

"Because they like it in there."

"But they're wet all the time. I don't think I'd like to be wet all the time. Why are ice cubes so cold?"

I turned to Jack. "Feel free to help out at any time."

"You seem to be doing just fine." He grinned.

"Why, Mummy?"

"Because the freezer is cold. I think Buddy wants to play ball." Buddy looked at me and shook his head. "Look, he's really eager."

Florence picked up the reluctant Chihuahua and went out into the garden.

"Thanks for all your help, Jack."

"I figured you had it covered, what with you being a crossword master and all." He laughed.

"I'm glad you think it's funny. There are tons of things I'd like to do this Sunday; taking part in a crossword competition isn't even in the top thousand."

"Why did you agree to do it, then?"

"You know why. Grandma blackmailed me. If I hadn't agreed, she wouldn't have told me where I can find the goose that lays the golden eggs."

"You still haven't told me where that is."

"That's because part of the deal was that I had to promise not to tell anyone."

"That doesn't include me. I'm your husband."

"Grandma made a point of saying especially not to tell you."

"Whisper it. She'll never know."

"That's what Winky thought and he ended up with a wig stuck to his head. Do you really want to take that risk?"

Jack ran his hand across his head. "Perhaps not. By the way, before you came downstairs, Florence was asking about that Kids' Music Fest thing. It's this weekend, isn't it?"

"Yeah. On Saturday."

"Florence reckons you said Wendy could go with us. Am I supposed to be asking Donna?"

"Don't mention anything about it to her yet. There's something I need to check out first."

"Do you want to tell me what that is?"

"No. This is on a strictly need-to-know basis."

"Fair enough."

"Have you seen my handbag?"

"It's on the sofa where you left it."

"Hey there!" Wanda shouted. I pretended not to hear her, grabbed my bag, and made for the door. "Hey, cloth ears, I'm talking to you."

"Oh, sorry, I didn't hear you, Wanda. Actually, I'm just on my way to work."

"I'm not happy." She made a bubble-sigh.

"Whyever not? You have this lovely tank and all these fantastic ornaments, colour coordinated to your exacting standards."

"I'm lonely."

"It's just a phase you're going through. You'll be as

right as rain later."

"I'm in this tank all day with no one for company."

"Jack and I are in the lounge with you most evenings."

"That's no consolation. Listening to you two droning on about nothing much in particular is worse than the silence."

"Gee thanks."

"So, what do you intend to do about it?"

"What do you expect me to do?"

"Get some friends for me to talk to."

"Friends? Plural?"

"Yes."

"This tank isn't big enough for more than two fish, so how about I just get you one friend?"

"That would be better than nothing, I suppose. When?"

"It might take a while."

"But I'm *ever* so lonely."

"Okay, okay. I'll get you a friend today."

"Do you promise?"

"I promise."

I was just on my way out when Jack called to me from the kitchen.

"What is it? I need to get going."

"I was just wondering what this is in the bin?"

"Can't you tell?"

"It looks like a bottle full of bits of wood and cloth."

"Then you'd be wrong. That masterpiece is the Cutty Sark."

"Really?" He examined it from a number of different angles. "Are you sure?"

"According to Mrs K. She was the one who made it."

"What's it doing in the bin?"

"Would you prefer it was on the mantlepiece?"

"Definitely not." He dropped it back into the bin.

***

There was no point in going directly to the pet shop because it wouldn't be open. As I made my way upstairs in the office building, I wondered which of Mrs K's many hobbies I would have to deal with today. I couldn't hear any music, so hopefully that meant I'd seen the back of the Morris dancing.

When I walked through the door, I almost jumped for joy because sitting behind the desk was a Mrs of the V variety.

"Mrs V!" I rushed around the desk and gave her a hug. "You're back!"

Clearly uncomfortable with my over-the-top show of affection, she managed to wiggle free. "Jill, whatever has got into you?"

"Sorry. I'm just so happy to see you. How is your sister?"

"Much improved, I'm pleased to say. I'm not sure I could have taken another day down there. I trust Kay did a satisfactory job in my absence?"

"Mrs K? Yeah, she did a great job. Except—err—"

"What happened?"

"Nothing really. It's just that she has so many hobbies."

"Kay always has had a lot of interests."

"She was Morris dancing in here yesterday."

"Oh dear. That's hardly appropriate."

"It was my own fault. I did say she was free to indulge

in her hobbies when things were quiet. Anyway, never mind that now, you're back and that's all that matters. Can I get you a cup of tea?"

"I wouldn't hear of it. That's my job. I'll bring it through to you."

"Can I give you another hug."

"I'd rather you didn't."

"Okay."

"Mrs V is back!" I announced to Winky.

"Big whoop!" He scowled.

"I've missed her so much."

"I haven't." He pulled out several sheets of paper. "This is for you."

"What is it?" I took it from him. "A petition to bring back Jules?"

"Yes, and as you can see, the demand is overwhelming."

"I don't recognise any of the names on here except for yours. Who are they?"

"People who care about my welfare. They know that being in the same office as the old bag lady is detrimental to my health."

"These signatures have all been written by the same person."

"No, they haven't."

"Yes, they have. It's obvious. And they've all been written with the same pen too."

"Are you going to act on this petition or not?"

"Not." I tore it into a dozen pieces and deposited it in the bin.

Half an hour later, Winky was still grumbling to himself. "Do you know how long it took me to write — err — I mean collect all those signatures?"

"I neither know nor care. Anyway, I have to nip to the pet shop."

"What are you buying for me? A new collar would be nice. Velvet, preferably."

"I'm buying a goldfish."

"I thought you already had one?"

"I do, but Wanda is lonely and wants a friend."

"So that's how it is, is it? She just has to snap her fins, and you go out to buy her a friend. What about me? I get lonely too."

"Rubbish. You have lots of friends. Goodness knows how."

"That would be my charismatic personality."

***

"Back again?" Rupert was busy updating the window display at Rue Pets.

"I need a goldfish."

"Don't tell me Goldie has passed away? Your poor daughter must be distraught."

"Who's Goldie? Oh wait, did you say *Goldie*? I thought you said Rodney. No, Goldie is still going strong." More's the pity.

What? Of course I was joking. Sheesh!

"Thank goodness for that." Rupert sighed with relief. "You had me worried there."

"Goldie is lonely. I mean, I think she is. Obviously, I can't know that for sure, but she gives me that impression."

"The tank you bought is certainly large enough to accommodate two goldfish without any issues. Would you like to come over here, to pick one out?"

"Pick one? Aren't they all the same?"

"Absolutely not. They all have their own distinct personality."

"O—kay." I watched the goldfish swimming back and forth while trying to decide which one would be a good match for Wanda. "I'll take that one."

"That one?"

"No. The one behind it."

"This one?"

"No. It's over there now."

"This one?"

"Yeah, that's it."

"Good choice." He popped the net into the tank and scooped out the fish. "I'm sure they'll get on like a house on fire."

I wanted to pay another visit to Harry's sister's house, but I could hardly do that with a goldfish in my hand. I didn't like the idea of leaving it in the car, so I found a quiet alleyway and magicked myself back to the old watermill.

"Jill?" Jack was at the kitchen table, tapping away on his computer. "Where did you spring from?"

"I needed to bring this home." I held up the goldfish.

"Why did you buy that? Wanda isn't dead, is she? She looked okay earlier."

"No, she's fine, but she was complaining about being lonely."

"Did you drive all the way home, just to bring that back?"

"Not exactly."

"You used magic, didn't you? I thought you said you wouldn't do that unless it was absolutely essential?"

"It *was* essential. I have to check out a house this afternoon, and I can't afford to draw attention to myself. If I walked around carrying a goldfish, I'm pretty sure someone would notice me."

"Is it a boy or a girl?"

"I've no idea. I never thought to ask." I pulled open the drawstring on the plastic bag. "Excuse me, fish?"

"What?"

"I was just wondering, are you a boy or a girl?"

"What does it look like?"

"I—err—what do I call you?"

"Mabel."

"Right."

"How long are you planning to leave me in this awful bag?"

"Not much longer." I turned to Jack. "I think she and Wanda are going to get on just fine."

***

When I'd been with Harry's sister, Gloria, something had felt off. It had started even before I got through the door when I'd heard raised voices. There was no doubt in my mind that Gloria had been arguing with someone, but she'd insisted that she was alone in the house. Gloria had told me that her brother was looking forward to the wedding, and that there hadn't been any signs of stress between Harry and Lorna. She'd been less than forthcoming when I'd asked how she and Lorna had got along. There was a strong possibility I was barking up the wrong tree, but I still wanted to find out who had been in the house with her the previous day.

Could it have been Harry? Was he hiding there?

For once my luck was in because I'd no sooner turned onto the road where she lived than I saw her climb into her car and drive away. I gave her a few minutes and then made my way along the street, looking out for CCTV cameras. Bingo! The house directly opposite Gloria's had cameras mounted just below the roof.

If I just turned up at the neighbours' door and asked to view their CCTV footage, I'd no doubt get short shrift, so I popped around the back of Gloria's house, and used magic to change my attire.

"Hello, constable," said the man who answered the door. I could barely see his face behind the huge plume of smoke coming from his pipe.

"Good morning, sir." I coughed. "I noticed you have CCTV cameras on the front of your house."

"I do indeed. Those are Maxview CT35As. The man in the shop tried to fob me off with Maxview CT34s, but I told him that I didn't want yesterday's technology."

"Right. There was an incident on this street yesterday, and I believe it may have been caught on your cameras."

"An incident, you say?" He blew out another huge cloud of smoke. It smelled like he was smoking dung. "What kind of incident?"

"A young woman had her phone snatched."

"Disgraceful. What is the world coming to when you

can't walk down the street without some yob stealing your property?"

"Quite. That's why I was hoping to take a look at the footage from your cameras."

"If it helps you to put Johnny Thief behind bars, Algernon Allegory is only too happy to help."

"That's very kind of you Mr Allegory."

"Call me Algernon, please. Come inside, young lady. The command centre is in my study." The hall reeked of tobacco smoke. On the walls were a number of framed photographs, all of Algernon, sporting different pipes. "I'm the founder member of WADPA."

"Of what?"

"It stands for Washbridge And District Pipe Aficionados. Have you ever tried a pipe, young lady?"

"No, I don't smoke." The smoke in the hall was growing thicker and I lost sight of him. "Algernon, where are you?"

"This way. Follow my voice."

I did as he said and found him in his office, sitting in front of a bank of screens.

"If you're busy, Algernon, you can leave me to it. I'm quite familiar with CCTV controls."

"I'm never too busy to help the long arm of the law. Now, you said the incident took place yesterday, I believe. What time would that have been?"

I'd originally arranged to meet Gloria at two o'clock, but I'd arrived thirty minutes early. Whoever was in the house with her must have arrived some time before that.

"Could we start at one o'clock, please?"

"Absolutely."

Algernon certainly knew his stuff, and within a matter

of minutes, the timestamp showed one o'clock. Just as I'd hoped, the camera had captured images of the road, and the houses on the opposite side of the street.

The two of us watched the screen intently. For most of the time, the street was deserted. Occasionally, a car would drive past, and a few pedestrians walked in either direction. At one-thirty, a figure approached the house opposite, and knocked on the door. A few moments later, she disappeared inside the house. Thankfully, Algernon didn't seem to notice that the person on screen was me. A few minutes later, a man appeared from behind the house and hurried away down the street.

"Are you sure you have the right time?" Algernon paused the tape.

"Positive. Maybe it happened further down the street."

"The Browns, three doors down have CCTV. It isn't up to the standard of the Maxview CT35A, obviously, but it might have captured what you're looking for."

"Thanks, Algernon, I'll go and check with them."

I didn't bother going to the Browns' house because I'd already got everything I needed. Not long after I'd entered Gloria's house, I'd heard a door close. The man I'd heard arguing with Gloria had obviously made a quick exit, and he'd been caught on Algernon's CCTV. It wasn't her brother, Harry. It was Robert Tonking, the best man.

Why had Gloria denied there was anyone in the house with her, and what had they been arguing about?

***

According to Mad, the ghouls had something truly

awful planned, and I believed I now knew what it was. Fortuitously, I'd overheard the men working on the stage for the Kids' Music Fest. They'd said the ghouls would be arriving on Friday evening, ahead of Saturday's show. The workmen had appeared to be human, but for all I knew, they may have been undercover ghouls. Either way, I had to warn Mad, so that she and her people could take action. Otherwise, there could be a bloodbath on Saturday.

I made a call.

"Mad's phone. Brad speaking."

"Hi, Brad, it's Jill. Is she around?"

"She's just nipped across the road for coffee. Shall I ask her to call you when she gets back?"

"Could you ask her to meet me in Washbridge Park, near the east gate?"

"Sure. When?"

"Straight away. Tell her it's urgent, would you?"

"Okay. Will do."

Chapter 15

While I was waiting for Mad at the park gates, I made two phone calls: the first to Gloria, the next to Robert. I didn't mention to either that I had called the other, but I had a feeling that I didn't need to. They both agreed to meet me the next day in Coffee Animal. When they asked what it was about, I was deliberately vague. I was hoping that the uncertainty would put them off-balance.

Mad appeared, coffee cup in hand; she looked out of breath.

"Brad said it was urgent."

"It is. I think I may have a lead on your ghouls."

"Tell me."

"I overheard them talking about it."

"Overheard *who*?"

"Two guys who were assembling that stage."

"Were they sups?"

"Not as far as I could tell."

"What exactly did they say?"

"That the ghouls are going to be here on Friday night."

"They must have been droids; there have been unsubstantiated reports of ghouls using them in the human world."

"It's the Kids' Music Fest here on Saturday."

"I know, and ghouls really love children's young flesh. If you're right, and the ghouls are going to target the music fest, it will be an absolute bloodbath."

"You'll need to call for backup, I assume?"

"Yeah, but not until I know more." She started towards the stage.

"Mad, what are you going to do?"

"I have no idea."

"That's okay, then. For a minute there, I thought you didn't have a plan."

I caught up with her and we headed towards the portacabin that was behind the stage.

"Mad, I think—"

"Shush!" She put her finger to her lips, and then mouthed, "There's someone in there."

"Can you hear what they're saying?" I whispered.

She shook her head. "I'm going in."

"You can't. Not alone. I'm coming with you."

"No. Stay here. If I'm not out in ten minutes, go to GT and tell my boss what's happened."

"I can't let you go in—"

"Jill, please! For once in your life do as I ask."

"Okay, but be careful."

This did not sit well with me at all, but what she said made sense, so I stayed back while she went inside the portacabin.

I couldn't hear what was being said inside, but there were no screams, which I took as a good sign. Eight minutes later, and there was no sign of Mad. Nine minutes and still no sign. Another twenty seconds and I would magic myself to GT. Hopefully, I'd be back with reinforcements in time to rescue Mad.

The door to the portacabin opened, and she stepped out. On first glance, she didn't appear to be injured. In fact, she had a huge grin on her face.

"Are you okay?" I rushed over to her.

"I'm fine." She chuckled.

"What happened?"

She produced a rolled-up poster from behind her back, opened it up, and held it out for me to see. "Look who's headlining on Saturday." She laughed.

"The ghouls are a *band*?"

"Apparently."

"I've never heard of them."

"Neither have I, and I run a record shop."

"I feel like an idiot. I'm sorry, Mad."

"Don't be silly. I'm glad you were wrong. At least there won't be a bloodbath in the park on Saturday. I'd better get back to the shop because Brad has a meeting with the accountant later."

***

I couldn't believe that I'd been so stupid.

What do you mean, you could? Cheek.

I should have realised that if the ghouls (the real ones, not the band) had been planning to attack the spectators at the music festival, their accomplices wouldn't have been discussing it so openly. At the very least, they would have used some kind of code name instead of referring to ghouls. They would probably have said the *hens* were expected on Friday evening. Or the lemons.

Yes, I do realise that someone saying the lemons were expected on Friday would have been weird, but I'm just trying to make a point here. Sheesh, give a girl a break!

After that little diversion, which Mad would probably never allow me to forget, I figured I deserved a cup of tea and a cupcake, so I magicked myself over to Aunt Lucy's house.

"You're lucky to catch me in," Aunt Lucy said. "I've been spending most of my time at the cork museum."

"Is it still drawing in the crowds?"

"It certainly is. Yesterday was the busiest day so far. My wrist is still aching from all the autographs that I signed."

"Who would have thought there were so many corkers?"

"Jill!"

"Sorry. I meant cork enthusiasts."

"Another cupcake?"

"I shouldn't really. Go on, then. Just one."

"I think the twins might be regretting their decision to open the museum."

"Because no one is buying any food or drink?"

"Yes. What makes it even worse is that some people are bringing their own drinks and snacks with them. I thought Pearl was going to have a fit yesterday when she saw one group who had all brought their own flasks."

"Oh dear." I laughed. "Those girls can't buy a break. They should have charged an entrance fee for the museum."

"It's too late for that now."

"Aunt Lucy, do you happen to know where Candle Casino is?"

"Why on earth do you want to know?"

According to Grandma, I would find the goose that laid the golden egg at the casino, but I didn't want Aunt Lucy knowing about my search for the compass stones because she would worry about Florence.

"It's in connection with a case I'm working on."

"Are you sure, Jill? You may think a little flutter is harmless, but gambling can be addictive."

"I won't be gambling, I promise. It's just part of my investigation."

"Alright, then. Do you know Big Pie Lane?"

"I've never heard of it."

"Do you know Small Pie Avenue?"

"No."

"What about Mash Road?"

"Are you making these up?"

"Of course not. You know where the fire station is, don't you?"

"Yes."

"That's Mash Road."

"Okay."

"Walk past the fire station until you come to Small Pie Avenue, then stay on Small Pie Avenue until you reach Big Pie Lane."

"And the casino is on there?"

"Yes, about halfway down the road."

If I'd had any sense (no input from you required, thank you), I would have jotted down the directions. I found the fire station easily enough, but I was unsure which direction to take from there. I opted to go left, and sure enough I came to Small Pie Avenue and then Big Pie Lane.

Mission accomplished!

Or so I thought. After walking from one end of Big Pie Lane to the other, I could see no sign of Candle Casino. Thoroughly exasperated, I approached an elderly vampire who was sitting on a bench, eating a bag of peanuts.

"Excuse me."

He turned away and popped something into his mouth. "Sorry about that. I can't eat peanuts with these in." He tapped his teeth, which I gathered by his previous manoeuvrings must have been dentures (complete with fangs), which he'd just put back into his mouth.

"I'm sorry if I startled you."

"That's okay." He held out the bag. "Would you like some?"

"No, thanks. I was wondering if you know where I can find Candle Casino. I was told it was on this street."

"You don't want to get into that gambling malarky. A friend of mine, Bobby Breeze, lost everything he had on the blackjack."

"I'm not going there to gamble. It's just business. Have they moved?"

"No. They're still where they've always been." He pointed down the road. "Do you see the Pie and Mash shop?"

"Milly's Mash? Yeah, I walked by there. The pies smell delicious."

"They are, especially the chicken and mushroom. The casino is in the basement below Milly's."

"I didn't see a sign."

"There isn't one. I think they try to keep a low profile."

"Right, thanks very much."

"Are you sure you wouldn't like some peanuts?"

"No, thanks." I started down the road, but made the mistake of glancing back, just as the vampire was removing his dentures again.

On my first walk up the street, I hadn't noticed the steps next to the pie and mash shop; they led down to a green door. I pressed the buzzer and moments later, a werewolf opened the door.

"Good afternoon, madam." His high, squeaky voice didn't match his huge frame.

"Hi. Is this Candle Casino?"

"It is indeed." He stepped to one side. "Please come inside. Would you like to check your coat?"

"No, thanks. I'll keep it on."

"Very well. If you need to buy any chips, the cash desk is to your left."

"I thought I'd just take a look around first."

"Of course, madam. If you need anything, just ask one of the hosts."

"Thank you."

The lights were so bright, and the sounds so loud that they stopped me dead in my tracks. The room was way bigger than I'd expected; it must have extended below the adjoining properties. To my left were tables offering roulette, craps and all manner of card games. On the opposite side of the room, was line after line of slot machines, but where was the goose that laid the golden egg? If this turned out to be another dead end, I would not be a happy goosey.

It occurred to me that maybe one of the slot machines had a goose theme, so I walked down the lanes of machines, studying each one as I passed by.

"Are you trying to find the winning machine?" An old witch, bent double with age, cackled to herself. Her stoop was so pronounced that I couldn't see her face at all, just her ridiculous purple hair.

"Actually, I'm looking for one that features geese, but there doesn't appear to be one."

"You want Golden Eggs."

"What's that?"

"It's over there, behind those curtains." She pointed with a crooked finger.

Leaving the witch still cackling behind me, I made my way to the far end of the room and slipped between the red velvet curtains. The Golden Eggs slot machine was ten times larger than the others. On the wall behind it was a banner that announced that three golden eggs on the winning line would pay to the winner a solid gold egg. The wizard who was already playing the machine was grumbling to himself under his breath. I watched as he fed a pile of coins into the machine. Occasionally, he managed to get two golden eggs on the win line, but he never managed to get three. Eventually, empty-handed, he turned away from the machine.

"Don't waste your money on that thing," he said. "It never pays out. I don't know why I bother to play it."

I had only four pound coins in my purse, and I figured I could afford to risk those. With my first attempt, I got zero golden eggs. With my second I got one. The third revealed two golden eggs. And on my final attempt—wait for it—I got none.

Great. What was I supposed to do now?

"Unlucky." The purple-haired, wizened old witch had crept up behind me, but I still couldn't see her face. "Why don't you have another go?"

"I don't have any more pound coins."

"Here." She held out a coin. "This is a lucky one. I can feel it in my bones."

"I can't take your money."

"Go on. Give it a try."

"Okay, thanks." I took the coin, fed it into the slot and pressed the play button.

One golden egg.

Another golden egg.

Three golden eggs!

Bells began to ring, lights began to flash, and something clattered into the tray. It wasn't a golden egg; it was the compass stone.

"Yes!" I punched the air, then turned around to the old witch, but she had disappeared.

***

"Mummy, Wanda has a friend," Florence said, as soon as I walked through the door.

"I know, darling, I bought her this morning."

"Daddy says her name is Mabel, but I want to call her Clementine."

Jack came up behind her and shrugged his shoulders.

"She's your goldfish," I said. "You can call her whatever you like."

"Why don't you tell Mummy what Thomas did at school today, pumpkin?" Jack rolled his eyes at me.

"He turned the board duster into a snake." Florence giggled. "The teacher and all the other kids ran out of the class. I didn't, though, because it was funny."

"It *isn't* funny, though, is it, Florence? Sups shouldn't do magic when there are humans around, should they?"

"I didn't do it, Mummy."

"I know you didn't. What happened afterwards?"

"When everyone else had left the classroom, he turned the snake back into a board duster. When the teacher came back, his face was really funny because he didn't know what had happened."

"Okay. Why don't you stay in here and watch Wanda and Mabel while—"

"Clementine."

"Sorry. Why don't you watch Wanda and *Clementine* while Daddy and I go through to the kitchen?" I grabbed Jack by his arm and led the way. "This nonsense with Thomas has to stop!"

"What can we do about it?"

"First thing tomorrow, I'm going to have a serious chat with Cindymindy and Ricky." I fished the compass stone out of my pocket. "Look what I've got."

"You got it. Brilliant! Where was it?"

"In a slot machine, in a casino in Candlefield."

"What does that have to do with the goose that laid the golden egg?"

"The slot machine is called Golden Eggs. I won this by getting three golden eggs on the winning line."

"How much did you have to spend before you won?"

"Not much. Just a few pounds. I'd actually run out of cash when a strange old witch gave me a coin for another go. That's when I won."

"That was lucky."

"I didn't even get the chance to thank her because she'd slipped away."

"Where are you going to put it?"

"With the other one."

"Which is where?"

"Somewhere no one will ever find them."

Chapter 16

The next morning when I came downstairs, Jack and Florence were already tucking into their breakfast.

"We're reading a camel book at school," Florence announced.

"That's nice, darling." I planted a kiss on her head.

"I want a camel."

"Camels can't be pets."

"Why not?"

"They're too big."

"It could live in the garden."

"No, it couldn't. No one is allowed to have a camel for a pet."

"They have them in the zoo."

"Yes, but that's different."

"It isn't fair."

"It's just the way it is, I'm afraid."

"Camels have humps. I wish Buddy had a hump."

"That dog has always got the hump," Jack said.

"Not helpful." I shot him a look.

"What does Daddy mean?"

"Take no notice of him. Daddy is just being silly, aren't you?"

"Yes, I was just joking, pumpkin. Before you get your breakfast, Jill, I think you'd better take a look at the goldfish."

"They're not—" I mouthed the word *dead*. "Are they?"

"No, but they're clearly agitated about something. There are so many bubbles in that tank it looks like the water is boiling."

"Great."

Jack wasn't kidding. Both fish were clearly distressed, swimming around and around while filling the tank with bubbles.

"Hey, you two, what's going on?"

"I want her gone!" Wanda pointed a fin in the direction of Mabel, just in case I was in any doubt about who she was referring to.

"I need my own bowl!" Mabel demanded.

"You said you were lonely, Wanda. You asked me to get someone to keep you company."

"Yes, but I didn't anticipate that you'd lumber me with this obnoxious individual."

"Can't the two of you at least give it a go? It's been less than twenty-four hours."

"I can't possibly spend another day with her," Mabel said. "She could bore for England. She spent two hours talking about the colour of that arch."

"I was just trying to be friendly," said Wanda. "I wish I hadn't bothered."

"So do I." Mabel swam over to the side of the fish tank where I was standing. "You have to get me out of here or I won't be responsible for my actions."

"Okay, okay. I'll be back in a minute." I hurried into the kitchen.

"Is everything alright in there?" Jack asked.

"Everything is peachy. Just peachy."

"What are you looking for?"

"This."

"What do you need the mixing bowl for?"

"I thought I might bake a cake." I turned on the tap, filled the bowl, and then returned to the lounge.

"I'm not going in that thing," Mabel said.

"It's either this or you stay in there."

"But it's a mixing bowl."

"I know that, but it's all I have until I buy another tank later today. Do you want to go in here or stay in there with Wanda?"

"Put me in the mixing bowl."

I'd just finished transferring Mabel to her new, makeshift home when Jack and Florence walked in.

"Why is Clementine in there?" Florence put her nose up against the glass.

"Who's she calling Clementine?" Mabel said.

"Shush! Not you, darling. I was talking to Mab— Clementine. She and Wanda don't seem to like each other."

"Why not?"

"I don't know. Because they both hate me, probably."

"But that's not a proper goldfish bowl, Mummy."

"I know, but it will have to do until I buy a new one later today. Now, does anyone mind if I get my breakfast?"

Florence had gone up to her bedroom to play.

"I'm sorry about the whole goldfish thing," Jack said. "Not the best way to start your day."

"And it's only going to get worse. I have to have a word with Cindymindy, so that'll be fun."

"What are you going to say to her?"

"I have no idea, but I'm done being nice, that's for sure."

"Don't do anything you might regret."

"And, as if that wasn't bad enough, I have to go to the launch of Grandma's wig shop later."

"What's it called again?"

"WiFY."

"Which stands for?"

"Wigs For You. I could get one for you while I'm in there if you like. You're starting to go a bit thin on top."

"I am not." He ran his fingers through his hair, to reassure himself, presumably.

Snigger.

***

As I walked across the village to Cindymindy's house, I mulled over what Jack had said. There was no sense in going in all guns blazing; I'd only end up doing something stupid. A more diplomatic approach was called for. I would calmly explain what had happened, ask her what she was going to do about it, and even offer to help.

Cindymindy and Ricky, who had a cigarette stuck in the corner of his mouth, were sitting in front of the house, eating what smelled like bacon cobs.

"Hi." I made a point of smiling as I walked down the path.

"Morning." Cindymindy managed through a mouthful of cob.

Ricky blew smoke from his nose.

"Fancy a bacon cob?" Cindymindy offered.

"No, thanks. I've just had breakfast. I wanted a quick word about something that happened at school yesterday."

"You mean Tommy and the snake?" She laughed, spitting out a chunk of bread in the process. "Hilarious, weren't it?"

"Actually, no, it wasn't. Don't you realise he's putting us all in jeopardy? If the rogue retrievers get wind of this, we could all end up back in Candlefield."

"I looked you up," Cindymindy said. "It says you're the most powerful witch in Candlefield, so what are you doing living here?"

"I—err—that's not what I'm here to discuss."

"Think you're better than the rest of us, do you?"

"No, of course not."

"So, what gives you the right to come around here, telling us how to raise our boy?"

"I wasn't trying to tell you how to—"

"Why don't you sling your hook?" Ricky spoke for the first time.

"Yeah." Cindymindy nodded. "And don't come back."

"Are you going to stop your son using magic in class? Yes or no?"

"We might." Cindymindy shrugged.

"Or we might not." Ricky laughed. "Shut the gate on your way out."

I left without another word, but only because if I'd stayed, I would definitely have done something I would later regret. This wasn't the end of this particular matter, though. Not by a long chalk.

The day before, I'd eaten the last of the custard creams from my office stash, and I couldn't face the prospect of a whole day without one, so I called in at the village store.

"Are you okay, Jill?" Marjorie Stock was behind the counter. "You're very red in the face."

"I'm fine, thanks. You haven't moved the custard

creams again, have you?"

"No, they're still in the same place. We may need to have a bit of a shuffle around later, though."

"Another one?"

"We have to make room for more blood oranges. Ever since the hotel opened, we seem to have had a run on them. I can't understand it."

"That is strange." I grabbed a couple of packets of custard creams and took them to the counter.

"Anything else, Jill?"

"No, just these, please."

"Are you looking forward to the crossword competition?"

"I'm counting the minutes."

"And getting in plenty of practice, I hope?"

"Every spare minute I have."

***

I was back in what was rapidly becoming my second home: Rue Pets.

Unsurprisingly, Rupert's face lit up when he saw me.

"Hello again. What is it you're after today? More ornaments for those two fish of yours?"

"I need another fish tank."

"Did you drop the other one? Are the fish okay?"

"They're fine. The tank is fine. They just can't stand the sight of one another."

"What makes you think that?"

A good question. I could hardly tell him they had told me so. "Err, I can just tell."

"Fair enough. Any thoughts on which tank you'd like?"

"I'd better have the same tank and ornaments again, otherwise one of them is bound to complain."

He gave me first a puzzled and then a sympathetic look. He no doubt had me down as some kind of crazy goldfish woman.

"I wish I'd been born a goldfish," Winky said. "You can't spend enough money on those fish of yours. Whereas me, I don't even get a new bowl."

"Stop moaning. You have the life of Riley."

"It's Kylie."

"What is?"

"The saying. It's you have the life of Kylie, not Riley."

"Says who?"

"Every feline in the world, that's who."

"Riley, Kylie, whoever — you have their life."

"And yet, I still have this grotty old bowl."

"If you want a new bowl, you'll have to come up with the cash."

"I will."

"Good."

For some reason, Mrs V seemed to be ring-a-ding dinging when she brought through my much-deserved cup of tea. "I found this in the bottom drawer of my desk, Jill. Any idea what it is?"

"It's one of Mrs K's Morris dancing leg pads."

Mrs V gave it another shake. "It's quite a pleasing sound, don't you think?"

"Not really, no."

"Armi is always saying that he and I should find a hobby that we can share. I'm going to suggest that we take up Morris dancing."

"Just as long as you don't want to practise in the office."

"You needn't have any worries on that score. You and Jack should do it too."

"With Jack's two left feet? I don't think so."

My phone rang.

"Jill, it's me."

"You and Peter should take up Morris dancing, Kathy."

"What are you talking about?"

"You're always saying you'd like a shared hobby."

"I've never said that. I see far too much of Pete as it is."

"Okay. Bye, then."

"Hang on. I haven't told you why I was calling yet."

"Oh yeah. You rang me, didn't you?"

"I worry about you, Jill. I just wanted to confirm the arrangements for Saturday."

"What's happening on Saturday?"

"Give me strength. It's the Kids' Music Fest."

"I knew that. So, what are the arrangements?"

"I thought we could meet at the park gates at one o'clock."

"What time does it start?"

"Two."

"Do we need to be there so early?"

"Definitely. From all accounts, they're expecting a big crowd because of the headliners. Not that you'll have heard of them."

"You mean The Ghouls."

"Wow, I'm impressed."

"I like to keep abreast of contemporary music."

"If you say so. See you on Saturday."

"Good one." Winky laughed. "You? Keep abreast of contemporary music? That's a laugh. Now, me, that's a different story. I have my finger on the pulse of today's music."

"Go on, then, name me the top chart artists of today."

And he did. Or at least, he reeled off a couple of dozen names, none of which I recognised. I had no idea whether they were genuine or if he'd just made them up. Should I claim to be familiar with them all, and run the risk of looking stupid if he'd just picked names out of the air?

I decided to play it safe with a non-committal. "Hmm."

***

If I'd realised that it was hedgehog day at Coffee Animal, I would probably have suggested a different venue. Dot and her nomadic beauty spot were behind the counter.

"Hey, Dot, I'm supposed to be meeting a couple of people in here, but I'm a bit late. I don't suppose anyone has asked for me, have they?"

"Yeah, they're over there in that far corner."

"Great, thanks." I ordered my drink and took it, together with my hedgehog, over to join Gloria and Robert. There was only just enough room on the table for the three cages and the drinks.

"This place is weird with a capital W," Robert said. "Why would they hand out hedgehogs?"

"Think yourself lucky it isn't crocodile day."

"When you called yesterday, you didn't mention that you were going to ring Robert too," Gloria said.

"I figured I didn't need to. Seeing as how you two are so

close."

"What's that supposed to mean?"

"When I came to your house, you told me you were alone, but that isn't true, is it, Gloria?"

"Why would I lie?"

"That's what I'd like to know. Look, let's cut to the chase. I know Robert was in the house that day and that he sneaked out while we were talking. And before you think about denying it, I probably should mention that I've seen CCTV from the house across the road."

The two of them exchanged a glance, then Robert spoke. "It's true. I was at Gloria's, but so what? It's not like it's important, is it?"

"I would have agreed with you if you hadn't sneaked out, and if Gloria hadn't lied. It strikes me that you'd only do that if you had something to hide."

"That's nonsense!" He was losing his cool now.

"It's no good. We have to tell her, Rob," Gloria said.

"No."

"We have to." She turned to me. "Harry couldn't go through with it."

"The wedding?"

"Yeah. He does love Lorna, but he wasn't ready to settle down."

"Why did he agree to get married, then? Never mind, that doesn't matter now. Where is he?"

"We don't know." Gloria sighed.

"Come on. You might as well tell me now."

"We honestly don't know," Rob said.

"You'd better tell me everything that you *do* know. And no more lies."

"Okay." He took a sip of coffee. "The closer it got to the

big day, the more depressed Harry became. I told him he needed to tell Lorna how he felt."

"So did I," Gloria said. "But it didn't do any good. He couldn't bring himself to do it."

Rob picked up the story. "That's when he came up with the idea of disappearing."

"And you didn't think to try and talk him out of it?"

"Of course we did!" he snapped. "We both tried, but it didn't do any good."

"How did he get off the island?"

"We don't know that either. Harry reckoned the plan would only work if we were as in the dark as everyone else there."

"I'll ask again. Where is Harry?"

"We've already told you that we don't know."

"How can you *not* know?"

"He said it would be best if we didn't know where he planned to go. That way, we wouldn't be able to tell anyone."

"This is probably the most ridiculous thing I've ever heard. The least you two can do is tell Lorna the truth."

"We will. Of course we will," Rob said. "But we're worried."

"About telling her? I should think you are."

"No, not that. About Harry. He promised he'd contact us within forty-eight hours to let us know he was safe, but we haven't heard a word from him."

"If he was willing to walk away from his bride-to-be on the eve of her wedding, by faking his own disappearance, you surely can't be surprised if he doesn't follow through on his promise to call you."

"Harry wouldn't leave us hanging like this," Gloria

insisted. "He knows we'll worry."

"I'm sorry, but I don't buy it. He's dumped you two in the same way he dumped Lorna. I suggest you go and tell her everything you know right now because I intend to call her first thing tomorrow."

I grabbed the cage with my hedgehog and headed back to the counter.

"Hey!" the hedgehog shouted.

"What?"

"How about some food for me?"

"I don't have time."

"Well, you're a complete waste of space, aren't you?"

"There's no need to be so spiky."

Chapter 17

I couldn't help but feel sorry for Lorna. She would be devastated when she discovered that Harry had deliberately engineered his own disappearance because he was too cowardly to tell her he didn't want to go through with the wedding. I doubted she would realise it, but in my opinion, she had actually had a lucky escape. Far better to discover his true character now than to spend a lifetime with someone like that.

For now, though, I had problems of my own to deal with. Namely, having to attend the grand opening of Grandma's new wig shop, WiFY. In the past, Grandma had always demonstrated exceptional business acumen, but I couldn't help but think this time she may have misjudged the market. Just how much demand could there be for wigs in Washbridge? I had a horrible feeling that the so-called grand opening could prove to be a non-event. It would be pretty embarrassing if I was the only one who turned up. Snigger.

The queue stretched all the way down the road, which just went to show how much I knew. The majority of those waiting for the shop to open were women, including a few sups. Just as when I'd jumped the queue at the cork museum, I again drew a few angry comments when I walked past those waiting, and knocked on the door.

"Hey, I've been queuing since nine o'clock."

"Can't you see the queue?"

"I'm staff," I lied, desperately hoping Grandma would let me in before I was attacked by the mob.

Fortunately, I didn't have long to wait because she appeared from the back of the shop, opened the door, and ushered me inside.

"Looks like a good turnout," she said, clearly pleased with herself.

"I knew there would be." I glanced around. "You must have spent a fortune stocking this place."

"One has to speculate to accumulate, Jill."

"You've got some wild and wonderful creations in here."

"Do you see anything you fancy?"

"I don't want a wig."

"What about one for that human of yours? He's starting to go a bit thin on top."

"Rubbish. Jack has a full head of hair. Where are the refreshments?"

"There aren't any. I don't want people spilling wine all over the merchandise". She glanced up at the clock. "It's time to let them in, I think. You'd better step back unless you want to be trampled underfoot."

I did as she said, and it was just as well because within a minute the shop was packed. Claiming that I was a member of staff had backfired on me because customers kept approaching me for advice. To escape, I forced my way through the crowd, some of whom were fighting over the same wigs, to the room at the back. I'd just made myself a cup of tea when the door opened, and Grandma walked in.

"I thought I'd find you hiding in here. It's going rather well, don't you think?"

"Very. Shouldn't you stay out front?"

"No need. My new assistant has just arrived."

"She's a bit late, isn't she?"

"Her bus was delayed. I see you haven't purchased anything yet."

"I told you. I don't want a wig."

"I think I have one that will change your mind."

"I doubt that."

"Look in that box." She pointed to a pink and white box on the chair.

"I don't want a wig, Grandma."

"Take a look."

"Okay, anything for a quiet life." I took off the lid and looked inside.

"Take it out." She cackled. "Do you recognise it?"

I pulled out the purple wig and stared at it in disbelief. The last time I'd seen it, it was on the head of the wizened old witch in Candle Casino; the one who had given me the lucky coin.

"I don't understand."

"Take my lucky coin," Grandma said, but not in her own voice.

"It was you. In the casino."

"Give the lady a coconut. I should be on the stage, don't you think?"

"But how did you—?"

"How did I *what*? Look so good in my purple wig? Make the three golden eggs appear on the winning line?"

"I don't believe it. I told you that I didn't need your help."

"And how has that worked out for you so far? The last I heard you'd been on a wild goose chase to, of all places, Goose Island."

"I would have worked it out in the end."

"Hmm. You may as well accept the fact that I'm going to help you whether you want me to or not."

"Okay, but we work together. I won't have you going off and doing your own thing."

"Agreed. Now, shall I wrap that wig up for you?"

***

No, I didn't buy the wig.

I was still in shock at having discovered Grandma had been the mysterious witch in the casino, and I wasn't sure how I felt about her insisting on helping me from then on. On the one hand, it was a relief to share the burden with someone else. On the other hand, it was *Grandma* — enough said.

I was about to head back to the office when my phone rang; it was a very desperate sounding Orlando Song.

"Jill, it's happened again. This is insane. What am I going to do?"

"Take a deep breath and tell me exactly what's happened."

"Troy came over to run through the edits we discussed, and when I played back the recording it was just like the others. It's ruined."

"Sit tight. I'll be over there as quick as I can."

Twenty minutes later, I pulled into the car park of Wash Sounds. The young woman behind reception introduced herself as Claire.

"Orlando will be through in a minute," she said. "He's very upset."

"I'm not surprised."

"I know it's silly, but I feel like this is all my fault somehow."

"Why would you say that?"

"The problems started not long after I began to work here. Orlando has never said anything, but I reckon he must think I'm cursed."

"Don't be silly. I'm sure he thinks no such thing."

Just then, the man himself appeared in the doorway, and beckoned me to follow him.

"Your receptionist thinks you blame her for what's happening," I said.

"That's silly, but I probably have been a little short with her. It's just the stress of all this. Troy is in the studio and he isn't very happy. And to make matters worse, Roy hasn't turned up. I've tried calling him, but he's not picking up."

"What are you going to do about this mess?" Troy looked like he might implode at any moment.

I was puzzled that Troy had directed his question not at Orlando, but at me.

"I told Troy that you are a P.I., Jill," Orlando said, by way of explanation.

"So?" Troy glared at me. "How could you let this happen again?"

Before I could respond, Orlando came to my defence. "To be fair to Jill, she has only been working on the case for a few days."

"Can I listen to the recording?" I said.

"I can't bear to hear it again." Troy started for the door.

"Hold on," Orlando called after him. "Don't you want to schedule a date to rerecord it?"

"Are you kidding? I'm never working here again. In

fact, you can expect a bill from my lawyers for all the time I've wasted." And with that, he left, slamming the door behind him.

Thoroughly demoralised, Orlando sank into the chair. I gave him a couple of minutes before I said, "If you'll take my advice, you'll close the studio until we get to the bottom of this."

"But I've never closed before. Except for at Christmas."

"What's the point in staying open? You just run the risk of alienating more artists and generating even more bad publicity."

He sat in silence for a couple of minutes, then said, "You're right. What choice do I have? You have to find out who's behind this quickly, Jill, or the studio may never open again."

No pressure, then.

***

Florence greeted me at the door. "Buddy is hiding in the bushes, Mummy."

"Maybe he's playing hide and seek."

"He won't come out."

Jack came through from the kitchen. "That's because this little madam has been trying to get him to wear a hump that she made from some old fabric."

"Florence, is that true?"

"He would be my little camel."

"Buddy doesn't want to be a camel," Jack said. "He's obviously quite happy being a dog."

"He's a spoilsport!" Florence huffed.

"Did Thomas do anything naughty at school today?" I

asked, as much to change the subject as anything else.

"He didn't come to school."

"Is he poorly?"

"Don't know." She shrugged. "Can you put the hump on Buddy, Mummy?"

"No, I can't, and I don't want to hear any more about it."

"Not fair!" She stomped off.

"Kids!" I rolled my eyes. "Don't you just love them?"

"You don't think she'll —" Jack hesitated.

"She'll what?"

"Turn Buddy into a real camel."

"No, of course not."

"Are you sure?"

"Not entirely." I hurried after her. "Florence, come here."

Before Florence went to bed, I'd secured a promise from her that she wouldn't turn Buddy into a camel. More importantly, I'd satisfied myself that such a spell was far beyond her capabilities.

Until I went into the lounge, and saw the mixing bowl, I'd totally forgotten about the new goldfish tank, which I'd left in the car.

"Where's my new home?" Mabel demanded. "Don't tell me you forgot about it."

"No, I didn't forget. I'll go and get it." I hurried out to the car, grabbed the fish tank, and transferred Mabel to her new home.

"Happy now?"

"Yes, this will do nicely."

"How come she gets the new tank?" Wanda

complained.

"Be quiet. I don't want to hear any more from either of you tonight."

"Come and sit down here." Jack patted the sofa.

I didn't need telling twice. "I'm ready for this. It's been one heck of a day."

"Do you want to talk about it?"

"I got no sense out of Cindymindy or that husband of hers. They seemed to think Thomas' antics were funny."

"I hope you didn't do anything stupid."

"I wanted to, but I walked away."

"Good. Do you think your visit had anything to do with him not going to school today?"

"I highly doubt it. Knowing those two, they probably forgot to take him. And of course, I had the joy of attending the opening of WiFY."

"Did anyone actually show up for that?"

"The place was chock-a-block. They were fighting over some of the wigs."

"Like it or not, you have to admit your grandmother has a brilliant head for business."

"While I was there, I discovered that Grandma was the wizened old witch who pointed me in the direction of the casino, and gave me the coin which won the stone."

"You really have had a bad day. Still, you can relax now and forget all about it." He'd no sooner said that than my phone rang. "Don't answer that."

"I have to. It's one of my clients." I pressed the talk button. "Lorna?"

"Jill, I can't believe it." She was in floods of tears, no doubt having spoken to Gloria and Robert.

"I'm really sorry, Lorna. It must have been tough to

hear the truth."

"I never expected this."

"You probably don't want to hear this right now, but you deserve better."

"What are you talking about?" she snapped.

"Have Robert and Gloria spoken to you?"

"No, just the police."

"The police? What did they want?"

"To tell me they'd found Harry."

"They have? Where is he?"

"I don't know. They just said he was dead."

"*Dead*? How? Where?"

"They found his body washed up at the lake."

Chapter 18

The next morning, Jack and Florence had only just come downstairs when I was ready to leave the house.

"You're going in early, aren't you?" Jack stifled a yawn.

"I said I'd go and see Lorna first thing."

"Have you had any breakfast?"

"No, I'll grab something later." I gave him a peck on the cheek.

"Bye bye, Mummy." Florence was clearly still only half awake.

"Bye, darling. Have a nice day at school."

All the lights were blazing at Lorna's house. The woman who answered the door introduced herself as Lorna's mother. She showed me to the bedroom where Lorna was lying on the bed, dressed in jeans and a tee shirt. Unsurprisingly, she looked shocking.

"Do you want me to stay with you, Lorna?" her mother said.

"No, it's okay."

"I'm so sorry for your loss, Lorna." I took a seat next to the bed.

"I was sure he would turn up." She sobbed. "I never expected this."

"When did you find out?"

"Two policemen came to the house while I was eating dinner yesterday. As soon as I saw them at the door, I knew he was dead."

"Have you spoken to Gloria or Robert?"

"No. I suppose I ought to tell them, didn't I?"

"Don't worry about that just now. Someone will let

them know." This put me in something of a predicament. Should I tell her that Harry had staged his own disappearance because he'd decided, rather late in the day, that he didn't want to get married? Somehow, now didn't seem the right time; she was already in too much pain. "What did the police actually say?"

"I don't remember. I kind of blanked out after they told me they'd found Harry's body." She threw a tissue into the bin, which was already close to overflowing. "I need to get my cheque book to pay you for the time you've spent on this."

"Don't be silly. That can wait. You need to focus on yourself for now."

"Okay, thanks."

By the time I left, Lorna was on the verge of falling asleep, which was probably the best thing for her.

As soon as I was back in the car, I called Robert.

"It's Jill."

"Have you heard about Harry?" he said.

"Yes, I've just come from Lorna's."

"How is she?"

"How do you think? How did you hear about Harry?"

"It was on the local news."

"Robert, did you tell her about — you know what?"

"Gloria and I had intended to go over there first thing this morning to tell her. Do you think we should still do it?"

"No. She needs to rest. Are you sure Harry didn't tell you how he planned to disappear?"

"No, honestly. I don't think he trusted me to keep my mouth shut. The radio said he was found at the lake. Do you think he tried to swim back from the island?"

"I have no idea. Sorry, I have to go. Bye."

***

I hadn't had anything to eat and I was ravenous, so I popped into the first café I came across, which was called On A Cob. From the outside, it didn't look very impressive, so I was pleasantly surprised to find the place was spotless inside. The notice on the counter read 'Table Service', so I took a seat next to the window, and waited for someone to come and take my order. I didn't have long to wait before a grey-haired man appeared behind the counter. As soon as he saw me, he came over to my table.

"Welcome to On A Cob. Is this your first visit?"

"It is."

"I thought so. I never forget a face. What can I get for you?"

"I couldn't find the menu. What do you have?"

"Bacon cobs, sausage cobs, egg cobs, bacon and sausage cobs, bacon and egg cobs, sausage and egg cobs, and bacon, sausage and egg cobs."

"Right. I'll have bacon, sausage and egg, please."

"A bacon, sausage and egg cob, it is."

"Actually, I'd just like the bacon, sausage and egg. No cob."

"Sorry, we don't do that."

"But you do have bacon, sausages and eggs, right?"

"On a cob, yes."

"Couldn't you do them without the cob?"

"Sorry, no can do."

"O–kay. In that case I'll have a bacon, sausage and egg cob, please."

"Coming right up. And to drink?"

"A latte, please."

"No latte, I'm afraid."

"Cappuccino?"

"Sorry."

"What *do* you have?"

"Tea."

"Okay, tea it is."

"We only do pots."

"Okay, I'll have a pot of tea, please."

"A pot of tea for *one*?"

"Err, yeah. It's just me."

"Right you are." He put his pen behind his ear and made his way back to the counter.

When he brought over my food, I was tempted to take the bacon, sausage and egg off the cob, but I was afraid of the consequences if I did. To be fair, it was all delicious and certainly hit the mark. By the time I left, I was feeling much better.

"Hey, Jill, I didn't realise this was one of your haunts." Daze was looking in the window of the adjoining sportswear shop.

"Hi. It's the first time I've been in there. The food is nice enough, but it's a bit of a weird set-up."

"You mean the whole, *it has to be on a cob* thing?"

"Yeah."

"We're both barred because Blaze had the temerity to take his sausage and bacon off his cob. When Joe spotted him, he marched us both off the premises."

"Wow! That's a bit extreme. Where is Blaze?"

"He had to go to the chiropodist. In-growing toenail."

"Nasty. Mrs K told me you'd both dropped by the office the other day."

"We did, yes. What happened to Mrs V?"

"She was visiting her sister, but she's back now."

"It wasn't urgent. We just wanted to give you a head's up about Cuddles."

"Who?"

"He's a notorious shifter. I'm surprised you haven't heard of him."

"The name doesn't ring a bell."

"He's pretty much a one-off. Shifters normally transform into animals of one kind or another, but Cuddles can transform himself into a soft toy, usually a teddy bear."

"That's a weird kind of ability."

"True, but he puts it to good use. Before he was imprisoned last time, he'd managed to rob over a dozen properties here in the human world."

"By posing as a teddy bear?"

"Mostly, although he did once pose as a cuddly bunny rabbit."

"I take it he's no longer in prison. Did he escape?"

"No, he served his time and was released. The authorities insist he's a reformed character and is unlikely to reoffend. I'm not totally convinced, so I thought I'd better put the word out that he was back on the streets. If you hear anything on the grapevine, let us know, will you?"

"Of course. I hope Blaze's toe is okay."

"Even if it is, he'll still be moaning about it for weeks.

You know what men are like."

***

The discovery of Harry's body should have signalled the end of the case for me; Lorna had even offered to pay my bill. Before I filed it under closed, though, I wanted to pay another visit to the lake, to see what I could find out about the discovery of the body. It seemed crazy to me that it should have taken so long to wash up.

Matty was reading the same book as the first time I'd met him.

"Back again, young lady? Your name is on the tip of my tongue."

"Jill."

"That's it. I should have remembered because that was my first girlfriend's name. Do you want to go over to the island again?"

"Not today, thanks. Did you hear about the body they found?"

"I was the one who found it. Gave me a right scare, I can tell you."

"Whereabouts was it?"

"I'll show you." He put his book down and led the way around the edge of the lake. "Just over there, on that bank."

"What did you do?"

"Called the police. There wasn't much point in calling the ambulance because he was obviously dead and had been for some time."

"What did the police say?"

"Not much. They just asked when I'd found him, then

took my details in case they wanted to contact me. I assume it's that young fella who went missing?"

"Yeah, it was."

"Figured it must be, seeing as he was wearing a suit."

"He was fully clothed?"

"As far as I could tell, but I didn't get too close."

"What I don't get, Matty, is why his body would only turn up now. The police were supposed to have searched the lake."

"That search was a joke." He scoffed. "They spent barely any time on it. I reckon they'd already decided he'd done a runner. The lake looks harmless enough but it's deep in parts, and thick with reeds and the like. If that young fella tried swimming, dressed in his suit, he was asking for trouble."

"What do you think happened to him?"

"He probably tried to swim back across the lake, got into trouble and drowned. His body was probably caught up in the reeds until now."

"Okay, Matty, thanks."

"I was just about to have a cuppa. Do you fancy one? There's plenty in my flask."

"Thanks, but I need to get going."

***

As I drove back to Washbridge, I reflected on what Matty had said. It was certainly possible that Harry could have drowned while trying to swim back to the shore, but why would he attempt to do it fully dressed? It didn't make any sense. He'd obviously planned the disappearance in advance, so why not leave a change of clothing hidden on shore? That way he could have stripped off on the island before attempting the swim. Harry was either reckless, stupid or there was more to this than met the eye.

As I approached the office building, I noticed lots of small flyers blowing around the pavement. Which inconsiderate idiot would dump them all over the street like that? It was only when I got closer to the building that I realised the flyers were coming out of a window. And not just any window — my window! I grabbed one and couldn't believe what I saw.

"Jill? Are you okay?" Mrs V was clearly startled by my dramatic entrance.

"I'm fine. Can't stop, sorry." I went charging past her and burst into my office, to find Winky standing by the window, casting flyers into the breeze. "What on earth are you playing at?"

"I'm doing what you told me to do."

"What are you talking about? I didn't tell you to litter the street with your stupid flyers."

"You said I should raise money to buy my own bowl, so that's what I'm doing. I've set up a GoFundMeow page, and now I'm getting the word out."

"By throwing flyers out of the window? What's wrong with sending an email?"

"No one likes spam."

"Stop! Don't throw any more of those out of the window."

"What about my bowl?"

"I'll buy you one."

"I don't want any old bowl. I want two top-of-the range

bowls."

"Two?"

"One for my food and the other for the milk."

"Okay, I'll buy you two. Now give me the rest of those flyers."

He'd no sooner handed them to me than the office door opened, and a worried-looking Mrs V appeared. "This officer would like a word with you, Jill."

A uniformed policeman stepped into the room.

"Good morning, madam."

"Morning, officer. What can I do for you?"

"You can begin by explaining why you have chosen to litter the Queen's highway with these." He held up a handful of flyers.

"Err, that wasn't me."

"Really? And what are those in your hand?"

"These? Err, I can explain."

"I'm listening."

"It was an accident."

"I see. You accidentally threw a few hundred flyers out of your window. Is that what you're telling me?"

"Yes. I was walking past the window when I tripped over Winky."

"Who?"

"My cat." I pointed to Winky who was now sitting on the sofa, clearly enjoying the show.

"He only has one eye."

"Yes. Hence the name."

"Do I take it that Winky is the subject of this?" He waved the flyer in front of my face.

"That's right."

"Do you really think it's appropriate to canvas

donations, just to buy a couple of cat bowls?"

"The ones he wants are really expensive."

"I assume he told you that, did he?"

"Err, no. I just meant—"

"You do realise that it's a crime to deliberately throw litter onto the street, I assume."

"I'm sorry. It won't happen again."

"Fortunately for you, I'm in a generous mood today, so I won't charge you."

"Thank you, officer."

"On one condition."

"What's that?"

"You go outside and pick up every one of those flyers."

"But there are hundreds of them. It will take ages."

"You'd best make a start, then."

***

My back was aching because I'd just spent the last hour picking up all the flyers and depositing them in the bin. When I walked into Rue Pets, Rupert did a double take.

"Surely you're not after another fish tank?"

"Not today."

"More ornaments?"

"No, this visit is not fish-related. I need a couple of bowls for my cat."

"I didn't realise you had one. I hope you keep it well away from your fish."

"Don't worry. Winky lives in my office here in Washbridge."

"Isn't that a little unusual? What do your clients make of it?"

"No one has complained so far." That wasn't strictly speaking true. "So, where will I find the bowls?"

"Over there in that corner."

"Thanks."

After the ordeal Winky had just put me through, I should have bought him the cheapest ones I could find, but I was conscious of the fact that what he really wanted was to move into the house with me. If buying him a couple of expensive bowls took his mind off that, it would be a price worth paying.

"Have you seen anything you like?" Rupert appeared behind me.

"I'm looking for something *really* special, but these all look a little too plain."

"I have to say it's very refreshing to meet someone who is so devoted to their pets. I hope your little pussy cat appreciates you."

"Hmm."

"What you need is the Majestic Collection."

"Which ones are those?"

"The Majestic Collection has its own section. Follow me." He led the way to a small area, separate from the rest of the store. "What do you think of these?"

The first thought that went through my head was *how much*? "They're very posh."

"Only the best for the best. Just look at the quality of these bowls." He handed one to me. "Impressive, aren't they?"

"It's very nice. Quite heavy."

"You won't find better than these."

"Okay. Give me two of those, please."

Chapter 19

"Jill, thank goodness you're back," Mrs V said. "I thought that policeman had arrested you. I was just about to call Armi to ask him how to post bail."

"He didn't arrest me. It was all just a big mistake."

"That's a relief. By the way, I talked to Armi last night about Morris dancing and he seems quite keen. I'm going to give Kay a call later to ask about her group. Are you sure you and Jack wouldn't like to join too?"

"Positive. Incidentally, did Armi get the chance to look at my office lease?"

"He did, and it's not good news I'm afraid. He reckons there's nothing you can do about the proposed increase."

"Bummer. Okay, thank him for taking a look anyway."

"That's what I'm talking about!" Winky stood back and admired his new bowls.

"I hope you like them because they cost me a small fortune."

"I'm worth every penny. That copper was a bit officious, wasn't he? You should have told him to sling his hook."

"If I'd done that, I'd probably be behind bars now."

My phone rang with an unknown number.

"Is that Jill Maxwell?"

"Speaking."

"My name is Patsy Puggins. I work for P.I. Monthly, and I was just wondering if you'd be interested in placing an ad in our first issue."

"I've never heard of it."

"As I said, it's a new publication. The first issue comes

out in a few weeks, and pre-sales figures are very encouraging."

"How much does it cost to advertise?"

"A thousand pounds for a full-page ad, six hundred for a half-page, or three hundred and twenty-five for a quarter page."

"Is there anything smaller than that?"

"No, sorry. A quarter page is the smallest."

"How many copies do you expect to sell?"

"It's hard to be sure as it's the first issue, but it should be available in all high street newsagents. It's quite likely that subsequent issues will command a much higher ad price."

"Okay. Put me down for a quarter page."

"Excellent. The thing is, the deadline for copy is tomorrow, so I'll need yours by then."

"I'll never get an ad designed that quickly."

"There's no need to worry about the design. Our creative team will handle all that. We just need to know the wording you require. You can text it to me on this number."

"Okay."

"And remember, when it comes to adverts, less is more."

"Right."

"I look forward to receiving the ad copy later today. Bye."

"What have you signed up for now?" Winky said.

"An advert in P.I. Monthly."

"That sounds like a riveting read. Remind me to take out a subscription."

"I need to come up with the wording for the ad."

"How about, *Jill and Winky, ace investigators. No case too big or too small?*"

"What about, *Jill Maxwell, Private Investigator. Experienced in all manner of investigation work, both personal and commercial. Call today for an obligation-free discussion?*"

"I prefer my version."

Ignoring him, I shot off a text with my copy to Patsy Puggins. I'd been looking for ways to increase business. This new magazine could be just what I needed.

***

When I'd asked Orlando Song if there were any ex-employees who might hold a grudge against the studio, he'd mentioned Joyce Keys who had worked as a receptionist until she'd been caught stealing petty cash. I planned to pay her a visit, but first I was gagging for a coffee, so I magicked myself over to Cuppy C.

One of the assistants was behind the counter, but there was no sign of the twins.

"Hi, Jill, your usual?"

"Yes, please." It was a little disconcerting that I didn't even recognise this particular assistant, and yet not only did she know my name, but also my usual order. Maybe the twins included my photo and details in their induction training. "Where are the twins?"

"Upstairs."

"In the cork museum?"

"In what *was* the cork museum. They closed it yesterday. They're just packing away all the corks."

I grabbed my coffee and muffin, and made my way upstairs. The twins were so busy that neither of them noticed me standing there.

"Good afternoon, girls."

"If you've come to say you told us so, you can go back downstairs." Amber wiped her arm across her forehead.

"I wouldn't dream of it." I grinned. "But I did."

Pearl opened one of the cabinets, slid her arm inside, and scooped all the corks into the box at her side. "I'll be glad to see the back of these stupid things."

"Does Aunt Lucy know you've closed the museum?"

"Yeah, she tried to talk us into keeping it open, but *she* isn't the one losing money hand over fist."

"Does she know you're just slinging the corks into those boxes? It's going to take her ages to sort them all out."

"If you're so concerned, Jill, why don't you do it?"

It was clear that the twins were in a foul mood, and that anything I said would only make things worse. I made my excuses and went back downstairs where I found *me* sitting by the window. When I say *me*, I mean my doppelganger, Linda, who I'd met once before. Sitting next to her was a little girl who looked about the same age as Florence. Linda spotted me and beckoned me over.

"Hey, Jill, how are you?"

"Fine, thanks."

"Why don't you join us? Unless you're waiting for someone?"

"Thanks, I will."

When I sat down, the little girl looked at me and did a double take. "You look like my Mummy."

"I know. You must be Eliza."

"I'm five."

"My little girl, Florence, is five too."

"Does she like pandas?"

"I'm not sure. She really likes unicorns, though."

"Pandas are better than unicorns." She declared and then went back to looking at her book.

"That's me told." I laughed. "How's business, Linda?"

"Pretty good, thanks to your popularity. Are you sure you wouldn't like me to pay you a percentage of my fee?"

"Don't be silly. You and I were supposed to be getting together some time, weren't we?"

"I'd love that, but I imagine you're very busy."

"That's true. Even my weekend is booked solid."

"Actually, I'm taking Eliza on her first visit to the human world this weekend."

"Really? How exciting for you, Eliza. Are you looking forward to it?"

"Yes. I'm taking Andy with me."

"*Andy?*"

"That's the name of her favourite panda," Linda said.

"I hope you and Andy have a wonderful time, and we really must make the effort to all get together soon."

***

Orlando had given me an address for Joyce Keys, which turned out to be a flat above a shop that sold pogo sticks.

"Hi." A man stuck his head out of the shop door. "Are you thinking of buying a pogo stick?"

"Err, no. Actually, I'm just about to visit someone in the flat above your shop."

"Joyce?"

"That's right."

"I sold her a PG125 last year."

"Really? That's nice."

"*Nice* doesn't adequately describe the PG125. State of the art would be more accurate. Are you sure you wouldn't like to take a look inside?"

"Yes, thanks."

The stairs leading to the flat were uncarpeted, and the walls were in desperate need of a lick of paint.

A woman holding a cat answered the door. She eyed me suspiciously—the woman, that is—the cat appeared to be asleep.

"Joyce Keys?"

"Yeah?"

"My name is Jill Maxwell. I wonder if you might spare me a few minutes?"

"You're wasting your time. I don't have money to buy anything."

"I'm not selling anything. I wanted to talk to you about your time at Wash Sounds."

"What about it? Who are you, anyway?"

"I'm a private investigator."

"I didn't take that cash. It was all lies."

"That's not what I wanted to talk to you about."

"What then?"

Before I could tell her the purpose of my visit, her phone rang. "Hold Betty, would you?" She put the cat into my arms, and stepped back inside the flat.

The cat opened her eyes. "Who are you?"

"Jill."

"Have you got anything for me to eat?"

"No, sorry."

"You're not much use then, are you?" The cat jumped out of my arms and headed down the stairs.

Joyce hadn't closed the door properly, so although I

couldn't hear everything that was being said, I did hear the caller's voice. It was a voice I recognised.

"I told you," Joyce said. "She's here now. Right. I'll get rid of her. Yeah, I'll see you in a few minutes." She ended the call and then came back to the door. "Where's Betty gone?"

"She ran down the stairs."

"Great. It'll take me ages to find her now. Thanks for nothing."

"Sorry about that. Now, about Wash Sounds."

"I don't have anything to say about that place." And with that, she closed the door in my face.

***

"Changed your mind, I see," said the funny little man in the pogo stick shop.

I'd only popped back in there because it had started to rain, and I needed to be somewhere that I could keep an eye on the comings and goings from the flat.

"Err, yeah. Maybe."

"You'll never regret it. Once someone buys their first pogo stick, they're in it for life. Have you seen anything that caught your eye?"

"Not yet, but I'll keep on looking."

"These in the window are the more expensive models for the advanced user. You should really take a look at our beginner's range over the other side of the shop. They're much less expensive."

"Err, no. I think I might like one of these." I didn't want to move from the window in case I missed Joyce leaving the flat.

"As you wish. Would you like me to demonstrate them for you?"

"Maybe in a few minutes. I'll just take a closer look at them for now."

"Okay, give me a shout if you need anything. I am a level five pogo stick master in case you were wondering."

"Right, thanks."

The rain was coming down much heavier now, and there was a limit to how long I'd be able to keep up the pretence of being interested in the stupid pogo sticks. Sooner or later the pogo stick master would expect me to put up or get out.

I'd examined each of the pogo sticks at least three times when I caught a break. Running across the road, with his coat pulled up over his head, to shield him from the rain, was a familiar figure.

I waited until he'd entered the door to the flat, then I made for the exit.

"Did you decide which one you'd like to try?" The pogo stick master appeared from behind a column.

"Not yet. I'll call in again tomorrow with my husband. Thanks. Bye."

I hurried out of the shop, and up to the flat where I thumped on the door; there was no answer.

"Joyce! I know you're both in there." I hammered on the door again. "If you don't open the door, I'm going to the police."

I could hear voices inside, and moments later, Joyce opened the door.

"What do you want?"

"I'd like to talk to you and Roy."

"There's no one else here. Just me."

"I guess I'll go to the police, then."

"Let her in, Joyce," Roy shouted.

"Come in." She stepped to one side.

A couple of minutes later, the three of us were in the lounge, Joyce and Roy on the sofa, me in a rocking chair which had clearly seen better days.

"This is not what it looks like," Roy said.

"It looks like you two are an item. I assume you sabotaged the recordings as revenge for what happened to your lady friend here."

"That's not what happened," Roy insisted. "Yes, Joyce and I are an item. We started seeing each other while she was working at Wash Sounds."

"You can't have been very happy when she lost her job."

"I wasn't, but only because I knew she hadn't taken the money."

"Why didn't you tell Orlando that?"

"I should have, but he didn't even know we were seeing each other."

"So you did nothing?"

"What could I do? Walk out on my job too? What good would that have done?"

"You had the access and the means to sabotage the recordings."

"I can't blame you for assuming it was me, but think about it for a minute. If these incidents continue, Wash Sounds is likely to go out of business. Why would I risk putting myself out of a job?"

He had a point. "If it wasn't you, then who was it?"

"Isn't it obvious? Roger Tunes has the most to gain from the demise of Wash Sounds."

"I've already spoken to him. He didn't strike me as the sort."

"He can be very convincing when he wants to be. Are you going to tell Orlando? About me and Joyce, I mean?"

"Not unless I discover you are behind the sabotage."

"You won't, I promise."

I wasn't sure what to make of all that. Although Roy had reason to be angry with Orlando for the way he had dismissed Joyce, I wasn't convinced it was reason enough to undertake a campaign of sabotage against Wash Sounds. To have done that would have meant cutting off his nose to spite his face.

***

As soon as I walked through the door, Florence came running up to me.

"Look what Great-Grandma bought me."

"A toy camel. That's nice."

"I'm going to call him Humpy."

"That's a brilliant name, darling."

Jack came through from the kitchen. "You've met Humpy, then?"

"I certainly have. When did Grandma bring him over?"

"She didn't. She was waiting by the school gates when I got there. How did she know that Florence was into camels?"

"That woman knows everything."

Chapter 20

The next morning, I was on my way downstairs when I heard Florence yelling in the kitchen. "Where is he, Daddy? Where's he gone?"

"Where did you leave him, pumpkin?" Jack was clearly searching the kitchen for whatever it was that Florence had misplaced.

"Where is who?" I said.

"Humpy has gone." Florence was on the verge of tears.

"He can't be far away. When did you see him last?"

"He was on there." She pointed to the kitchen table.

"Are you sure?"

"Yes!" She stomped her foot. "Where is he?"

"We'll find him," Jack said. "Won't we, Mummy?"

"Of course we will. Jack, you search down here; Florence and I will look upstairs."

I sent Florence to double-check her bedroom while I checked ours. I was looking inside the wardrobe when I heard Jack call me. I assumed he had found the stupid camel, thank goodness.

"Have you got him?" I shouted from the top of the stairs.

"You'd better come down here and see for yourself."

I didn't like the sound of that one bit. Had Buddy got hold of the soft toy and ripped him to pieces?

"Where is he?" I couldn't see any sign of the camel.

"I don't know."

"Why did you shout me, then?"

"My watch has gone."

"What do you mean, *gone*?"

"I left it on the coffee table and it's not there."

"Are you sure?"

"I'm positive."

"It can't have just disappeared."

"Humpy has."

"What are you saying? That we've been burgled, and they stole your watch and a soft toy?"

"It looks like it. Unless anything else is missing?"

It was only when I glanced around that I realised my handbag had gone. "My bag's gone."

"What was in it?"

"My cards and a bit of cash."

"How did they get in?" Jack was already headed back to the kitchen.

"I can't find him, Mummy." Florence was back downstairs and in tears.

"We'll buy you another one at the weekend."

"But I want Humpy."

"We'll find you one just like Humpy, I promise."

After Jack had finished checking the kitchen, he took a look upstairs. When he came back down, he shook his head. "I don't get it. There's no sign of a—"

"It's okay, Daddy." I interrupted him before he could spook Florence. I didn't want her to realise there had been a break-in. "We're going to buy Florence a new camel this weekend."

"Just like Humpy," Florence added.

"That's right. Just like Humpy."

We all ate breakfast as if nothing was wrong. It was only when Florence had gone upstairs to get ready for school that Jack and I discussed what had happened.

"I don't get it. How did they get in?" Jack said.

"No idea."

"And why take the camel? I can understand them taking my watch and your handbag. But why take a soft toy?"

That's when the penny dropped. "Maybe they didn't."

"What do you mean?"

I jumped up and headed for the door. "I won't be long."

"Where are you going?"

"To see Grandma."

If steam had been coming out of my ears, as I walked over to the hotel, I would not have been at all surprised. I was beyond livid.

"Are you okay?" the receptionist asked—perhaps she could see the steam.

"Where is she?"

"Your grandmother is in the sauna. She should be out in about fifteen minutes."

"That's too long." I started towards the spa area.

"You can't go in there."

"Just watch me."

The small glass window in the sauna was steamed up, so I had no idea who else might be in there, but frankly I didn't care.

"You can't just barge in here like this," Grandma said. Thankfully, she was alone in there.

"Can you put your robe on?" I averted my eyes.

"No, I can't. If you're going to stay, you'd better undress or you'll melt."

"I am not undressing."

"What do you want, anyway? This is one of the few chances I get to relax during the day."

"I'm here about the camel you gave to Florence."

"Cute, isn't it?"

"How did you know Florence wanted a camel—never mind, it doesn't matter. Where did you get it from?"

"What do you care? She likes it, doesn't she?"

"She did until it disappeared."

"Surely she hasn't lost it already?"

"She didn't lose it. It did a runner."

"I think you've been overworking."

"I'm serious. It's gone, along with Jack's watch and my handbag. Where did you get it from?"

"It wasn't easy to find. I tried several toy shops, and none of them had one, but then I struck lucky. The guy in the last shop I visited said they didn't have a camel, but that he could get hold of any soft toy animal within twenty-four hours."

"Did he now? And how do you think he managed that?"

"I don't know, and I have no idea why you're so angry. I could have simply magicked one up, but you're always telling me I shouldn't use magic in the human world. And now, when I've gone to the trouble of searching the shops to find one, you're still on my case."

"Cuddles."

"Pardon."

"I take it you haven't heard of him."

"I don't have the first clue what you're talking about."

"He's a shifter."

"So?"

"Unlike other shifters, Cuddles specialises in transforming into soft toys. He has just been released from prison where he was serving time for robberies committed here in the human world."

"Are you telling me that—?"

"That's precisely what I'm telling you. The soft toy you gave to Florence was actually a common thief who has stolen Jack's watch, and my handbag."

"I'll kill him. Slowly and painfully." She stood up, put on her robe (thankfully) and headed for the door.

"Make sure it's very painful." I turned to leave.

"Hold on. Give this to Florence." She handed me a camel that was identical to Humpy. "I should have just used magic in the first place."

"You found him, Mummy!" Florence grabbed the camel. "Where have you been, you naughty little camel?"

"He was sleepwalking," I said. "Why don't you take him upstairs and put him in your bed? He must be tired."

"Okay, Mummy."

"Why are you so sweaty, Jill?" Jack said.

"It's a long story."

***

I figured I'd better update Daze on recent events, so when I arrived in Washbridge, I gave her a quick call.

"Daze's phone. Blaze speaking."

"It's Jill. Is Daze there?"

"She's had to pop to the dentist. Lost filling."

"Oh dear. Poor Daze. I'm ringing about Cuddles."

"Are you feeling a bit neglected, Jill? I'll be happy to give you a cuddle."

"I meant Cuddles, the shapeshifter."

"Of course, sorry. What about him?"

I told Blaze the sorry saga of Humpy, and explained

that Grandma was now on his case.

"If he finds out your grandmother is after him, he'll probably hand himself in to the authorities. If he has any sense, that is."

"If you hear anything, will you let me know, Blaze?"

"Of course."

"And tell Daze I hope her tooth is okay."

"It's only a filling; she'll be fine. Although, she does have a tendency to make a big deal of these things."

"How is your toenail, Blaze?"

"Oh, Jill, you can't imagine the pain. I could barely walk. I'm still getting twinges."

***

I arrived at the office building at the same time as Farah.

"Good morning, Jill."

"Hi."

"I know you must think I'm losing my mind, and I don't blame you, but those dogs really did disappear."

"Don't worry about it, Farah, we all have weeks like that. I have more than most. Hopefully, none of your dogs will *disappear* today."

"I really shouldn't say this, but I have one dog coming in today that I wish *would* disappear."

"How come?"

"She's a Pomeranian called Angel. Never has a name been less appropriate. Delilah and I call her Killer because she's so vicious. One of these days, I'm sure she'll take one of my fingers off."

"Good luck. I don't envy you."

When I walked into the office, I found Mrs V tutting to herself. "Men!"

"Oh dear. What has Armi done now?"

"I told you that we'd decided to take up Morris dancing, didn't I?"

"You did. Don't tell me he's changed his mind already."

"No, he's still very keen, but Armi got talking to our gardener, Walter, and it turns out he's also a Morris dancer."

"I'm not sure I see the problem."

"Walter is a member of the Wash Crew."

"That sounds like some kind of hip-hop gang."

"I agree, but it's actually a Morris dancing group. Kay is a member of The Washbridge Dancers. The two groups are fierce rivals, apparently."

"I still don't understand what you're so annoyed about."

"Armi insists he wants to join Walter's group."

"The Wash Crew? Couldn't you join them too?"

"No, because I've already promised Kay that we'd join her group."

"I'm sure you can convince Armi to change his mind."

"You overestimate my influence over him, Jill. I spent most of last night trying to get him to join the Washbridge Dancers; I even threatened to stop dusting his cuckoo clocks, but he simply won't budge. That man is so stubborn."

Winky was on the sofa, looking rather distressed.

"What's wrong?"

"We've been robbed."

"What do you mean?"

"Someone must have sneaked in during the night while I was asleep. They stole my bowls."

"Are you sure?"

"See for yourself." He pointed to the spot where his bowls should have been.

I took a quick look around. "They don't seem to have taken anything else."

"To be fair, there's nothing worth stealing in here, is there?"

"How did they get in?"

"Through the window, I guess."

"Well, you'll just have to make do with your old bowls now. I can't afford to buy any more."

"C'est la vie." He shrugged.

***

I was pleasantly surprised by how well Winky had taken the loss of his prized bowls. I'd fully expected him to throw a tantrum and demand that I replace them. It just went to show that he could be reasonable when he tried.

Although I had an address for the new recording studio, Kaleidoscope, I hadn't been able to track down a telephone number, so I had no choice but to turn up at the door and hope that I'd get to talk to someone.

First signs were not promising. The brick building had clearly once been a plumbers' merchant. How did I know that? Because the rusting sign had not been taken down. The only clue to its new occupants was a small sign on the door, which was locked. There was no bell or buzzer, so I knocked on the door as loudly as I could. When there was no answer, I took a walk around the building to see if I could find another entrance. The only other door was a fire exit, which offered no means of entry. I was considering whether to use magic to get inside when a man appeared from the next building: a wholesale nut merchant.

"You won't get any joy there, love." He cracked open a walnut with his bare hands.

"How do you know?"

"There's never anyone there during the daytime. They do all their work during the night."

"Really? Are you sure?"

"Positive. The only time I've ever seen them is when I work late." He held out his hand. "Walnut?"

"Yes, please. How do you do that with just your hands."

"It's easy when you know how." He grabbed a couple more from his pocket and demonstrated.

"Very impressive."

"Are you a singer, then?"

"Me? No. I just wanted a word with the owner of the studio."

"I could give them a message when I next see them if you like?"

"It's okay. I'll call back again one evening."

What a colossal waste of time that had proven to be. What kind of studio only worked during the night?

***

Back at the office building, I'd just started up the stairs when an almighty commotion broke out. I was used to hearing the occasional bark from down the corridor, but this sounded like the hound of the Baskervilles. As well as the barking, I could hear Farah and Delilah shouting at the top of their voices. Something was clearly amiss, so I sprinted up the rest of the stairs, and down the corridor.

When I entered the salon, I found the two women, standing behind the counter; they were both clearly agitated about something.

"Is everything okay? I heard a terrible noise coming from in here."

"Sorry about that, Jill. It was Killer."

"The Pomeranian you told me about earlier?"

"Yeah. She just lost her mind."

"While you were trimming her?"

"No, that's the weird thing. I hadn't even made a start on her, had I, Delilah?"

"No," Delilah said. "We were just standing in here when she went absolutely crazy."

"Any idea why?"

"None," Farah said. "When we went through there, she was barking her head off at nothing, apparently. She's calmed down now, thank goodness. I'm not looking forward to trimming her, though."

"Okay, I'll leave you both to it."

There was no sign of Mrs V, but she had left a note on her desk to say she'd popped out to pick up a prescription. There was no sign of Winky either, but then he shot in through the window. He looked in a state of shock.

"Are you okay?"

"Err, yeah. I'm fine."

"You could have fooled me. What's going on?"

"Nothing. Nothing at all."

"Hang on. Where have you just been?"

"Me? Nowhere."

"It was you, wasn't it?"

"What was?"

"The missing dogs."

I didn't need to hear his response because it was written all over his face.

"What missing dogs? I have no idea what you're talking about."

"You took those two dogs out of their cages, and then put them back again, didn't you?"

"Why would I go anywhere near a dog? I hate them."

"Precisely. You've never liked the idea of having Bubbles just down the corridor, have you? You've been trying to drive them out."

"Rubbish."

"That's why you always picked the small dogs, but you didn't reckon on little Angel, did you?"

"That dog is insane. It nearly took my paw off."

"I knew it was you."

"So what if it was? They should never have been allowed to open."

"How on earth did you manage it? How come they didn't just chase you away?"

"Most dogs are simple creatures. Offer them a few treats, and they'll do whatever you want them to. Even if you're a cat."

"This has to stop right now. Farah has enough to contend with without having to worry about her dogs disappearing."

"That Pomeranian should be locked up permanently."

"Do I have your word that this will never happen again, or do I have to go and get Angel, and bring her down here to see you?"

"Don't do that."

"I won't if you give me your word that you won't try to sabotage Bubbles again."

"I promise."

Chapter 21

It was almost time for my interview with the representative from WWW, and I have to admit I was really excited. They didn't include just anyone in Witch Who's Who, so once the new edition was published, I would be well and truly on the map.

"Mrs V, do we still have the china cups and saucers?"

"Yes, of course."

"Would you mind giving them a quick wash. I'd like to use them for my two-thirty appointment."

"I didn't realise you had anyone coming in. There's nothing in my diary."

"Sorry, I must have forgotten to mention it."

"Who is it?"

"Err, someone from the tax office."

"Not that Betty Longbottom again?"

"No, not Betty. Someone else."

"Are you sure you want to use the best cups for someone from the tax office?"

"Yes, please. It always pays to make a good impression, don't you think?"

"I suppose so. I'll go and get them."

"What are you up to?" Winky said.

"What do you mean?"

"I heard you ask the old bag lady to get out the posh cups. What gives? And don't give me that rubbish about it being someone from the tax office. Loony tunes next door might buy that guff, but I know better."

"I'm not supposed to tell anyone, but as you're just a cat, I don't suppose that matters."

"*Just* a cat?"

"You know what I mean. If I tell you, do you promise not to breathe a word to anyone? Not even another cat?"

"I promise."

"Okay. It's all very exciting. I'm still in shock."

"You're giving this quite the build-up. It had better be good."

"I'm going to be in WWW."

"You? A wrestler? They'll wipe the canvas with you."

"I'm not going to be a wrestler. WWW stands for Witch Who's Who. You know you've made it when you appear in there."

"That's it?" He couldn't have looked any less impressed if he'd tried. "I thought you said it was something exciting."

"It is, and I don't want you messing things up for me. Why don't you go and see one of your lady friends for a couple of hours?"

"Have you seen the weather? It's raining rabbits and dogs out there."

"Okay, but you have to stay out of sight. I don't want to hear a squeak from you while I'm being interviewed."

"No self-respecting cat would ever squeak. We leave that to the mice."

"You know what I mean. Just behave yourself."

At two o'clock precisely, Mrs V came through to my office and closed the door behind her.

"Your visitor is here, Jill."

"Excellent. What's her name?"

"It's a *he*. He says his name is Vincent Beaucoup. Are you sure he's from the tax office?"

"Yes. Didn't he say he was?"

"Yes, he did, but he doesn't dress like a tax man."

"Show him in, would you, please?"

"Very well."

"Jill Maxwell, how absolutely fabulous to meet you." The man was dressed in a yellow suit, yellow shoes and a red dicky bow—with yellow spots. "I've long been a fan of yours."

"Thanks. Do have a seat, Mr Beaucoup."

"Call me Beau. All my friends do, and I know we're going to be great friends, Jill."

I made the mistake of glancing over at Winky who was pretending to put his paw down his throat.

"Tell me, Beau, how many new entries will there be in the next edition of WWW?"

"Very few, Jill. Just you and ten others, I believe. You'll be joining a very exclusive club, but I'm sure you already know that."

"Absolutely."

Mrs V came through, carrying a silver tray.

"What adorable crockery," Beau gushed. "Are those china?"

"Yes, they are." Mrs V picked up the teapot. "How do you take yours, Mr Beaucoup?"

"Just a splash of milk, please."

"Sugar?"

"No, I have to watch my figure."

Mrs V rolled her eyes at me while pouring the tea. Thankfully, Beau didn't seem to notice.

"So, Beau, what exactly would you like to know about me?"

"Absolutely everything. After all, yours is something of a unique story. As I understand it, you were raised in the human world and didn't even discover you were a witch until you were—what?"

"In my mid-twenties."

"And now you're considered to be one of, if not the, most powerful witch alive."

"Some people say that."

Winky was continuing to mock me from under the sofa; that cat was so dead.

"Why don't we start at the beginning with your childhood and take it from there."

Some people just love to talk about themselves. Not me of course. I find it all too embarrassing.

"Goodness, is that really the time?" Beau looked at his watch. "The last two hours have flown by. Still, yours is quite the story."

"I haven't quite finished yet."

"I think I have more than enough." He put his notebook into his briefcase. "I just need to take your order."

"For what?"

"Copies of the new edition when it's published."

"I didn't realise I had to buy any."

"You don't. There's certainly no obligation to do so, but most people like to have a copy to give to their family and friends. Obviously, you won't be able to give them to your human acquaintances."

"Of course not."

"So, do you want me to put you down for any?"

"Err, yes, definitely. Let me see. I'll want one for Aunt Lucy, then there's the twins, they'll want a copy each. One for Grandma. That's it, I think."

"Will you want one for yourself? You wouldn't be able to let your husband see it of course."

"I can keep it here at the office."

"Okay. I make that five copies in total."

"Maybe I should add a couple more, just in case."

"Seven, then."

"Make it eight."

"Eight it is. At fifty-five pounds a copy equals—"

"Fifty-five pounds each?"

"They are leather-bound."

"Of course."

"So, that will be four-hundred and forty pounds in total."

"Okay."

"Would you like to pay by card or cheque?"

"You need the payment, now?"

"I'm afraid so. It's a cashflow thing. Being a businesswoman yourself, I'm sure you understand."

"Of course." I took out my credit card.

"Sorry, debit cards only."

"Oh, okay." I handed it over, and he produced a card reader from his briefcase.

"There, that's all done."

"When will I receive my copies?"

"Within a few months. I'll deliver them to you personally." He stood up and offered his hand. "It's been an absolute pleasure, Jill."

"Thanks for coming in, Beau."

"Have you finished talking about yourself yet?" Winky yawned as he came out from under the sofa.

"Beau said he wanted to know everything about me."

"I bet he regretted that. The man was practically comatose by the time he interrupted you."

"Rubbish. It's important to get all the details correct in such a prestigious publication."

"Are you even sure Witch Who's Who exists?"

"Of course I am."

"Did you actually check online?"

"There's no internet in the sup world."

"But you did your research?"

"Of course. I'm not stupid."

"Says the woman who has just handed four-hundred pounds to a man dressed like a banana."

***

When I'd asked Orlando Song if he could think of any acts who might hold a grudge against him and his studio, he could come up with only one: Arnold and the Armchairs. Tracking them down had proven to be quite difficult, but I eventually discovered that the band had split up not long after they'd recorded their ill-fated album at Wash Sounds. In the course of my research, I'd also discovered that the band was essentially just Arnold Arbuthnot and a number of session musicians, who rarely lasted more than a few months. Once I knew that, I focussed my attention on tracking down Arnold. It turned out that he had made quite a career change. Instead of fronting a rock band, he was now an independent rodent exterminator, working under the name of The Rat Man.

I gave him a call.

"The Rat Man. Arnold speaking. How can I be of service today?"

"Hi, my name is Jill Maxwell. I wondered if I might pop over and have a word with you. Are you in your office?"

"Yes, I am, but if you give me your address, I'm more than happy to come to you. That way, I can get a first-hand look at your rat problem."

"I don't actually have a rat problem."

"Cockroaches?"

"No, I'm a private investigator. I've been hired by Orlando Song, and I was hoping to talk to you about Wash Sounds."

"I thought you said you didn't have a rat problem. Orlando is the biggest rat walking on two legs."

"I'd really appreciate it if you would talk to me."

"Okay, but I have to go out on a call in ten minutes. I should be back in an hour or so. You can come over then if you like."

"That would be great. I'll see you then."

***

After the trick Winky had just pulled with Bubbles, I shouldn't even care, but I couldn't help but feel a little sorry for him after some toerag stole his new bowls. What can I say? I'm just a big softie.

I had a little time to spare before going to see The Rat Man, so I paid another visit to Rue Pets where Rupert greeted me enthusiastically.

"You really should sign up for our loyalty card. There are lots of offers every month for cardholders."

"Thanks, but I think this will be my last visit for a while."

"Something for your fish?"

"Not this time. I'm shopping for the cat."

"A nice new collar? A scratching post?"

"Actually, I'd like a couple more of those bowls which I bought from you the other day."

"I'm afraid you're out of luck. I sold the last one yesterday, and I won't have another delivery until late next week."

"Oh well, never mind. I'll try again then."

I took a slow walk over to The Rat Man's office, grabbing a takeaway coffee en route. I arrived just in time to see him pull up in a white van with a cartoon of a rat on the side.

"Are you the private investigator?"

"Yeah. Jill Maxwell."

"You'd better come in." I followed him into the tiny office, which had faux-wood panelling on all the walls. "Would you like a drink?"

"No, thanks, I had one on the way over here."

"Grab a seat. You said you wanted to talk about Wash Sounds."

"That's right. I understand from Orlando that you and your band recorded an album there."

"We did, and a total waste of money that turned out to be."

"Why do you say that?"

"Did Orlando play you our album?"

"No, he didn't, but he did say you weren't happy with the result."

"That's the understatement of the year. The recording made my voice sound terrible. There was no way we could release that album, and I didn't have the money to record another one, or to continue to pay the rest of the band. That sad episode proved to be the final straw; the band split up and I set up this business."

"Does that mean your music career is over?"

"Definitely not. As soon as I've saved enough money, I'll get the band back together and head to the studio. Not Wash Sounds, though."

"How many albums have you made?"

"That would have been the first. We always focussed on gigging before. Anyway, why does Orlando need a P.I?"

"There have been a few unexplained problems at the studio."

"You're telling me. I was on the receiving end of them."

"What's happening now is totally different. Perfectly good recordings are being corrupted."

"He surely doesn't think I had anything to do with it, does he?"

"Err, no, of course not."

"Then why did he suggest you talk to me?"

"He gave me the names of all the bands who had recorded there in the last year," I lied. "Have you been back to the Wash Sounds studio since you recorded that album?"

"No, why would I? I never want to see that place again. What kind of music are you into?"

"Oh, you know. All sorts."

"Would you like to hear one of mine?"

"Err, sure." I figured that if I feigned interest by listening to one of his tracks, he'd be more likely to open up to me.

"Okay, here goes." To my surprise, he opened a cupboard and took out a guitar. "This is one I wrote myself; it's called Rock Baby Girl."

And with that, he burst into song. There aren't words to adequately describe just how bad it was. He could certainly play the guitar, but his voice was the worst; it was so bad it made me want to cut off my ears. Somehow, though, I managed to smile and nod approvingly.

"What do you think?"

"It's — err — a classic."

"Isn't it just? And Orlando had the nerve to say my voice was the problem. Can you believe that?"

"You said that you were primarily a gigging band?"

"That's right."

"Did you get many gigs?"

"Enough, yeah."

"Did you have a regular circuit of venues?"

"Nah, we didn't get many repeat bookings, but that suited me. It's much more exciting to play at different places each week."

"I guess so."

Arnold didn't offer to play any more of his songs, which was just as well because I'm not sure my ears could have withstood it. The man was clearly deluded; he really did believe that he had a great voice. No wonder his band never got any repeat bookings.

Chapter 22

It was Saturday morning, and I was exhausted after a busy, but mostly unproductive week. There was still no sign of the church hall re-opening because the water damage had, apparently, been quite extensive. With no dance class or basket-weaving, I planned on having a nice lazy morning ahead of the Kids' Music Fest that afternoon.

Jack was out in the garden, playing with Buddy; Florence was upstairs playing with Humpy, so I settled down in the lounge with a book. I rarely got the chance to read these days, but Kathy had given me this one, which she swore was the best thing she had read for years. The title: Two Gnomes for Harriet didn't inspire me with confidence.

I'd only read a couple of pages when an almighty crashing sound came from upstairs. Dropping the book, I hurried to the foot of the stairs.

"Florence? Are you okay?"

"Yes, Mummy."

"What was that banging noise?"

"Nothing."

Hmm. A likely story. I knew that little madam was up to something, so I dashed up to her bedroom.

"What's going on, Florence?"

"Nothing." She was standing directly in front of her wardrobe.

"I heard a crashing sound."

She shrugged and gave me that innocent little look of hers. I was just about to give her the benefit of the doubt when…

"Atishoo!" The sneeze came from inside the wardrobe.

"Who's in there, Florence?"

"No one."

"Step aside, please."

I pulled open the door, half-expecting to find Wendy inside. She must have come over while I was having my shower.

But it wasn't Wendy.

"Hi," said the pink dragon with green spots.

"Who are you?"

"Bobby."

"What are you doing in Florence's wardrobe?"

"She told me to hide in here."

"Florence? Would you care to explain?"

"It was an accident." She pointed towards her bed. It was only then that I spotted the spell book, which was open at a spell called Make Your Own Dragon. "I didn't think he'd be so big."

Who came up with such ridiculous spells?

"He can't stay here. You'll just have to reverse the spell."

"I tried, Mummy, but it doesn't work."

"I'll do it. Sorry, Bobby, but I have no choice."

"That's okay." He was starting to well up.

I felt bad, but it had to be done.

Except that I couldn't make it work either. It was only then that I spotted a note, in tiny writing, at the bottom of the page which read: Please be aware this spell cannot be reversed.

Great! Just great!

"Why won't it work, Mummy?"

"Because this spell can't be reversed, apparently."

"Does that mean I can keep Bobby?"

"No, it doesn't. We don't have room for him, and besides you can't have a dragon in the human world."

"What are we going to do with him?"

"I don't know. I need to think about it."

"Can I play with Bobby while you think?"

"Yes, but try not to break anything, Bobby."

"Okay." He jumped out of the wardrobe.

Back in the kitchen, I gave Grandma a call.

"Is this urgent? I'm having my pedicure."

"I just have a quick question. Hypothetically speaking, if you had a dragon you needed to get rid of, what would you do?"

"A lightning bolt to the head is as good as anything."

"I don't mean kill it. I mean if you wanted to find a home for it, for example, what would you do?"

"Why do you have a dragon?"

"Florence magicked it up."

"That little one is coming on in leaps and bounds. You must be so proud."

"Yeah, but back to the dragon."

"You'll need to take it to Dragon Rescue."

"Where will I find them?"

"They're behind the bakery on Loaf Street."

"Okay, thanks."

Just as Jack walked into the kitchen, there was another almighty crash from upstairs.

"What on earth was that?"

"That's Bobby."

"Who's Bobby?"

"A dragon, obviously."

"Why is there a dragon upstairs?"

"Florence magicked him up."

"O—kay. Where's he going to live?"

"Not here. Florence and I are going to take him to Dragon Rescue in Candlefield."

"I thought you were going to have a lazy morning?"

"So did I."

***

"That sign says it's closed, Mummy."

Unfortunately, Florence was correct. The notice in the window of Dragon Rescue showed that the centre was only open Monday to Friday.

"Great!"

"Where am I going to go?" Bobby said.

"We'll have to take you to Aunt Lucy's house. I'm sure I can persuade her to look after you until Monday morning."

"Is she nice?"

"Yes, she's very nice. Come on. Let's go."

"Jill! Florence! What a lovely surprise." Aunt Lucy beamed. "Who's that with you?"

"This is Bobby."

"Hi." He waved a paw.

"Hi, Bobby." To my surprise, instead of inviting us inside, she stepped out and closed the door behind her.

"I was hoping that Bobby could stay with you until Monday morning when the Dragon Rescue centre opens."

"I'd love to have him stay, but it would never work."

"Why not?"

"Have you forgotten about Barry?"

"Oh yeah. That could get messy."

"Very."

"I have no idea what I'm going to do with him."

"No one wants me." Bobby sighed.

"Of course they do," Aunt Lucy reassured him; she was clearly feeling a little guilty. "I've got an idea. The upstairs room in Cuppy C is empty now the girls have closed down the cork museum. He could stay there until Monday."

"Do you think the twins will mind?"

"Are you familiar with the phrase, sometimes it's better to ask for forgiveness than permission? I think this is one of those occasions."

"But how do we get him in there without them seeing?"

"Don't worry." Aunt Lucy grinned. "I have a plan."

***

When the twins spotted Florence and me, they beckoned us to come into the shop. I shook my head and indicated that they should come outside to us.

"Why don't you come inside?" Pearl said.

"Florence has a cold. We wouldn't want to give it to your customers."

Right on cue, Florence pretended to sneeze. That little girl of mine was a natural thespian.

"Poor you," Amber said. "Are you okay?"

"Yes, thank you." She snuffled.

"I bet I know what will make you feel better," Pearl said. "How about a yummy cupcake?"

"Okay, thank you." Florence forced a smile.

Before Pearl could go back into the shop, Aunt Lucy appeared behind them at the door.

"Where did you spring from, Mum?" Pearl said.

"We came in the back way."

"*We?*"

"Me and your new house guest."

"What *house guest*?" Amber said.

"Why don't you come and meet Bobby?"

Aunt Lucy led the way.

"I thought Florence had to stay outside?" Pearl said, as we made our way upstairs.

"Her cold has cleared up, hasn't it, Florence?"

"Yes, I'm all better now."

When they saw Bobby, I was expecting to face the twins' wrath, but I needn't have worried because they both immediately fell in love with him.

"Can I stay here until Monday, please?" Bobby said.

"Of course you can." Amber was clearly smitten.

"Do you like cake?" Pearl asked him.

"You managed to get rid of the dragon, then?" Jack said when we reappeared in the kitchen.

"He's staying at Cuppy C," Florence said.

"How come?"

"The dragon rescue centre doesn't open at the weekend. Aunt Lucy couldn't have him because of Barry, so he's staying with the twins until Monday." I turned to Florence. "No more magicking up strange creatures."

"I won't."

"Promise?"

"I promise."

"Good. If no one minds, I'm going back to my book.

What time do we have to leave for Kids' Fest?"

"I said we'd pick up Wendy at twelve."

***

Jack was driving, I was in the passenger seat, and the two girls were in the back, laughing and giggling about Bobby the dragon. We were halfway to Washbridge when Kathy called.

"Jill, where are you?"

"On our way."

"On your way where?"

"To the park of course."

"I don't understand."

"It isn't a difficult concept, Kathy. We're in the car driving towards Washbridge."

"So you aren't here in the park already?"

"Have you been at the wine?"

"Lizzie said she saw you near the gate, but when we went to look for you, you weren't there."

"That's because we're *in the car*. We should be there in about twenty minutes."

"Okay. See you soon."

"I take it that was Kathy," Jack said.

"Yeah. I think she may have finally lost the plot."

As soon as we arrived at the park, Florence and Wendy both begged for an ice cream, so Jack took them to get one while I waited by the gates. I'd not been there for very long when Mad appeared, accompanied by Lizzie.

"Hello, you two. Where's your mum and dad, Lizzie?"

"I'm not sure." She shrugged. "Mum said I could hang

out with Mad. Auntie Jill, can I ask you something?"

"Of course."

"Have you been chased by any ghouls recently?"

The two of them burst into laughter.

"Thanks for sharing that with her, Mad."

"Sorry, Jill." Mad wiped a tear from her eye. "You have to admit it was funny."

"Hilarious. What's the latest on the ghouls, anyway? The real ones, that is."

"We've been told to stand down. It seems there was an over-reaction at HQ because someone misinterpreted the intel."

"That's a relief. How come Brad isn't here?"

"We couldn't both leave the shop, so I took a vote and won." She grinned.

"Have you heard any of The Ghouls' stuff, Auntie Jill?"

"No. Are they any good?"

"They're okay, but most of their fans are much older, like you and Mad."

"Cheek." Mad gave Lizzie a friendly punch on the arm.

"Give her one for me."

"We'd better get going, Lizzie," Mad said. "We want to try and get near the front. Catch you later."

"Mummy!" Florence came running over, ice cream cone in hand. "We just saw you."

"I saw you too. That's a big ice cream."

"No, I mean we saw you over there, near the ice cream van, didn't we, Daddy?"

"She's right," Jack said. "There's a woman in the queue who is the spitting image of you."

"Really?"

"Yeah, she has a little girl with her. Why don't you go

and take a look?"

"Okay, I will." Even before I reached the queue, I knew who it would be. "Linda, hi."

"Jill? Fancy seeing you here."

"When you said you were visiting the human world this weekend, it never occurred to me that you might be coming here. My husband and daughter just told me they'd seen my doppelganger."

"I'm sorry. If it's going to cause a problem for you, we can leave."

"Don't be silly. Get your ice creams and I'll introduce you to Jack and Florence."

Totally bemused, Jack, Florence and Wendy looked back and forth between Linda and me.

"This is Linda and her daughter, Eliza," I said by way of introduction.

"I can't believe how much alike you two are," Jack said. "You could be identical twins. Do you live around here, Linda?"

She hesitated, clearly unsure what to say in front of my human husband, so I came to her rescue, "Err, no they're from Sheffield, aren't you?"

"That's right," Linda said.

Fortunately, Eliza was busy showing Florence her panda, so she didn't contradict her mother.

Just then, I spotted Kathy and Peter in the distance. If Kathy saw Linda and me together, it might not be so easy to explain.

"Sorry, Linda, my sister and her husband are here. We'd better get going."

"Okay, but you and Florence must come and visit us

soon."

"We will, I promise." I grabbed Florence by the hand. "Let's go and see your Auntie Kathy."

"Bye, Eliza," Florence shouted over her shoulder.

"Are you sure you're *you*?" Kathy said.

"What are you talking about?"

"There's another *you* here somewhere."

"Has she been at the wine, Peter?"

"She did have a glass before we came out."

"It's true," Kathy insisted. "I saw her."

"I didn't." Peter shrugged.

"That's because you'd gone to the loo."

"We'd better get inside." Jack took out our tickets.

The organisers had erected a fence along the length of which were gates numbered one to six.

"Which gate are we in?" I said.

"Six."

"It's over there," Kathy pointed.

Just beyond gate six was another gate marked Performers and VIPs only. It was the only one without a long queue.

"Can't we sneak in there?" I said.

"No, we can't. Have some patience, Jill." Kathy scolded me. "We're almost in."

As we waited our turn, I spotted a familiar face coming out of the VIP gate; it was Joyce Keys. I was about to call to her when Kathy dragged me through the gate.

There were no reserved seats, so once inside it was a scramble to grab them. We were lucky enough to get two sets of three. Florence, Wendy and Jack took one set; Kathy, Peter and I took the other.

"Why don't you sit down, Kathy."

"I'm looking for Lizzie. She's here with that friend of yours."

"Yeah, I saw them earlier."

"What's her name? I know it's something weird."

"Mad."

"That's it. The two of them have become very close since Lizzie took an interest in music. She's always visiting that record shop of hers. She asked if I minded if she hung around with Mad, but now I'm freaking out because I can't see her."

I stood up and scanned the crowd. "They're over there. Near those speakers."

"Oh yeah. Do you think I should go and get her?"

"She'll be fine with Mad."

I thought the two support bands were terrible, but Florence and Wendy clearly approved because they were happily boogying along to them. I was, however, pleasantly surprised by the headline act. The Ghouls played music that was much more to my taste.

"These guys aren't bad," I said.

"They're really boring." Florence pulled a face.

"This is like the stuff my mum likes," Wendy said.

"We're getting old." Kathy looked at me and sighed.

"Isn't that the truth."

"Aren't you going to wish me luck?" Kathy said when we were walking back to the cars.

"Good luck with what?"

"Trust you to forget. It's the Washbridge Businesswoman of the Year awards tonight. I'm starting to get really nervous."

"Best of luck."

"I'll call you tomorrow to let you know how I fared."

"I'll be waiting with bated breath."

Chapter 23

Jack, Florence and I had just sat down for breakfast. Florence was eating her muesli while reading the book that Donna had given her the day before, as a thank you for taking Wendy to the Kids' Music Fest. Appropriately, it was called Ronald, the Biggest Dragon in the World.

For some unknown reason, Jack was grinning like a Cheshire cat.

"What's tickling you?"

"Nothing."

"Come on. Something obviously is. Spit it out."

"I'm just glad we have such a strong marriage."

"Err, right?"

"What I mean is, unlike some couples, we never have a *cross word*." He dissolved into laughter.

"How long did it take you to come up with that little gem?"

"You're not five-*across* with me, are you?"

"That's terrible."

He was in hysterics now.

"What is Daddy laughing at?" Florence looked up from her book.

"Nothing, darling. Your daddy is just being very silly."

"It's better to be happy than six-*down*," Jack quipped.

"Is that it? Have you exhausted all your crossword jokes?"

"Yeah, that's it, I promise. No more *cryptic* comments from me."

Jack was still chuckling to himself when it was time for me to leave.

"Bye, Mummy." Florence gave me a kiss. "Have a nice time. I hope you win."

"Thanks, darling, but I don't think that's very likely."

I'd arranged to meet Grandma outside the village store. We were travelling to the crossword competition with the Stock sisters, who had taken the unprecedented decision to close the shop for the day. Grandma was already there when I arrived.

"Late as usual." She tapped her watch.

"I'm bang on time. You must have been early."

"I hope you've put in plenty of practice for this competition."

"When do I have time to practise? I have a business to run and a little girl to look after."

"Excuses, excuses. I have a hotel to run and a wig shop to manage, not to mention all the other demands on my time, and yet I've found time to put in hours of practice."

"What does it matter, anyway? If I come last, which I won't, it's not like it's any skin off your nose."

"Of course it is. You and I are playing as a team."

"Since when?"

"Since always. It's a team competition."

"I had no idea."

"You'd better be on your best form. I don't want your performance to drag us down."

Fantastic! This day had just got ten times worse. Although I hadn't been looking forward to the competition, I'd assumed I'd be able to cruise along with no pressure, but now, with Grandma breathing down my neck, the stakes were suddenly much higher.

"Good morning, Jill. Good morning, Mirabel." Marjorie stepped out of the shop. "What a wonderful day for it."

"Wonderful," I said through gritted teeth.

"Where's that sister of yours?" Grandma snapped. "I don't want to be late."

"Don't worry. She's just picking out a few snacks for the journey."

It was then, for the first time, that it occurred to me that I had no idea where the competition was being held.

"Where exactly is it we're going today?"

"Bristol."

"I thought it was being held here in Washbridge."

"It's a national competition," Grandma said. "Why would it be held here?"

"Bristol is miles away."

"Which is why Cynthia had better get a move on." Grandma looked pointedly at the shop.

"I'll go and hurry her along." Marjorie disappeared back inside.

"How are we getting to Bristol?" I asked Grandma.

"In your car of course."

"Why *my* car?"

"Because you're the only one who has one. Why do you think I put your name down for the competition?"

"I assumed it was for my high IQ and incredible intellect."

"That's very funny." She laughed. "Are you going to fetch the car or not?"

"It doesn't look like I have much choice." I ran back to the old watermill, dashed in the door and grabbed my car keys out of the bowl.

"Jill?" Jack came out of the kitchen. "Is everything alright?"

"Everything is just dandy. I've just found out that this

stupid competition is being held in Bristol, and muggins here is the chauffeur."

"Oh dear."

"You haven't heard the half of it. It's a team competition and guess who I'm partnered with?"

"Not—"

"Yes, Grandma. This is going to be a very long day."

We'd been travelling for just over an hour when Marjorie, who was sitting in the back with her sister, leaned forward. "I'm sorry to be a nuisance, but do you think we could pull into the next services. I need a tinkle."

"Can't you hold it?" Grandma snapped at her.

"I'm afraid not. I shouldn't have had that second cup of tea this morning."

"It's okay," I said. "The next services are only a couple of miles away."

We'd been back on the motorway for about thirty minutes when Cynthia said, rather sheepishly. "I'm really sorry, but I need to tinkle now. Could we stop at the next services, please?"

"Couldn't you have gone when your sister did?" Grandma looked as though she was about to explode.

"Sorry. I didn't need to go then."

"It's okay, Cynthia," I said. "We're not far from the next services."

By the time we came off the motorway at Bristol, Marjorie and Cynthia were both fast asleep.

"Can you bring the satnav up on your phone?" I asked Grandma.

"Why?"

"To direct us to the competition venue."

"We don't need satnav."

"Of course we do. You don't know your way around Bristol."

"I don't need to. I'll cast the 'WitchNav' spell."

"The what?"

"Please don't tell me you've never heard of it."

"I haven't."

"Do you ever read that spell book of yours?"

"Err, occasionally."

"There's more to being a witch than just being extremely powerful. You also need to constantly add to your repertoire of spells. I bet Florence spends more time learning new spells than you do."

I'd never admit it, but Grandma was right.

"Rubbish. You'd better cast that spell of yours or we'll never find this place."

Grandma cast the 'WitchNav' spell and the image of a strange-looking creature appeared on the windscreen in front of her.

"I'm Navvy," he squeaked. "Where would you like to go today?"

"Take us to the Topmast Centre, would you?" Grandma instructed him.

"It will be my pleasure."

And that's just what he did. The weird little creature not only gave clear verbal directions, he also overlaid the map onto the windscreen.

"Thanks, Navvy," I said when we pulled up into the car park.

"My pleasure, ladies." And with that, he disappeared.

"Marjorie! Cynthia!" Grandma yelled. "We're here."

"Oh my." Cynthia wiped the sleep from her eyes. "I must have dozed off."

"Me too." Marjorie yawned. "I need the loo."

Inside, the huge hall had been furnished with hundreds of small tables, each with two seats next to it.

"Hand over your smartphones and smartwatches, please." The woman at the door stopped us.

"I need my phone," I objected.

"Sorry, but you won't be allowed to compete unless you give it up. It's the only way to stop people cheating by going online." She held open the bag, and reluctantly I placed my phone inside. Grandma did the same. Neither of the Stock sisters possessed a smartphone; they both claimed not to understand new technology.

The crossword competition was obviously very popular because almost all of the tables were occupied. Grandma and I were allocated a table near to the cloakroom. The Stock sisters were seated a couple of tables away.

"Ladies and gentlemen, can I have your attention please." The MC was standing on a makeshift stage located at the opposite side of the hall. Once the crowd had fallen silent, he continued. "Welcome to the thirty-seventh annual Cross-swords crossword competition."

"*Cross-swords*?" I mouthed to Grandma.

"It's a magazine for crossword nuts."

The MC continued. "For those of you new to the competition, I'll quickly run through the rules."

And he did, in tedious detail. The Cliff notes version was that there would be three rounds. In each round, every team had to complete their crossword, and raise their hands once they'd finished. The first ten teams to finish in each round would be awarded points. The first team to finish would receive ten points, the next would receive nine, etc. There was, however, one big catch: If a team's crossword was found to have been completed incorrectly, that team would be eliminated from the competition altogether. Wow, this was much tougher than I'd expected it to be.

A number of officials handed out the crosswords for the first round, placing them facedown on the tables. Once everyone had one, the MC did a quick countdown, and the competition was underway. Grandma immediately began to fill in answers while I could only stare hopelessly at the clues.

"Five down," I said triumphantly. "Angry."

"It's only four letters."

"Oh yeah. Seven down, then. Cheese."

"The first letter has to be a W."

"Are you sure?"

"Positive."

And that's how it continued. Grandma kept adding the answers while I made suggestions which she shot down in flames.

It was less than twenty minutes since the MC had given us the go ahead when a man and a woman, at a table in the centre of the hall, stood up and shouted *Finished*. An official collected the crossword and took it to the stage where it was quickly verified.

"We have our winner of the first round. Table sixty-three gets ten points."

Not long after, a second table declared that they'd finished. Their crossword too was verified as correct.

Table seventy-five tried to claim the eighth place, but they were eliminated because one entry was found to be incorrect.

Two familiar voices were the next to call out. Marjorie and Cynthia were on their feet; Marjorie was holding their crossword aloft. After verification, they were awarded eighth place and three points. Table twenty-four took ninth place, and then Grandma stood up.

"Finished!" She turned to me. "Stand up, Jill."

I did as she said and waited nervously while the crossword was checked. Moments later, it was verified.

"We won a point!" I said.

"I think you'll find *I* won the point. You didn't complete a single clue."

"I still think cheese was the correct answer."

In the second round, the Stock sisters did even better, finishing a creditable third. Grandma improved on our previous position by finishing sixth, but she was clearly not happy.

"We can't let those drippy sisters beat us."

"Cynthia and Marjorie aren't—okay, maybe they are a bit drippy, but they're always doing crosswords, so they're forced to have an edge."

"Ladies and gentlemen." The MC was back onstage. "This is the third and final round. As you can see from the scoreboard, the competition is still wide open, so there's everything to play for."

"If we don't beat those sisters, I'll never be able to hold my head up in the village again," Grandma said. "I need you to pull your weight this time."

"I'll do my best."

"You'll need to do a lot better than that."

Five minutes into the final round, and I had at long last managed to enter an answer. "Look, Grandma. I got one."

But she didn't look. Instead, she seemed to be staring across the room. "Those cheating little so-and-sos."

"Who?"

"The Stock sisters. Look at them."

I did as she said, and saw that Marjorie seemed to be fiddling with something under the table.

"What is she doing?"

"She's got a smartphone."

Sure enough, Marjorie was tapping away on the phone. I was gobsmacked. I never would have believed it of them.

"Right, that does it." Grandma was livid. "It's time to fight fire with fire."

"You're not going to set their crossword ablaze, are you?"

"Of course I'm not. I didn't want to do this, but they've left me with no choice but to use the 'WitchWord' spell."

"The what?"

"You really must start to study that spell book." She closed her eyes, cast the spell, and the next thing I knew, our crossword had been completed. Grandma got to her feet and shouted, "Finished."

Everyone looked around in astonishment. It was easily the quickest anyone had completed a crossword all afternoon. Judging by the mumbling from all around us, everyone expected it to be incorrect and for us to be eliminated. But it was verified, and we were awarded ten points.

Even those ten points weren't enough for us to win the competition overall, but we did finish in fourth place, ahead of the Stock sisters who finished sixth.

"That was a remarkable performance that you and Jill put on, Mirabel," Marjorie said as we drove home.

"Thank you, Marjorie." Grandma was looking very pleased with herself. "You two did very well too."

"Thank you, Mirabel." Cynthia beamed. "We have been practising a lot."

Grandma looked at me and rolled her eyes. I half-expected her to confront them about the hidden phone, but she must have mellowed in her ancient age because she never mentioned it.

When we arrived at the village, I dropped the sisters off first, then drove over to the hotel.

"I hope you're going to heed what I said about spending more time studying the spell book, Jill," Grandma said.

"I will, I promise. I'm going to make a concerted effort to expand my repertoire of spells."

"Good." She was just about to get out of the car when she hesitated. "I assume you heard about Madge Pearpots?"

"Who?"

"She's the head of WOW. She was elected last year."

"Is that organisation still going? I haven't heard much about them recently."

"Apparently so, but their numbers have dropped dramatically. Anyway, it seems that Madge was the victim of a scam recently. Poor dear." Grandma could not have sounded any less sincere if she'd tried.

"What happened?"

"The conman played on her vanity, of which she has plenty. From what I hear, they posed as a representative for Witch Who's Who."

"WWW?"

"Sorry?"

"Err, isn't that what they call it?"

"They don't call it anything because it doesn't exist. Anyway, Madge fell for it hook, line and sinker. The silly woman handed over hundreds of pounds to the conman. Can you believe it?"

"I—err—no, that's terrible."

"Bye, then, Jill. Give my love to Florence."

"Bye."

Bum and double bum!

"Mummy, you're back." Florence threw her arms around me.

"Hello, darling."

"Are you okay, Jill?" Jack said. "You look a little pale."

"I'm fine. It's just been a long day. What have you two been up to?"

"We went to a new park," Florence said.

"I took her to West Chipping Park for a change."

"Daddy got his feet wet." She giggled.

"How did you manage that?"

"We went on a pedal boat, and just my luck, they gave me the one that was letting in water."

"Did it sink?"

"No, thank goodness. It stayed afloat long enough for me to get us back to the shore, but my feet were underwater."

"It was so funny!" Florence laughed. "Daddy had to

squeeze the water out of his socks."

Chapter 24

It was Monday morning, and I didn't feel as though I'd had a proper weekend break after spending Saturday dealing with a dragon and then going to the Kids' Music Fest, followed by the crossword competition on Sunday.

"I can't believe the Stock sisters would try to cheat like that," Jack said, as we ate breakfast. "They look like butter wouldn't melt."

"I know. I thought Grandma was going to blow a fuse when she saw what they were up to."

"Instead, she resorted to cheating as well," he said.

"Using magic isn't really cheating."

"Of course it is. I'm surprised you didn't get in before her."

"I would never do such a thing."

"Says the woman who cheats at snakes and ladders every time we play."

"Rubbish. Grandma did say something yesterday that got me thinking, though. She pointed out that I never spend any time studying the spell book."

"Why would you need to? Aren't you supposed to be the most powerful witch in Candlefield?"

"Yes, but as Grandma rightly pointed out, I rarely learn new spells."

"I thought you were able to conjure up your own spells."

"I can, but it seems silly trying to re-invent the wheel. Anyway, I've decided that I'm going to take time out to study the spell book for a few hours each week."

"Just don't go magicking up any more dragons."

"Speaking of which, I wonder how the twins coped

with Bobby over the weekend."

"Florence and I had a great time at West Chipping park. We should all go there one weekend. There's much more to do there than in Washbridge Park."

"I heard you get your socks washed free of charge with every boat ride."

"Ha ha. At least it gave Florence a good laugh."

"That's not the only thing it did. It's given me an idea related to one of my cases."

"How come?"

"I'll tell you tonight if my hunch pays off."

"Do you think Bobby is alright, Mummy?" Florence was doing her least favourite job: feeding Buddy (while holding her nose).

"I'm sure he is. I bet the twins have been spoiling him. They've probably been feeding him cake all weekend."

"What is Dragon Rescue like?"

"I don't know."

"What if Bobby doesn't like it? What if he's really sad there?"

"He won't be."

"How do you know?"

"I — err — just do."

"But it might be horrible."

"How about I go and check it out? Would that make you happy?"

"Yes, but if it's horrible, you'll have to find somewhere else for him to stay."

"Okay."

***

"Morning, Mrs V."

She yawned. "Sorry, Jill. Good morning."

"Are you okay?"

"I didn't get much sleep last night."

"Dare I ask why not? I'll understand if you don't want to share the intimate details."

"It was nothing like that. Our burglar alarm went off just after midnight, and neither of us could remember how to disable it. It was still going when I came into work this morning."

"What set it off? Not burglars, I hope."

"There wasn't a break-in. Armi said he thought it might have been a squirrel. It's lucky we don't have any close neighbours, or we'd be very unpopular. The man is coming around this morning to sort it out, and to show Armi what to do if it happens again." She yawned again.

"If you want to go home and catch up on your sleep, you can."

"No, I'm fine." More yawns.

"You should sack her for sleeping on the job," Winky said.

"Mrs V was only yawning. She's been up most of the night."

"Please don't give me the lurid details."

"It was just the burglar alarm."

"That's what she told you, but who knows what kind of kinky stuff her and Arni get up to."

"It's Armi, and you're just being ridiculous."

"I've been thinking." He jumped onto my desk.

"Whatever it is, I'm not interested."

"Passive income."

"What about it?"

"That's what you need."

"I just need *income*. Of any kind."

"In which case, you'll be pleased to know that I have the perfect solution to your money problems."

"I'm still not interested."

"You'll change your mind when I tell you about this once in a lifetime opportunity."

"Which part of *I'm not interested* don't you understand?"

"It gives me great pleasure to present to you Feline Fortune." He passed me a glossy brochure.

I gave it a quick skim. "This stuff is cheap and tacky."

"No, it isn't. It's all top quality."

"Are you kidding? I can buy all of this stuff at Rue Pets for a third of these prices."

"Yes, but it wouldn't be the Feline Fortune brand."

"Who cares? Cat food is cat food. Cat litter is cat litter. And who needs aromatic oils for their cat?"

"Everyone who cares about their feline companion. Would you like to place your first order?"

"No chance, and if you've got any sense, you'll forget all about this rubbish. You haven't actually ordered any stock yet, have you?"

"Of course I have."

"Then you're an idiot."

"It's only a small order. I won't have any difficulty selling it, you'll see."

My phone rang; it was Kathy.

"Jill?"

"Just a second." I put my hand over the phone. "If you've got any sense, you'll cancel that order now."

"It's too late." Winky shrugged.

"Kathy, sorry about that. I was trying to talk someone out of buying a load of cheap junk."

"Who?"

"Err, Mrs V."

"I thought she had more sense."

"Me too."

"Where were you yesterday, Jill? I must have called you a dozen times."

"Sorry, I was out with Grandma all day."

"Aren't you going to ask me how I got on?"

"How you got on with *what*?"

"With the Washbridge Businesswoman of the Year award of course."

"Oh yes. How did you get on?"

"I was runner-up."

"Unlucky, sorry."

"What do you mean *unlucky*? It's a fabulous achievement for a business as new as mine. I'm over the moon."

"Of course you are. Congratulations. That's brilliant."

"Peter is taking me out for a meal tonight to celebrate. He says he's very proud of me."

"Actually, Jack is taking me out to celebrate too." He just doesn't know it yet.

"Oh? What are you celebrating?"

"You know me. I don't like to brag."

"Yeah, okay." She laughed. "So, why is Jack so proud of you?"

"Grandma and I took part in a national crossword competition yesterday."

"You? In a crossword competition? You were never any

good at crosswords."

"Not as a kid, but now, without wishing to toot my own trumpet, I'm something of a grandmaster."

"You don't toot your trumpet. You either toot your own horn, or blow your own trumpet."

"Pedantic much."

"So, how did you get on in the competition?"

"We came fourth, but like I said, it was a national competition with hundreds of teams taking part."

"You and your grandmother played as a team, then?"

"Yeah."

"How many answers did you personally get correct?"

"I wasn't keeping count, but definitely the lion's share. Grandma is getting on and her mind isn't as sharp as it used to be."

"Is that so? The next time I bump into her, I'll make a point of asking her all about it."

"I wouldn't do that. It'll only embarrass her. Anyway, I have to get going. Enjoy your meal."

"You entered a crossword competition?" Winky laughed. "You're useless at them. You couldn't even work out the golden goose clue, and that was really simple."

"Didn't you hear what I said? I came fourth in a national competition."

"I heard what you said, and I also watched your nose grow another six inches."

"I don't have time to waste on you. I have work to do. Go and cancel that order."

"No chance."

I made a call to Norman Bagshot.

"Mr Bagshot? It's Tuppence Farthing. I came to see you

the other day."

"I'm hardly likely to forget someone with such a delightful name. What can I do for you?"

"I've more or less decided to have my wedding on the island, but I really would like to get a proper look at your launch. Do you know when the repairs will be finished?"

"Good news. They're all done and she's back in business."

"Excellent. When can I pop over and take a look at her?"

"You can come over now if you wish."

"Great. I'll be over there as soon as I can."

"Okay. See you shortly."

***

Mrs V came through to my office, yawned, and then said, "Farah is here. She wondered if you were free."

"She hasn't lost another one of her dogs, has she?"

"I don't think so."

"I have to go out soon, but I can spare her a few minutes. Send her through, would you."

"Hi, Jill," Farah said. "Sorry to bother you like this."

"Don't be silly. Grab a seat."

"Thanks. I just wanted to let you know that I've decided to move out."

"You're leaving this building?"

"That's right."

"Surely not because of what happened with the *disappearing* dogs?" I glared at Winky; this was all his fault.

"No. Well, that's part of it, I guess. And then there's the

upcoming rent increase."

"I'm really sorry, Farah. I promised I'd do something about that, but it turns out there's nothing I can do about it."

"It's not your fault. I know you tried your best. I've realised it was a mistake moving here, and that's down to me. The location is all wrong. For a start, there's no parking nearby which puts a lot of people off. And what was I thinking taking a unit at the top of a flight of stairs?"

"What will you do? Go back to mobile grooming?"

"Not likely. I've had my fill of that. I've fallen really lucky. I found a ground-floor unit just a few miles from where I live. It has parking and is the ideal size. And even better, the rent is half of what I'd be paying if I stayed here. It's perfect."

"I'll be sorry to see you go, but at least it sounds like you've landed on your feet. When will you be moving out?"

"Next week."

"So soon?"

"No point in delaying." She stood up. "I hope you'll still bring Barry to see us."

"Of course I will."

When she'd left, I turned my glare on Winky.

"What?"

"This is your fault."

"It sounds to me like I did her a favour. She should be thanking me."

***

When I arrived at the lake, the launch was back in its

moorings. Norman Bagshot was busy polishing its brass fittings when he saw my approach.

"Hello again, Tuppence. Would you care to step onboard?" He held out his hand and helped me onto the launch.

"It's bigger than it looked in the photographs."

"I decorate her with flowers and satins sheets for the wedding parties."

"How many can you take across the lake?"

"There's room for twenty-four guests at a time, which means a maximum of two trips because, as Warren may have already told you, the chapel can only accommodate forty-five guests. What do you think?"

"It's lovely. Much better than I was expecting. What if it rains, though?"

"That's not a problem. There's a full-size canopy which encloses the whole of the passenger section."

"What about storage? Some of the guests who are travelling by train may have cases with them."

"They can leave them in the boathouse or if it's stuff they need to take with them to the island, there's some storage room under the seated area." He walked to the rear of the launch and tapped a square hatch with his foot.

"Can I see inside?"

"Of course." He pulled open the hatch.

I bent down to take a closer look. "Excellent, that puts my mind at ease on that score."

"Do you have any more questions for me, Tuppence?"

"Just the cost, I suppose."

"It's five-hundred pounds for the day; that includes up to two trips in both directions. If you want to use the launch for the rehearsal, I usually do that for one hundred, but that's restricted to one trip each way, and of course, I don't bother decorating the boat."

"Okay, thanks. I think that's everything."

"Here, let me help you to get out."

"Thanks. I'll give you a call when I've booked the chapel."

Chapter 25

On a purely commercial basis, it would have made sense for me to find cheaper premises, and there were plenty of vacant offices in and around Washbridge. But my office was my connection to my adoptive father; even now, I still felt his presence around the place, so I would just have to suck up the rent increase. I desperately needed to up my income, but all my efforts at marketing had failed miserably. What I needed was passive income. What I needed was Feline Fortune.

Just kidding.

I'd promised Florence I would check that Bobby had settled in at Dragon Rescue, so I magicked myself over to Cuppy C, where the twins were both behind the counter, looking rather down in the dumps.

"What's wrong, girls?"

"Mum was in here just now." Pearl sighed. "She gave us a right tongue lashing."

"I've not seen her that angry since we were kids and we spilled a can of paint on the living room carpet," Amber said.

"And I can guess why. Corks?" They both nodded. "I did tell you not to just sling them in a box. She'd spent ages categorising them."

"We told her we were sorry. It's just that we were so disappointed that the cork museum didn't work out. Your usual, Jill?"

"No, thanks. I can't stay. I promised Florence I would check how Bobby was settling into Dragon Rescue."

"He isn't there," Amber said.

"How come? Don't tell me it was closed again today?"

"It's not that."

"What then? Where is he?"

"Upstairs."

"Wouldn't they accept him?"

"We didn't take him there."

"Why not? You're not exactly run off your feet, are you?"

"We kind of like having him here."

"What do you mean, *you like having him here*? He's a dragon."

"Thanks for pointing that out." Amber rolled her eyes. "Here we were, thinking he was a rabbit."

"When *are* you planning on taking him to Dragon Rescue?"

"There's no hurry, and besides, we have a plan."

"Coming from you two, those words fill me with dread."

"Show her," Pearl said to Amber.

"She'll only make fun and criticise like she always does."

"No, I won't. Unless it happens to involve corks."

"This is only a rough copy. We're going to get it printed properly." Amber reached under the counter, and then placed a makeshift poster in front of me.

Come and meet Bobby the dragon. Five pounds per person. Ten pounds for a selfie with Bobby.

"You can't do this! It's exploitation."

"No, it isn't. This was Bobby's idea."

"A likely story."

"It was, wasn't it, Pearl?"

"Honestly, Jill. He loves being here with us, and he

asked if there was any way he could stay longer."

"So you said, *sure as long as you don't mind becoming our cash-dragon.*"

"That's not what happened. We said he was welcome to stay for as long as he liked. It was when he said he wanted to pay his way, that the three of us put our heads together and came up with this plan."

"Hmm."

"If you don't believe us, why don't you ask him yourself?"

"I will." I started for the stairs and the twins began to follow. "No, you don't. You two stay down here, so I can get to the bottom of this without you putting pressure on him."

"Hey, Jill!" Bobby came bounding across the room to greet me. For a horrible minute, I thought he was going to knock me straight back down the stairs, but he put the brakes on just in time.

"Hi, Bobby. I thought you were going to Dragon Rescue today?"

"Didn't Amber and Pearl tell you? They said I can stay here."

"That's nice, but don't you think you might like it better at Dragon Rescue? There'll be lots of other dragons there."

"No, I really like it here. The twins said I can meet their customers and have my photo taken with them."

"So I hear, but did you know they're going to charge the customers cash to meet you?"

"Yes, that was my idea. Isn't it great? I love it here, and the twins said I can have two free buns every day."

"That sounds fantastic, but if you change your mind, and want to go to Dragon Rescue, you know you can leave at any time, don't you?"

"I know, but I want to stay here."

"Okay, Bobby. I have to get back."

"See you again soon, Jill."

The twins were waiting for me at the foot of the stairs. They had their hands on their hips, and were both smirking fit to burst. They had clearly been listening to my conversation with Bobby.

"Well?" Amber said.

"I think you owe us an apology," Pearl snapped.

"I'm sorry. I was wrong."

"*Pardon.*" Pearl cupped her ear. "What was that you said?"

"I said I'm sorry. He clearly does want to stay here."

"And you accept that we aren't exploiting him?"

"Yes. When are you going to start letting people go and see him?"

"As soon as we've got the posters printed. It shouldn't take more than a couple of days. Hopefully, we can make back some of the money we lost on the cork museum."

"You should use some of that money to buy your mum some flowers."

"Good idea."

***

Mrs V was still yawning.

"Are you sure you don't want to call it a day and head home?" I said.

"No, I'm fine." Yawn. "Besides, Armi has just called to say the man is working on the alarm now, so I probably wouldn't be able to get any sleep if I did go home."

"Okay, but if you change your mind, it's not a problem."

Mrs V wasn't the only sleepy one in the office; Winky was flat out on my desk. He'd obviously been on my computer again, despite my forbidding him to use it. The screensaver was showing, so I moved the mouse to check what he'd been doing, expecting it to be something related to Feline Fortune.

I was wrong. The computer was logged onto eBay, and the photo on-screen was of two cat bowls. They were just like the ones that had been stolen. Bless his little paws; he must have been trying to find identical ones online. He was clearly upset at having them stolen so soon after getting them.

Wait a minute! I couldn't believe it! He hadn't been looking at bowls for sale. He was logged into his own listing.

"Winky!" I slapped the desk.

He jumped so hard that he almost fell off. "Where's the fire?"

"You are in *so* much trouble."

"Why did you wake me up like that? You could have given me a heart attack."

"What's this?" I pointed to the screen.

"Oh? I—err—that's nothing." He tried to grab the mouse, but I was too quick for him. "It's not what you think it is."

"It's *precisely* what I think it is. You're selling those bowls I bought for you. The bowls you claimed had been stolen."

"I'm not sure I actually said they'd been stolen."

"That's exactly what you said. How could you do it? I thought you liked those bowls."

"I did. I still do. It's just that I need all the money I can lay my paws on at the moment."

"What for?"

"To pay for my Feline Fortune starter stock."

"You, sir, are unbelievable. After your previous exploits, I wouldn't have thought anything you did could shock me, but you managed it. You really have plumbed new depths this time."

"I sense you're a little annoyed."

"A *little*? A *little*? I'm—I'm—I can't even find the words."

"If it's any consolation, the bowls look like they're going to go for a good price."

"It isn't a consolation. You're a despicable toerag."

"Jill? What are you doing with that stapler? Jill, put it down."

He made it out through the window just in time.

***

"Mr Song is here, Jill." Mrs V yawned. "Can you spare him a few minutes?"

"Sure. Ask him to come through, would you?"

Orlando seemed to have aged several years since I last saw him, only a few days earlier.

"Are you okay, Orlando?"

"Not really. Do you mind if I sit down?"

"Help yourself. Would you like a drink?"

"No, thanks. I don't suppose you've made a breakthrough on the case, have you?"

"I'm afraid not. I've spoken to all the people we discussed, but I've come up with nothing so far."

"I feared as much. I think it might be best if you stop working on the case."

"Not yet, surely? I haven't finished my investigation yet. There's still hope."

"I'm not sure that there is. I received a phone call this morning from the band that had booked the studio for the whole of next month. They cancelled."

"Why?"

"They made some silly excuse about looking for a different sound, but I'm sure it's because they've heard about my troubles. What makes it even worse is that they used the studio when they were just starting out in the business. They were strapped for cash back then, so I let them have a lower rate. Now they've made the big time, and can afford to pay, they've dumped me. Where's the loyalty, Jill? That's what I'd like to know."

"That's a horrible way for them to repay your kindness."

"That's just the way things are nowadays. And to think, I even sent them a bottle of champagne to celebrate their first headlining gig last weekend."

"Where were they headlining?"

"In Washbridge Park at the Kids' Music Fest."

"You're talking about The Ghouls."

"That's what they call themselves now." He laughed. "When they recorded their first album, they were called the Earwigs. I told them they'd never get anywhere unless they changed their name. Seems like they took my advice."

"How about this, Orlando? I'll stop the clock on your

case, so you won't get charged a penny for any work I do from now on, but I'll continue to investigate for a few days at least."

"I can't expect you to work for nothing, Jill. I don't want to be responsible for your business going to the wall too."

"A few days won't bankrupt me."

"Okay, then. That's very kind of you."

We chatted for a few more minutes, then Orlando left. He'd no sooner stepped out of the door, than he was back.

"Jill, I thought I should let you know that your receptionist is fast asleep out here. Do you think she's okay?"

"Yeah, she just had a bad night. Thanks, I'll see to her."

"Mrs V." I gave her a gentle nudge.

"Oh? Jill, I'm so sorry. Mr Song didn't see me asleep, did he?"

"No, I don't think he noticed, but you have to go home now."

"But—"

"No buts. Off you go."

"Okay, I suppose you're right. I'm really sorry."

"There's no need to apologise. In fact, you might just have done me a big favour."

***

"Is Bobby happy at Dragon Rescue?" Florence asked, as soon as I arrived home.

"He isn't there."

"Has he run away?"

"No, he's going to stay at Cuppy C with Amber and Pearl."

"Forever?"

"Probably not forever, but for a while at least."

"Does he like it there?"

"He seems to, and the twins give him cake."

"I'm glad Bobby is at Cuppy C. Will I be able to go and see him?"

"Yes, but the twins are charging five pounds to see him now."

"I don't have five pounds."

"It's okay. I'm sure they'll let you in for free."

Jack was busy making dinner. "Did I hear you say the dragon is staying at Cuppy C?"

"Yeah. It seems he and the twins have really hit it off. They're going to charge customers to see him."

"Those two don't miss a trick, do they?"

"You're right there. How long will dinner be?"

"About twenty minutes."

"I have to go out tonight."

"Why?"

"I have a lead on one of the cases I'm working on."

"Won't it wait until the morning?"

"I'm afraid not. It has to be tonight."

Florence had decided she wanted to take Humpy to bed with her.

"Wouldn't you rather have one of your other toys? Camels aren't very cuddly."

"No, I want Humpy."

"What about Ted? He likes to be cuddled."

"Ted's had lots of cuddles. It's Humpy's turn."

"Okay. What book would you like me to read to you

tonight?"

"Trixie And The Magic Worm."

"Really? I read that last time." And the time before that, and the time before that.

"Yes, it's my favourite."

"I know it is, but wouldn't you like something different for a change?"

"No, thank you."

I flicked through the pages for Florence's benefit, but I didn't need to look at them because I knew every word off by heart.

"Goodnight, Worm. Goodnight, Trixie. And the two friends were soon fast asleep. The end." I put the book down and gave Florence a kiss. "Night, night, darling."

"Night, Mummy."

"I hate that worm!" I said to Jack who was in the lounge, reading a golf magazine. "Even the title is misleading. He isn't magic; he's just lucky."

"Do you think maybe you're taking it a little too literally?"

"I should write children's books."

"You've said that before."

"They couldn't be any worse than Trixie and the Not-Really Magic Worm."

"Do you want a glass of wine?"

"I can't. I have to go out, remember?"

"Maybe when you get back?"

"Maybe, but I'm not sure what time that'll be." I stooped down and kissed him on the forehead. "I'll see you later."

"Be careful."

The building where Kaleidoscope was based appeared to be in darkness, but that was because all of the windows had blackout blinds fitted. To avoid being seen by passersby, I made my way around the back of the building, and then cast the 'listen' spell. I was hoping I might hear music inside, which would have suggested a recording session was in progress.

The spell worked perfectly, but it didn't pick up the sound of music. Instead, I heard two familiar voices in a heated exchange.

"I still say it was a mistake," the man said. "What if one of them remembers me?"

"They won't. It was years ago."

"But they might."

"Give it a rest. It'll be fine, you'll see. Anyway, I've told them everything is set."

My hunch had proven to be correct, so it was time to confront those inside. After magicking myself into the building, I followed the sound of the raised voices.

"I've already told you that I'm not doing it again," the man said.

"You have to. We've come this far."

"I can't."

"Good evening, Roy." I was standing in the doorway of the recording studio. "Hello again, Joyce."

The two of them stared at me, open-mouthed, for the longest moment before Joyce found her voice. "How did you get in? You're trespassing."

"The door wasn't locked," I lied. "I did shout, but I

guess you couldn't hear me over your arguing."

"Get out!" Joyce spat the words.

"I don't think so."

"Roy, tell her to leave!"

"What's the point? She clearly knows."

"She doesn't know anything."

"Actually, *she* does," I said. "*She* knows that you have been sabotaging the recordings at Wash Sounds. *She* also knows that you persuaded The Ghouls to move the booking they had at Wash Sounds to your studio. Is that why you were in the VIP section of Kids' Fest, Joyce? To finalise the details?"

"Does Orlando know?" Roy said.

"Not yet, but he will do when I leave here."

"You can't prove a thing," Joyce said.

"Shut up, Joyce!" Roy shouted at her, showing a side of him that I hadn't seen before.

"You can't talk to me like that! I'm leaving." She practically knocked me over in her rush to get out of the building.

Roy was staring at the sound desk, shaking his head.

"Would you like to tell me about it, Roy?" I said.

"I've been an idiot."

"That much I know already."

"I've always wanted my own studio, but I've never had the confidence to do anything about it. After I started seeing Joyce, she persuaded me that I should go for it."

"Without saying a word to Orlando?"

"I was going to tell him."

"Really? When? After you'd ruined his studio's reputation and stolen all his clients?"

"That wasn't part of the original plan."

"Are you denying that you sabotaged those recordings?"

"I didn't mean—I—err—" His head dropped.

"Roy, look at me. Did you sabotage the recordings at Wash Sounds?"

He looked up. "Yes, I'm really sorry."

"It was Joyce who persuaded you to do it, wasn't it?"

"I can't blame her. I was the one who did it. What happens now?"

"That'll be up to Orlando."

Chapter 26

"What time did you get in last night?" Jack asked, as he handed me the fry-up he'd just made.

"It was almost midnight; you were dead to the world. When I called Orlando to tell him what had been going on, he asked me to go over to his place. I was there for almost two hours."

"What's he going to do?"

"I honestly don't know. He was devastated when I told him that Roy was behind the sabotage. Those two have worked together for over a decade."

"He must have had an inkling?"

"He didn't, but then he had no reason to suspect a man he thought was a loyal employee."

"I don't understand how Roy thought he could get away with it."

"I don't think Roy was the one driving this. I'd wager anything you like that was his girlfriend, Joyce."

"Why? Because Orlando sacked her?"

"Maybe, but I reckon that's only part of it. She was the one who pushed Roy to open the studio in the first place. I doubt he would have taken the plunge otherwise. Then, she persuaded him to sabotage the recordings at Wash Sounds, but judging by the snippet of conversation I overheard last night, he was already beginning to regret his actions."

"I assume the sabotage was designed to get the bands to move to Kaleidoscope?"

"Partly, but I'm pretty sure Joyce just wanted to see Orlando's business ruined."

"She sounds like a nasty piece of work."

"She is."

"What will happen to them now?"

"That's up to Orlando, and whether or not he decides to bring charges, but it wouldn't surprise me to find that Joyce has already done a runner."

"But I thought she and Roy were an item."

"Only for as long as it benefited her."

***

"Morning, Mrs V."

"Good morning, Jill." She held out my handbag.

"Where did that come from?"

"That friend of yours, the one with the catsuit, came in a few minutes ago. She said she couldn't stay, but asked me to give you this, and to tell you that Cuddles is behind bars. At least, I think that's what she said. Does that mean anything to you?"

"Yes, thanks. It's just our little joke."

"I'm so sorry about yesterday, Jill, falling asleep like that was unforgivable."

"Don't give it a second thought. If you hadn't, I might not have been able to solve the Wash Sounds case."

"I don't understand."

"The sabotage at the studio was being carried out by the sound engineer, Roy. Seeing how tired you were reminded me that every time I'd seen him, he was either yawning or dozing. That's because he was working at Wash Sounds during the day, and at his own studio at night."

"I'm glad it helped, but I still feel bad about it."

"Make me a cup of tea and all will be forgiven."

"Will do. I wonder who our new neighbours will be?"

"Who knows. I'm really sorry Farah has decided to go, but it sounds like her new place will be a better fit."

"I'll go and make that tea."

There were two cat bowls on my desk, and if I wasn't mistaken, they were the two I'd purchased from Rue Pets.

"Where did these come from, Winky?"

"I felt bad about trying to sell them, so I cancelled the sale."

"Good. Did you also cancel your order with Feline Fortune?"

"Certainly not."

"You do realise that will all end in tears."

"Rubbish. This time next year, I'll be making bank while sitting on the sofa. Passive income, that's the way of the future."

"We'll see."

I was standing by the window, looking at the street below, when Winky suddenly shot under the sofa. I was about to ask what was wrong when I realised Grandma was sitting in my chair.

"Where did you spring from?"

"WiFY."

"What's wrong with coming through the front door like everyone else?"

"A: I'm not everyone else. And, B: it's raining out there."

"What if Mrs V walks in? How will you explain how you got here?"

"Don't worry about Annabel. She won't disturb us."

"What have you done to her?"

"Nothing painful. Or permanent. Why don't you take a seat? You're making the place look untidy."

"I prefer to stand."

"As you wish."

"What do you want, Grandma?"

"I want to know when we'll find out the identity of the third guardian."

"*We*? There's no *we* about it. I'm the one who has to track down the compass stones."

"We've been over this before. This is now a joint venture; you and I are a team. So, who is the third guardian?"

"I don't know. I haven't heard from Martin yet."

"Have you chased him?"

"I've called him a few times, but there was no answer. I've left messages, but so far, no word."

"Then I suggest you put a fire under that brother of yours. The sooner we have all four compass stones, the sooner you can go toe-to-toe with Braxmore."

"Hang on. What happened to the *we*? I thought we were a team?"

"We're a team when it comes to tracking down the compass stones, but you'll have to go up against Braxmore alone."

"How come?"

"Because that's just the way it is." She glanced at her watch. "I have to get back to the shop; I have a fitting in ten minutes." And with that, she was gone.

"That woman gives me the creeps." Winky slunk out from under the sofa. "Isn't there something you could do to stop her coming here?"

"Like what?"

"Put something in her tea?"

"Are you suggesting I put poison in my grandmother's tea?"

"It doesn't have to be her tea. Coffee would do."

***

On arriving at Wesmere Lake, I went to see Matty first.

"Hello again, young lady. I was just about to make myself a cup of tea. Would you like one?"

"No, thanks. I'm just on my way to see Norman Bagshot."

"Now you're making me jealous." He grinned. "What does he have that I don't?"

"It's strictly business, I promise. Do you happen to know what kind of car he drives?"

"Norman? Yeah, he's got a black SUV. A Peugeot, I reckon. Why?"

"I noticed a car with a flat tyre in the car park. I wondered if it was his, but it wasn't an SUV."

"It's not my little Ford Focus, is it? I've only just had a couple of new tyres fitted."

"No, it was an Audi. I'd better get going. See you."

Once I was out of Matty's earshot, I made a call.

"Mr Bagshot?" I put on my best posh voice.

"Speaking."

"I believe you drive a black SUV."

"That's right. Who's this?"

"My name is Drusilla Penpoint. I'm afraid I've just given your car a little knock."

"What do you mean, *a little knock*?"

"I was trying to reverse park and I must have misjudged the space. I have my insurance details ready if you could pop to the car park."

"How did you know it was my—never mind. I'll be straight over."

I gave it a minute and then hurried over to Bagshot's boathouse. I knew I wouldn't have long because, as soon as he saw that his car was okay, he would realise the phone call had been a ruse.

Getting in place turned out to be much trickier than I'd imagined, and a whole lot more uncomfortable, but I managed it. All I had to do now was wait.

When he returned, Bagshot was mumbling to himself. He was no doubt relieved his car was okay, but curious as to who had pranked him. I had to time this just right, which meant waiting until he boarded the launch. I just had to hope that would be sooner rather than later. If he decided to spend the next few hours in his office, I would be in deep trouble.

For once, the Fates smiled on me, and a few minutes later, the boat swayed as he stepped aboard. That was my cue.

As soon as I knocked on the underside of the hatch, the footsteps stopped dead.

I knocked again, and said, "Let me out."

"Who's that?" There was a tremble in Bagshot's voice. "Where are you?"

"Let me out, Norman. Open the hatch."

Nothing happened, and for a horrible moment, I feared he might jump off the launch and run away. But then, the hatch above my head slid slowly open.

"No! You're dead." Bagshot turned white, and took a step backwards, but he couldn't tear his gaze away from the face of Harry. The 'doppelganger' spell had clearly worked perfectly.

"You killed me, Norman." I didn't know what Harry's voice sounded like, so I had to hope my generic male voice would do the trick.

"No, it was an accident."

"Why didn't you let me out?"

"I didn't know. Honestly."

"You knew I was down here. You were the one who helped me inside."

"I didn't know you were drowning."

"I knocked. And I shouted."

"I didn't hear you. The engine was too loud. I honestly didn't know. Not until it was too late."

"The water came over my head and into my mouth."

"I know. I'm sorry. I'm so very sorry."

"I don't believe you, Norman."

"It's true. I'd do anything to change what happened."

"Why did you lie to everyone? Why did you hide my body?"

"I was scared. I didn't know what to do." He rubbed his eyes and then looked again into the hatch. "Why have you come back?"

"Because this isn't over."

"Please, just leave me alone."

"I can't do that until you tell the truth. You have to tell the police what really happened. Lorna deserves to know."

"If I do that, will you leave me alone?"

"Yes."

"Do you promise?"

"I promise." I cast the 'invisible' spell and disappeared.

Norman breathed a sigh of relief, believing the nightmare had ended.

But he was wrong.

"If you don't do the right thing, I will be back. That's a promise."

Hearing the disembodied voice, he shot off the boat like a bat out of hell.

***

That evening, Jack and I were enjoying a quiet night in front of the TV. After having given yet another rendition of Trixie and the stupid worm, I was on the verge of nodding off when my phone rang.

"Ignore it," Jack said.

"Sorry, I have to take this." I went through to the kitchen. "Lorna?"

"I'm sorry to call you so late, Jill."

"That's okay. What is it?"

"The police just came to see me. It seems that Harry *was* running out on me after all."

"How can they be sure about that?"

She explained that the police were now certain that Harry had been on the launch when it returned from the island.

"But how is that possible?"

"He hid in the luggage hold underneath the seating. That space flooded when the boat took on water. He died right there under my feet and I had no idea." She broke down and began to cry.

"That's awful. I'm so very sorry."

"I want to be angry with him for leaving without a word, but all I can think about is the horrible way he died. Despite what he was planning to do, he didn't deserve that."

"How did the police work out what happened?"

"Apparently, the guy who owns the launch went to the police station and confessed. Harry had paid him to smuggle him back across the lake. According to the police, the guy is distraught."

"If he was so upset, why didn't he say something earlier?"

"He was too afraid, I guess."

"What's going to happen to him?"

"I've no idea. I just wanted to let you know, and to ask you to send me your bill."

"I'm sorry things didn't work out better for you, Lorna."

"Thanks. Bye."

I noted she hadn't mentioned Gloria or Robert, so she probably didn't know that they had been in on Harry's plan to disappear. That was yet another nasty surprise waiting for her. Poor girl.

I was just about to go back through to the lounge when my phone rang. I thought maybe it was Lorna again, but it was an unknown number.

"Hello?"

"Jill, it's me."

"Martin? You've changed your number."

"Sorry, it's complicated."

"Are you okay?"

"I'm fine. I have the name of the third guardian."

"Good."

"No, it's not. It's very bad."

"What do you mean?"

"It's Ma Chivers."

Oh bum!

ALSO BY ADELE ABBOTT

The Witch P.I. Mysteries
(A Candlefield/Washbridge Series)

Witch Is When... (Season #1)
Witch Is When It All Began
Witch Is When Life Got Complicated
Witch Is When Everything Went Crazy
Witch Is When Things Fell Apart
Witch Is When The Bubble Burst
Witch Is When The Penny Dropped
Witch Is When The Floodgates Opened
Witch Is When The Hammer Fell
Witch Is When My Heart Broke
Witch Is When I Said Goodbye
Witch Is When Stuff Got Serious
Witch Is When All Was Revealed

Witch Is Why... (Season #2)
Witch Is Why Time Stood Still
Witch is Why The Laughter Stopped
Witch is Why Another Door Opened
Witch is Why Two Became One
Witch is Why The Moon Disappeared
Witch is Why The Wolf Howled
Witch is Why The Music Stopped
Witch is Why A Pin Dropped
Witch is Why The Owl Returned
Witch is Why The Search Began
Witch is Why Promises Were Broken
Witch is Why It Was Over

Witch Is How... (Season #3)
Witch is How Things Had Changed
Witch is How Berries Tasted Good
Witch is How The Mirror Lied
Witch is How The Tables Turned
Witch is How The Drought Ended
Witch is How The Dice Fell
Witch is How The Biscuits Disappeared
Witch is How Dreams Became Reality
Witch is How Bells Were Saved
Witch is How To Fool Cats
Witch is How To Lose Big
Witch is How Life Changed Forever

Witch Is Where... (Season #4)
Witch is Where Magic Lives Now
Witch Is Where Clowns Go To Die
Witch Is Where Squirrels Go Nuts
Witch Is Where Rainbows End
Witch Is Where Unicorns Cry
Witch Is Where The Lights Went Out

Susan Hall Investigates
(A Candlefield/Washbridge Series)
Whoops! Our New Flatmate Is A Human.
Whoops! All The Money Went Missing.
Whoops! Someone Is On Our Case.
Whoops! We're In Big Trouble Now.

Murder On Account (A Kay Royle Novel)

Web site: AdeleAbbott.com
Facebook: facebook.com/AdeleAbbottAuthor